PRAISE FOR DECLAN BURKE

'Among all of the recent crop of Irish crime novelists, it seems to me that Declan Burke is ideally poised to make the transition to a larger international stage.'

John Connolly

'Stop waiting for Godot – he's here. Declan Burke takes the existential dilemma of characters writing themselves and turns it on its ear, and then some. He gives it body and soul . . . an Irish soul.'

Reed Farrel Coleman, author of *Empty Ever After*

'Declan Burke has broken the mould with *Absolute Zero Cool*, which is actually very cool indeed. Funny, inventive and hugely entertaining crime fiction – I guarantee you'll love it.'

Melissa Hill, author of *Something from Tiffany's*

'If you want to find something new and challenging, comic crime fiction is now the place to go . . . Declan Burke [is] at the vanguard of a new wave of young writers kicking against the clichés and producing ambitious, challenging, genre-bending works.'

Colin Bateman, author of *Nine Inches*

'*Absolute Zero Cool* is a surreal rollercoaster of a read, full of the blackest humour, and yet poignant. An outrageously funny novel . . . The joy is in the writing itself, all sparky dialogue and wry observation, so smooth that when it cuts, it's like finding razor blades in honey.'

Deborah Lawrenson, author of *The Lantern*

'Burke has written a deep, lyrical and moving crime novel . . . an intoxicating and exciting novel of which the master himself, Flann O'Brien, would be proud.'

Adrian McKinty, author of *Fifty Grand*

First published in 2011 by
Liberties Press
7 Rathfarnham Road | Terenure | Dublin 6W
Tel: +353 (1) 405 5701
www.libertiespress.com | info@libertiespress.com

Trade enquiries to Gill & Macmillan Distribution
Hume Avenue | Park West | Dublin 12
T: +353 (1) 500 9534 | F: +353 (1) 500 9595 | E: sales@gillmacmillan.ie

Distributed in the UK by
Turnaround Publisher Services
Unit 3 | Olympia Trading Estate | Coburg Road | London N22 6TZ
T: +44 (0) 20 8829 3000 | E: orders@turnaround-uk.com

Distributed in the United States by
Dufour Editions | PO Box 7 | Chester Springs | Pennsylvania 19425

Copyright © Declan Burke, 2011
The author has asserted his moral rights.

ISBN: 978-1-907593-31-4
2 4 6 8 10 9 7 5 3 1

A CIP record for this title is available from the British Library.

Cover design by Graham Thew
Internal design by Liberties Press
Printed by Bell & Bain Ltd

The publishers gratefully acknowledge
financial assistance from the Arts Council.

MIX
Paper from
responsible sources
FSC® C007785

As a tiny token, offered in thanks for all the joy her gift of unconditional love has given us, this book is dedicated to our beautiful baby girl, Lily.

ABSO
LUTE
ZERO
COOL

Declan Burke

Graphomania (a mania for writing books) inevitably takes on epidemic proportions when a society develops to the point of creating three basic conditions:

(1) an elevated level of general well-being, which allows people to devote themselves to useless activities;

(2) a high degree of social atomization and, as a consequence, a general isolation of individuals;

(3) the absence of dramatic social changes in the nation's internal life. [. . .]

But by a backlash, the effect affects the cause. General isolation breeds graphomania, and generalized graphomania in turn intensifies and worsens isolation. The invention of printing formerly enabled people to understand one another. In the era of universal graphomania, the writing of books has an opposite meaning: everyone surrounded by his own words as by a wall of mirrors, which allows no voice to filter through from outside.

Milan Kundera, The Book of Laughter and Forgetting

Times are bad. Children no longer obey their parents and everyone is writing a book.

Marcus Tullius Cicero (106-43 BCE)

The man at the foot of my bed is too sharply dressed to be anything but a lawyer or a pimp. He is reading, intently, which leads me to believe he is a pimp, as these days lawyers are more usually to be found writing novels than reading them.

Above his head, close to the ceiling, a gecko in Irish racing green is the only splash of colour in a room that is otherwise entirely white. White walls, white tiles on the floor. The window blinds, bedside locker, sheets, wainscoting, the door – all white.

As it is a manuscript of a novel the man is reading, the page facing me is white.

His eyes meet mine.

'You're some man for one man,' he says. He lays down the manuscript, comes up with a newspaper. 'They're a day behind here,' he says, 'but you get the drift.'

The newspaper's front page is dominated by a charred hospital that appears to be teetering at an angle.

I reach for the pen and pad on the bedside locker, scrawl one word.

Rosie?

He gets up and comes around the bed, takes the pad.

3

'The wee girl's okay,' he says. 'Some smoke on her lungs, apparently, but nothing serious. She'll be fine.'

He unfolds the newspaper, leafs through. 'Reading between the lines,' he says, 'they reckon the best you can hope for is criminal damage. And that's claiming insanity. Start out full-blown, work your way down to temporary, you could be out in five years. But that's the best case scenario.'

A man cannot live tilted away from the world. The world will not permit it. Gravity will have its way.

He must live straight, upright, or not at all.

'Worst case,' he says, 'they'll be pulling out the big guns, offences against the State, terrorism, the works. I mean, there's no specific law against blowing up hospitals, but let's just say they've plenty of wiggle room to play with.'

He waits. The A/C hums. From beyond the shuttered window, faintly, comes the *burr-thrip* of cicadas.

'So that's the good news. The bad news,' he says, holding up the op-ed pages, tapping the editorial, 'is they're saying you couldn't have been working alone. They're saying you must have had help, maybe a whole cell.'

There is nothing to add to this. It would appear that all effort has come to naught.

He folds the newspaper and tucks it under my pillow. Retrieves the manuscript, which he places on the pristine sheet beside my hand. He lays a red pen on top so that it underlines the title, 'The Baby Killers'.

'Seeing as you won't be going anywhere for a couple of days,' he says, 'I thought you might like one last skim through. See if we can't kill a few more babies.'

My line for today comes courtesy of Samuel Beckett: *Ever failed. No matter. Try again. Fail again. Fail better.*

•

He just appears, as if wished for.

I'm out on the decking beside the goldfish pond, a fine hazy morning, one of those mid-spring bloomers, the sun on the rise and the day coming warm. Bees humming, the fountain burbling away like a baby dry and fed. Good coffee to hand. I'm just thinking that this is the life when a shadow falls across the pages. When I glance up, shading my eyes against the glare, he's standing there with a shy and slightly goofy grin.

'You don't remember me,' he says.

He's confusing me with someone else. We've nodded to one another in passing over the last couple of days, in the refectory up at the Big House or strolling around the grounds, and each time I had the impression he was waiting for me to recognise him, for a friendly smile to allow him jump in and start a conversation.

Not my scene. The whole point of being here is to cut myself off, shut down, focus on the work. Exile and silence, then hope for cunning.

Now I lean back in the chair, still shading my eyes, and admit that I don't remember him. I hear myself apologise, saying that I've always had a terrible memory for faces; names yes, I've never had any trouble recalling people's names, but faces just don't work for me. None of which is true, in fact it's the reverse, but even if it were true I think I'd have remembered this guy.

'It's probably the eye-patch,' he says. 'I wasn't blond then, either.' He has a platinum-blond crew-cut, one Newman-blue eye and a square jaw. I guess him to be mid-thirties. 'And I was about three inches shorter.'

He shuffles his feet. 'A man needs some stature,' he says.

I'd put him down for a poet if it weren't for the motorcycle boots. For some reason the poets here prefer comfortable shoes.

'I don't suppose there's any coffee going,' he says.

Just to be polite, and because I need a fresh coffee, I cross the lawn and go inside my chalet and draw two cups of coffee. Waiting for the kettle to boil, watching through the window as he filches a smoke, I make a bet with myself as to how long it'll be before he starts whining about how no one understands how hard it is to be him.

I'm thinking, Christ, maybe if you spent more time at your desk clarifying a few things, instead of roaming the grounds in search of fellow enablers and stealing other people's smokes . . .

The bet: if he bitches about the Arts Council inside ten minutes, I'm taking the afternoon off to go fishing on the lake.

Back out on the decking, he's staring down into the pond.

'Listen,' I say, 'this is kind of embarrassing, but . . .'

He turns to face me, a defiant jut to his chin. 'Karlsson,' he says.

'And we've definitely met,' I say, blowing on my coffee.

'In a manner of speaking.'

'I don't follow.' Except then I realise he knows me through the web, the blog I write that keeps tabs on the latest in Irish crime fiction. Karlsson doesn't ring any bells, but maybe I know him by another name, an avatar.

'I'd have remembered someone called Karlsson,' I say. 'Are you a writer?'

'Right now I'm an evil genius.'

'I get that, yeah, the eye-patch and all. But what were you when I knew you?'

'A porter.'

'A porter?'

'A hospital porter.'

I reach for the makings and roll a smoke. Sip some coffee and wait for a tic or flinch to give him away. He only stares.

'You're that Karlsson?' I say.

'Him, yeah.'

'Okay, I'll play along. You're Karlsson. So what can I do for you?'

'You can start by telling me what happened.'

'With Karlsson? Nothing.' I explain that first drafts get written and printed out and then go on the shelf for at least six months. No exceptions.

'Fair go,' he says. 'But it's been nearly five years now. I mean, I was twenty-eight when you wrote that draft. And I know you didn't stop writing. I saw your latest one, *The Big O*, it arrived on the shelf a couple of years back.'

'Things just went in a different direction, man. No offence.'

'I never thought you did it deliberately,' he says. 'But you should know, I'm in limbo here.'

He slips a forefinger under the eye-patch, scratches something away.

'Publish or I'm damned,' he says.

Karlsson was a hospital porter who assisted old people who wanted to die. His girlfriend, Cassie, found out. Then the cops got involved because Cassie contacted them anonymously before confronting Karlsson, except the cops wound up more concerned about where Cassie had gone.

'How's Jonathan?' I say.

'Jonathan?'

'Jonathan Williams. My agent, or agent as was. As far as I know, he's the only person who ever saw the manuscript. Unless he farmed it out for a reader's report.'

I'm presuming the guy is working on some kind of funky theatre piece that involves taking on Karlsson's persona, an unpublished character adrift in time and space. Not that I mind, it might even be fun to see it on stage, but I'd have preferred if Jonathan had asked permission before he handed over the manuscript.

'I've never met any Jonathan Williams,' he says. 'How could I? I'm in limbo here.'

'Right. And this limbo, does it preclude you from paying rights if you use the original story?'

A flash of something dark in the Newman-blue eye. 'You think this is a joke?'

'Actually, I think it's a bit comi-tragic. Not full-blown tragedy, mind, but poignant, yeah.'

'See, that's the problem right there,' he says. 'It's not full-blown anything.'

I'm liking the cut of his jib. Not only is he taking on Karlsson, he's critiquing the piece as he goes.

'Maybe you're right,' I say. 'If you want the truth of it, I'm not really sure I ever intended that one to see the light of day. It was just a bunch of stuff I needed to write at the time, get down on the page. These days I write comedy. It's easier, for one. And more fun. Life is shitty enough for people without asking them to waste their precious reading time on morbid stuff.'

'Hold up,' he says. 'Are you telling me you never even sent it away?'

'I didn't just bury it.' He has presence, I'll give him that, an intensity that leaves me feeling faintly, ridiculously, defensive. 'I mean, I gave it to Jonathan.'

'And what did he say?'

'He said he'd never read anything like it before. He reckoned he had to stop taking notes about halfway in, just read it through. I think the pervy sex stuff had him a bit freaked.'

'That's good, right?'

'Not in today's market. Freaking your agent isn't cool anymore.'

'And he never read it again?'

'He was about to but I stopped him. I was showing him *The Big O* that day.'

We sit in silence. The sun clears the hills to the south and the grounds come alive. Clematis buds starting to show, some pink apple blossom, snowdrops and daffodils nodding on the faint breeze off the lake. Now and again a quick flash of orange in the pond, the pair of golden carp, Jaws and Moby-Dick. The little fountain pootling away.

'So how'd *The Big O* do?' he says, gazing off up the hill at the hospital, its glass frontage ablaze as it mirrors the sunrise.

'It did alright, yeah. Got picked up in the States, a two-book deal, some decent wedge.'

'The States?'

'Yeah. Harcourt. Of course, then they went and merged with Houghton Mifflin and my editor got the boot, so it didn't get a lot of play over there. Still, the reviews were nice, enough to get them behind the second book.'

'And this is what you're working on now.'

'That's right.'

'So what happens to me?' he says. The cigarette, forgotten, burns down between his fingers.

'I've no idea.'

'You can't just leave me stuck here.'

'I hear you. But I'm already committed to this,' I nod at the pages scattered across the table, 'I've a deadline to meet. I can't just bunk off and start writing something new.'

'If it's good enough,' he says, 'they'll wait for it.'

'I doubt that. The industry's changed a lot in the last five years, you wouldn't believe how tight things have got. And I have other responsibilities going on. I mean, I'm married now. And we have a baby, Rosie.'

He congratulates me, grudging it.

'The point I'm making,' I say, 'is that I can't afford to spend any time on anything that isn't at least potentially commercial. Or to be perfectly frank, anything I don't enjoy doing. That dark shit is hard work. And if I don't like—'

'If it's dark,' he says, 'whose fault is that?'

'Mine, sure. But—'

'But schmut. If you made it dark you can make it funny. Just go back over it.'

'Make euthanasia funny?'

'Just listen to me a minute,' he says. 'Can you just listen? You owe me that much, at least.'

'I'm listening.'

'See,' he says, 'I'm just not that kind of guy. The Karlsson guy, I mean. I even changed my name when I dyed my hair. I'm called Billy now.'

'Billy?'

'I'm aiming to normalise things all round.'

'Then the eye-patch is probably too much.'

'That was just to get your attention.' He peels off the patch. There's an empty socket underneath, a puckered purple wound that puts me in mind of a sucked-out prune. He pats the pockets of his zip-up sweater and comes up with a pair of tinted shades, slips them on.

'What happened to your eye?' I say.

'You wouldn't believe me if I told you. Anyway, this Karlsson guy – I'm not him. Not anymore. And I don't think I ever was. I mean, I liked Cassie. Liked her a lot. And even if I didn't, I would-n't just kill her to get off on a euthanasia rap. I'd have done a flit. The old folks, they were one thing, they wanted to die and I was helping them out. But Cassie, no way.'

'I never actually said you killed her.'

'No, but you left it hanging.'

'As far as I can remember,' I say, 'I gave you a happy ending, you got away with it. The cop investigating, he turned out insane, had all these theories about population control. A big fan of the Chinese, if memory serves.'

'Even I didn't believe that,' he says. 'That ending was a mess.'

I allow that it was.

'You can do better than that,' he says.

'Not with you I can't.'

'*I'm* not the problem, man. The story's the problem.'

'The story's what it is,' I say. 'And it's told now.'

'I didn't hear any fat ladies singing.'

I stub out my cigarette. 'Listen, uh, Karlsson, I have to—'

'Billy.'

'Billy, yeah. Look, Billy, I have to go. Deborah's coming to visit today, and I've some pages to get straight before lunch. So . . .'

'The story was too freaky,' he says. He's holding up a hand to delay me. 'Too out there but not big enough. Plus you had me down as a total dingbat. These are things that can be changed.'

'I really don't know if they can.'

'Tell me this,' he says. 'How long have you spent thinking about me in the last five years?'

'I've thought about you, sure. And I wish—'

'I've got a way to make it bigger. Although you'd have to be more honest about me. If it was to work, I'd have to be more real. More *me*, y'know?'

'Right now you're sitting across the table smoking my cigarettes.' As much as he's a distraction, I'm intrigued by the guy's chutzpah. 'I don't know if I could handle you getting any more real.'

'That's because I'm Billy now. Karlsson never showed up, did he?'

'He never did, no.'

'Just as well. He'd probably have kidnapped little Rosie and tortured her until you'd rewritten the story the way he wanted it.'

'Y'know, I think Karlsson liked who he was. I don't think he'd have had any issues with what happened to Cassie.'

'Because the guy was a sociopath.' He shrugs. 'Who wants to live like that?' He leans in, drops the shades, pierces me with the Newman-blue eye. 'You think I wouldn't like a little Rosie to play with?'

'Do you?'

'I don't know.' He sits back, slipping the shades back in place. 'I'm not feeling it, if that's what you're asking. But they say men don't become fathers until their baby is born, maybe even a while after.'

'That was true for me, yeah.'

'Look, all I'm asking for is one more go, see if I can't make it out this time.'

'Out of this limbo.'

'Sure. Maybe if I was to get some kind of written permission from the old folks, so I'd have something to show Cassie when she found out about the euthanasia. That could help.'

'It'd help you and Cassie, maybe. But it wouldn't do much for the conflict in the story.'

'That's the other thing,' he says. 'I think you need a different kind of conflict. I mean, a hospital porter bumping off old people? You can get that stuff in the newspapers. Why would anyone want to read it in a book?'

'I guess it'd depend on how interesting the killer is.'

'Between you and me, you're no Patricia Highsmith.'

I allow that I'm not, although I remind him it's comedy crime I write.

'If you want my opinion,' he says, 'the conflicts that work best are between the reader and a character they like, okay, but who's doing stuff they wouldn't generally tolerate. Lear,' he ticks them off on his fingers as he goes, 'Raskolnikov, Hazel Motes, Long John Silver, Tom Ripley—'

'I take your point.'

'Your mistake,' he says, 'was to make Karlsson a total wackjob. No one who wasn't a complete fruit could like him.'

'Okay, so say I make you likeable. What then?'

'We blow up the hospital.'

After lunch, a picnic out on the decking, I tell Debs I'm half-thinking about having another go at the Karlsson story.

'Who?' she says.

I tape Rosie's nappy in place, snap the buttons on her baby-gro.

'Karlsson, the hospital porter.'

She frowns, remembering. 'The guy who killed all the old people?'

'I'm thinking of making it a comedy. But don't worry, I'll work on it in the evenings, once the other stuff is out of the way.'

'Your father's a space cadet,' she tells Rosie. The child, warm and dry again, gurgles like a faulty faucet.

'It's just a redraft,' I say. 'Nothing major.'

'I'll redraft the marriage licence,' Debs says. She tickles Rosie's tummy. 'But don't worry, it'll be nothing major.'

I

WINTER

The cancer counsellor waves a rolled-up newspaper to shoo us away from the windows so his clients won't have to watch us smoking. We are their bolted horses.

Some of my co-smokers drift away around the corner to where a breeze whips beneath the glass corridor connecting the hospital's old and new buildings. There they huddle together, shivering. It's a grey December day, sleet spattering the glass. The wind a cruel easterly.

The cancer counsellor raps on the window, jerks his head and thumb. I flip him the bird.

He opens the window and leans out, beckons me across. I stroll over. When I'm close enough, he mimes writing down the name on my plastic tag.

'Let me get this straight,' I say. 'You're *miming* a disciplinary action?'

This provokes him into taking out a pen and writing my name on the back of his hand. 'You're on report, Karlsson.'

'Ingrate. If we didn't smoke, you'd be out of a job.'

His face reddens. He doesn't like being reminded of his role as parasite. Not many do. 'Between you and me,' I say, 'stress is the big killer.'

He's fuming as he closes the window. I try to make the connection between the patients' cancer and my smoking but it can't be done. There's a fuzzy blurring of divisions, okay, and carcinogens either side of the wire. But I'm not finding the tangent point.

My line for today comes from Henry G. Strauss: *I have every sympathy with the American who was so horrified by what he had read of the effects of smoking that he gave up reading.*

•

'That's not very different from the first draft,' Billy says. We're out on the decking again, another beautiful morning. I'm hoping the good weather holds because I'm not sure I want to invite him inside.

'I think it works,' I say. 'I mean, you're going to have to be at least a little bit weird, otherwise no one'll believe it when you decide to blow up the hospital.'

'Fair go. But I don't know if I should flip him the bird. It's a bit, what, gratuitous? If it was me I'd be a bit more subtle than that.'

'I'll take it under consideration,' I say, making a note.

'What's next?' he says.

'You shave the skinny guy for his hernia operation.'

'Roll it there, Collette.'

•

Today I shave a skinny guy, Tiernan, for a hernia procedure. The latex gloves are cold but he doesn't seem to notice. I believe he's trying to pretend another man isn't fiddling around in his crotch.

Instead he tells me that a friend of his knows someone who died under anaesthetic. Tiernan says he doesn't want to die not knowing he's dying. What he's really saying is, he doesn't want to die. What he's really saying is, he has no one to confide in except the guy who shaves strangers' genitals.

'I do shaves,' I say. 'I push wheelchairs and lift the heavy stuff when the male nurses are busy. If you want a priest I'll see what I can do. But it's only a hernia op. Catch yourself on.'

He's shocked. I swab away the last of the cheap shaving foam. 'You think you have problems?' I say. 'I have to look at dicks all day. Want to swap jobs?'

He works in a travel agency and spends his day emailing pornography to friends who pretend to appreciate what he understands to be irony.

'You don't want to die?' I say. 'Then do something. If you do something you won't mind dying so much. Paint a picture. Have a kid. Then let it go. Dying isn't so different from just letting go.'

But he isn't listening. He's back thinking about this guy his friend knew, the one who died without knowing he was dying. I get a bang out of that. If there's one thing dead people know, it's that they're dead. And if that's anything like the way the living know they're alive, it's not such a big deal.

He watches me peel off the latex gloves.

'Pay attention,' I say. 'You might need to draw on this performance some day. You'd be surprised at how many people learn to live without dignity. Statistically speaking, you've every chance of becoming one of those people.'

The matron arrives. I wonder if they teach bustling at matron school. She throws back Tiernan's robe. Matrons don't usually check on hernia preps but I shaved the wrong side a couple of weeks ago.

'How are you feeling, Mr Tiernan?' she says. She says this so we can both pretend she isn't checking my work.

'I'm parched for a drink,' the guy says.

'It won't be long now,' she says. 'It'll soon be over.' She speaks to me without looking in my direction. 'Karlsson, I'd like you to take Mr Tiernan down to theatre at three forty-five.'

'Let's hope nothing funny happens on the way,' I say. But she's not listening.

•

He lounges back in the chair, tapping his lower lip with the butt of a pencil.

'You're still calling me Karlsson,' he says.

'Technically speaking,' I say, 'it's the other characters who call you Karlsson.'

'So have them call me Billy.'

'I could do that, yeah. Except if you become Billy, you're not Karlsson anymore.'

'I'm not Karlsson anymore.'

'Not to me, or you. But if the other characters start calling you Billy, they'll expect to see someone who looks like a Billy. And I'd have to go through the whole bloody thing changing your appearance every time it's mentioned. Your hair, your eyes, the way you walk . . .'

'Are we doing this,' he says, 'or are we doing this?'

I'm none too keen on his tone.

'No disrespect, Billy, but I'm doing you a favour here. Okay? And if we're going to do this on top of my own stuff, we can't be farting around worrying about every tiny detail.'

'What you need to do,' I say, 'is think of yourself as an actor. Yeah? Make like the story's a Mike Leigh movie, or one of those Dogme flicks, and you're contributing to Karlsson as he goes along, inventing dialogue for him, little tics and quirks. Making him you, eventually, but being subtle about it. How's that sound?'

He takes a while to consider.

'Okay,' he says. 'I'll give it a whirl.'

'Glad to hear it. Listen,' I say, 'I'm thinking of leaving out the Pope-Camus stuff.'

'What Pope-Camus stuff?'

'The goalkeepers bit.'

He shakes his head. 'I forget that one,' he says. 'What'd I say there?'

•

Albert Camus and Pope John Paul II were both goalkeepers in their youth. I like to imagine them at either end of a stadium, punting the ball back and forth while hooligans riot on the terraces.

As former goalies, Camus and Pope John Paul II may or may not have sniggered knowingly when they read about James Joyce's ambition to be both keeper and crucifier of his nation's conscience.

As for me, I was born. Later I learned to read, then write. Since then it's been mostly books. Books and masturbation.

Writing and masturbation have in common temporary relief and the illusion of achievement. Many great writers have been avid onanists, and many avid onanists have been great writers. Often the only difference, as a point of refinement, is whether the wanking or writing comes first.

Me, I write some, I tug some, I go to bed. Only a barbarian would wank first, then write.

My line for today comes from the Danish novelist, Isak Dinesen: *I write a little every day, without hope and without despair.*

•

Jonathan Williams is a jovial Welshman, albeit one who is a dead ringer for every kindly English professor you've ever seen in a Hollywood movie.

'No,' he says, 'I didn't give the Karlsson story to anyone.' His voice booms down the phone. 'I wouldn't do that without your permission.'

21

'Not even for a reader's report?'

'Not so far as I recall. And I believe I would have remembered,' he laughs, 'a reader's report on that particular gem.'

'That's what I thought.'

'Why?' he says. 'Is there a problem?'

'Not a problem per se.' I tell him I've taken a sabbatical, six weeks at the artists' retreat, and about Billy's idea of bringing Karlsson to life. 'I'm just wondering where he got his hands on the story.'

'I'm afraid I have no idea,' he says, 'but he certainly didn't get it from me.'

Jonathan is no longer my agent, but being a gentleman he asks how things are going. I tell him my editor at Harcourt is banging on about the deadline.

'Forget about him,' he urges. 'Get it right, that's the most important thing. In ten years' time, no one will care if you got it in by deadline or not.'

Sage words.

He says, 'If you don't mind me asking . . .'

'Go ahead.'

'Did you apply for Arts Council funding, towards the cost of the artists' retreat?'

'I did, yeah, but no joy. Apparently comedy crime doesn't qualify.'

'I don't suppose you used the Karlsson story as part of your application,' he says.

'I did, actually. They needed to see a couple of samples of my work, and Karlsson was just lying there doing nothing.'

'That's probably it,' he says. 'Someone at the Arts Council read the story and passed it on to your friend Billy. Utterly unethical, of course, but there you are.'

'And there's no way of finding out who might have read it?'

'Probably not. Those assessments are anonymous, so there's no chance of canvassing. But I can make some discreet enquiries, if you'd like.'

'No, you're grand.'

'Don't worry about it,' he says. 'The rights issue, I mean. If there's any doubt at any point down the line, I'll tell anyone who wants to know I read it in its original form and you're the sole author.'

'Thanks, Jonathan.'

'Don't mention it. Oh, and be sure to tell Anna I was asking for her when you see her next. Lovely woman, isn't she?'

Anna MacKerrig, daughter to Lord Lawrence MacKerrig, whose Scots-Presbyterian sense of *noblesse oblige* was fundamental to the establishing of the Sligo artists' retreat some twenty years ago.

'I haven't actually met her yet,' I say, 'but I'll certainly pass that on when I see her.'

'Very good. Well, I'll talk to— Oh, I knew there was a reason I rang.'

'Yes?'

'*The Big O*,' he says. 'An Italian publisher has made an offer. The money is little more than a token gesture, of course, but . . .'

'No, that's grand, we'll take it. It'd be nice to see it in Italian.'

'Wouldn't it just?' He chuckles. 'Maybe the advance will pay for a weekend in Rome.'

Maybe. If I swim there.

'Talk soon,' he says, and is gone again.

'Y'know,' Billy says, 'I don't think I should want to be a writer. I can see why you had it in there, to suggest Karlsson has some kind of depth. But now . . .'

'You've changed your mind since you've met me.'

I'm joking, but he nods. 'What I'm thinking,' he says, 'is that Karlsson wanting to be a writer, to be creative, that'll clash with him wanting to blow up the hospital.'

'The urge to destroy is also a creative urge.'

'Hmmmm,' he says. 'I'm not sure, if we want people to like me, that I should be throwing out nihilist sound bites. All that Year Zero stuff doesn't play too well in the 'burbs.'

'How about this?' I say. 'You want to be a writer at the start, except all you get are rejection letters. Then you get sour and decide to blow up the hospital.'

'Too narcissistic,' he says. 'Only a writer could be that self-absorbed.'

'But blowing up a hospital, that's not narcissistic at all.'

'It's an attention-grabber, sure. But you're the one who left me so's I need to do something drastic.'

'Leave me out of it, Billy. The hospital's your idea.'

'I didn't start out like this, man. If you'd have asked me way back when, I'd have told you my dream was to skipper a charter yacht in the Greek islands.'

'A hospital porter? Skippering yachts in the Aegean?'

His eyes narrow. 'What,' he says, 'the plebs aren't allowed to dream?'

'The plebs can dream whatever they want, Billy, but this isn't Mills and fucking Boon. Maybe if your dream was plausible, y'know . . .'

'A plausible dream?'

'Call it an achievable fantasy. Like, you can want whatever you want, and good luck in the cup, but if it doesn't play ball with the story's logic then it doesn't go in.'

'That's a bit limiting, isn't it?'

'You can't have unicorns in outer space, Billy.'

He grins. 'You could if they had specially designed helmets.'

'Fine. You want unicorns on Mars, hospital porters skippering yachts, we can do it all. But no one's going to buy it.'

'What you're saying is, you're not good enough to make it

convincing.' A faint shrug. 'Maybe that's why you're still slotting your fiction in around your day job, taking sabbaticals for rewrites.'

'Maybe it is. So maybe we should forget this whole thing so I can go back to actually enjoying what I write.'

He gets up. 'Let's take a break,' he says. 'We're obviously not going to get anything constructive done today.' He rolls a cigarette from my makings, lights up. 'One more thing,' he says, exhaling. 'You can't go threatening to pull the plug. You're either doing this or you're not, and if you're not fully committed then it isn't going to work. The start should be the easy bit. If you're finding it hard going now, it'll be a nightmare when we get into the endgame.'

He's right, but somehow apologising feels a step too far.

'Listen,' I say, 'I won't be here tomorrow. We're taking Rosie to see Debs's parents.'

'No worries.'

'I won't be back until Sunday evening.'

'See you Monday morning, so.'

'Monday, yeah.'

Debs is standing inside the chalet's patio doors with Rosie humped over her shoulder, patting the little girl's back to bring up wind. I put the manuscript and coffee mugs on the counter and hunch down to meet Rosie's gaze, but she's glassy-eyed, blissed out after a long feed.

'Y'know,' Debs says, 'it's just as well no one else can see what I can see. I'd hate for anyone to think my husband was a mentaller who needs to put in a couple of hours talking to his characters to get set up for the day.'

'Want me to take her?'

'Good timing.' She hands Rosie across, sniffing her as she goes. 'I think she has nappy issues. And change her baby-gro, will you? Put her little kimono outfit on.'

'The white one?'

'No, the pink one, the one your mother bought her. She's cute in pink.'

'Hey boopster,' I croon, rubbing Rosie's back. She burps up a little creamy sick that dribbles down onto my shoulder. 'That's my girl,' I say.

•

I have some sympathy for Orpheus. Perhaps this is why I am drawn to cellars, basements, caves and catacombs. There is, surely, a Freudian frisson to my fascination with vaults, crypts and bunkers. It occurs to me to wonder, on my regular perambulations through the hospital's cavernous underground car park, if my pseudo-gynaecological expeditions mask a benign desire to regain the original comfort of the womb or a more malign instinct to pierce and penetrate. Do I descend to the netherworld to liberate Eurydice, or to ensure my presumptive gaze annihilates her hope forever?

Orpheus had the good fortune to be created, by Apollonius Rhodius, an artist of sublime skill. In the original mythology, he is a valued member of the Argonauts who rescues his beloved wife from oblivion.

He subsequently had the misfortune to be redrafted by Virgil, Plato and Ovid, who between them not only contrive a tragedy from our hero's brave harrowing of hell, but in the process render Orpheus an ineffective coward who extinguished Eurydice.

Their justification was that Orpheus lacked a true commitment to his wife. In other words, they believed he should want to die in order to be with Eurydice forever, rather than simply resurrecting her from death.

Thus, as his love was not true, Orpheus was punished by the ever-mocking gods.

In the dark corners of my netherworld, prowling the shadows of the hospital's caverns, I wonder if any mortal should be expected to have the courage of the gods' convictions, who have all of eternity in which to debate the theoretical pros and cons of the ultimate in self-sacrifice.

Later, over dinner and a nice glass of red, I tease out the subtleties.

'So you're asking,' Cassie says, 'if I'd rather be rescued from hell or have you come join me?'

'That's pretty much it, yeah.'

'Hard to say, really.' She forks home some pasta and chews, considering. 'We couldn't just swap places?'

'I don't think Orpheus was offered that option.'

'Typical. I'm betting it was a bloke who wrote that story.'

'Actually there was more than one writer. But they were all blokes, yeah.'

'There's a shocker. So would you?' she says.

'Would I what?'

'Swap places with me.'

'That wouldn't make any sense. Better I stayed alive and tried to get you out, no?'

'No. I'm not offering that option. So would you?'

'I don't know.'

'Why not?'

'Well, it's hard to say, because you're not in hell.'

'K, we've just moved in together. How much worse could hell be?'

'Point taken.'

I met Cassie through a lonely hearts column. What I liked about her advertisement was that she required *asoh*. Most people specify a *good* sense of humour, but Cassie wasn't fussed. Laughs are laughs, she said.

Most people say they're first attracted by a sense of humour, the implication being that physical appearance is of secondary importance because beauty is ephemeral. The assumption here is that a sense of humour cannot age, that humour is immune to wrinkles, withering or contracting a tumour. People presume the things they cannot see – hope, oxygen, God – do not change, grow old or die.

A sense of humour is like everything else: it serves a particular purpose and then converts into a new form of energy. The trick is to be fluid enough to go with the flow and deal with each new manifestation on its own merits.

•

'You might want to scrap the next bit,' I say. 'It's an excerpt from that novel Karlsson was writing.'

'Any good?'

'Not really. Mostly they're just doodles, scraps of ideas.'

'Can we salvage any of it?'

'Not really. To be honest, they were meant to be rubbish, to point up Karlsson's delusions of grandeur. And as far as I know, they were the bits that put Jonathan off. With the pervy sex, like.'

'Colour me intrigued. Have on, Macduff.'

•

Sermo Vulgus: A Novel (Excerpt)

Cassie, my elbows skate in ungainly loops across the cheap varnish of this plywood desk as I write to unremember. The flat white sponge soaks up the words. Cassie, bury me in a cheaply varnished plywood coffin. Then look beyond the past. Train your eyes to see beyond the horizon of what we used to know, all the way back to where our future ends.

Cassie, we should have danced together, once at least, but you stumbled over words like 'imaginings'.

Did I hate you really? Did I choose you for the exaggeration of your form, for the overflow that allowed me to wallow in the cosy warmth of incestuous oblivion? Were you really the mother I never had? Withdrawal was always the sweetest relief as I slid out and away to limply drift back to the world.

Cassie, why did I want you only when you were lost?

•

'Dump it,' he says.

'Fine.'

'All that incest stuff, Jesus . . .'

'I already said, it's gone.'

'What's next?'

'You get your first official warning.'

•

The old new orders were, no smoking inside the hospital. The new new orders are, no smoking on hospital grounds. So the cancer counsellor makes an official complaint. If he had made a verbal complaint, I'd have received a verbal warning. An official written complaint results in an official written warning. My supervisor tells me this as he hands over the written warning.

'What about the rain forests?' I say. 'Don't cut down trees for the sake of an official complaint. If you have to make an official complaint, send me an email, or text it. Or recycle. Just send out the written warning on the back of the last one.'

'There's procedures,' he says. He wears a buttoned-up stripy shirt under a v-necked sweater, his hair greasy where it straggles over his collar.

'Get a haircut,' I say, 'you look like a sleazy monk. Smarten up, unbutton that top button. Being married is no excuse.'

I do not say this. What I say is, 'How about the far end of the

29

overflow car park, the one the cheap bastards use when they don't want to pay for parking in town?'

'Karlsson, there's no smoking anywhere on hospital grounds.'

'You can't even *see* the hospital from down there.'

'It's the rule.'

'Look, I can run with the logic of no smoking in the hospital, but—'

'Karlsson, if I catch you smoking anywhere on hospital grounds, you're fired.'

'Okay. So when do we stop the consultants *drinking* anywhere on hospital grounds? Like, when do we start testing the surgeons' coffee-flasks when they drive up in the morning?'

'It's for your own good,' he says. 'You'll live longer.'

This new ban has nothing to do with my health and everything to do with his, because he has a sickness for which orders obeyed are the placebo *du jour*. Who am I hurting by smoking in the overflow car park? I'm hurting me, sure, but I'm killing him.

'If you can tell a man how he should kill himself,' I say, 'you can tell him to do anything. You're just hanging around waiting for someone to tell you which window to jump out of.'

I do not say this.

'You've had your warning,' he says.

'Can I super-size that, with extra threat?'

But he's not listening. My line for today comes courtesy of Aristotle: *No excellent soul is exempt from a mixture of madness.*

•

'We should probably kill the Aristotle bit,' he says. 'I don't know if people respond all that well to insanity, not unless Russell Crowe is playing the lead. And the foul language, that should go too.'

'No lunacy,' I say, making the appropriate notes, 'and no swearing. Anything else?'

'Just one thing.' He reaches into his backpack and comes up with a sheet of paper. 'I took a stab at this last night. Something I remembered about Cassie. Want to try it?'

'Sure, why not?'

He makes to hand the page across.

'No,' I say, 'it's your stuff, you read it.'

'I don't have much of a reading voice,' he says.

'You want to be more real, don't you? More authentic?'

He crosses his eyes, mocking himself, then grins. 'Okay,' he says.

•

Sometimes Cassie sings in her sleep. The words are incomprehensible, the melody non-existent. There are moans, yelps and high-pitched squeals. None of these make sense in themselves. Nor do they make any more sense when heard in sequence. If a straight line exists between the static of the cosmos and a Mozart requiem, between pointless hiss and perfect design, then Cassie belongs in a choir of whales.

She might not sing for two months, then sing three times in one week. It might last for five seconds or minutes at a time. Why?

I have recorded her singing without asking permission. An unforgivable invasion. Except Cassie doesn't know that she sings. If I tell her, she might never sing again. What then?

I've slowed the tape down, speeded it up, played it in reverse. None of the manipulations yield any semblance of meaning. So far I have eliminated the following possibilities: hymns; pop songs; TV theme tunes; advertising jingles; nursery rhymes.

All I know is that her singing is not intended to be heard. It is not even the unselfconscious cries of a baby, because a baby is at least aware that it is crying, and that its inarticulate bawling signifies hunger, wet or pain.

In the darkness I wait for Cassie to sing. In the there and then of my waiting occurs the tangent point where I intersect with the human race, that unique breed aiming out along an arc designed to contradict nature's irrefutable logic.

•

'Well?' he says.

'You got the tone right,' I say. 'And I like the way you've made yourself sound like a tender pervert.'

'You don't mind?' he says. 'Me chipping in now and again, I mean.'

'Not at all. The more you write, the less I have to do.'

'Hey,' he says with that shy, goofy grin, 'wouldn't it be funny if I ended up writing about how I don't want to be a writer?'

'Get me a whalebone corset,' I say. 'I may have just cracked a rib.'

•

This morning a thick mist rolls down off the hills, a faint but pervasive drizzle. The kind that'd go through you without so much as a bounce. I stand well back from the window with the lights off, sipping my coffee and watching Billy read over something he has written, now and again glancing up at the chalet.

Around eight-thirty he leaves, slouching away around the stand of bamboo beyond the goldfish pond, shoulders hunched against the rain.

Something in the way he walks makes me realise that the extra three inches of height come from lifts he's had put into his shoes.

He hasn't even had a coffee. It was my turn.

•

In reverse order, the hospital's chain of command works something like this:

roaches
porters
porters' supervisors
nurses
ward sisters
matrons
interns
consultants
specialists
accountants
the board of directors
God

All these wondrous creatures need to defecate. Sooner or later, the works gum up. Everyone waits until the porter hoses out the Augean edifice. Then it all starts again.

I like to call this process 'Tuesday'.

Everyone has a thing about Mondays, but Mondays do their best.

Tuesdays are evil.

Tuesday is Monday's Mr Hyde, lurking in the shadows and twirling its luxuriant moustache. Tuesdays take Friday the 13ths out into the car park and set their feet on fire, just to see the fuckers dance. If Tuesday was a continent it would be sub-Saharan Africa: disowned, degraded and mean as hell.

Tuesdays are in a perpetual state of incipient rebellion. I can feel it. Tuesdays want to be Saturday nights, and a few pancakes once a year aren't going to keep them sweet forever. When it all blows up in your face, don't say you weren't warned.

We have chained Tuesdays too tightly, allowed them no time

off. We have taken no notice of Tuesday's concerns about working conditions. Tuesday is Samson, blind and furious, his hair growing back by imperceptible degrees.

You have been warned.

The union rep is on the phone, so it must be Tuesday.

'You got another official warning, Karlsson,' he says, 'and one member's shoddy work practices reflect badly on the entire union. You need to take that on board because we're all in this together. If enough people share the load it doesn't weigh anything. You know the cleaning contracts are up for review next month.'

'Aren't you supposed to be on my side?' I say. 'I'm being fucked up the arse, metaphorically speaking. What's the protocol for shouldering a metaphorical poke in the wazoo?'

'Rules are rules,' he says.

'There's such a thing as a bad law,' I say. 'Not only is the law an ass, it must be seen to be an ass.'

But it's Tuesday and he's not listening. 'One more infraction and you're suspended,' he says.

'One more and I'm fired. Where's the point in suspending me after I'm fired?'

'Consider yourself disciplined,' he says. 'You'll be receiving official confirmation within three working days.'

'Can I wait until the official confirmation arrives before considering myself disciplined? I have issues with imaginary manifestations of authority.'

I say, 'I'm an atheist, send a plague of locusts.'

But it's Tuesday. He's not listening.

•

'Again with the foul language,' he says.

'Duly noted.'

'And there's maybe a little too much Tuesday stuff. But,' he adds, 'that's just a suggestion. You're the writer here.'

'No, you might have a point. I'll take a look at it.'

'Okay. What's next?'

'Another excerpt from your Cassie novel.'

'I thought we were dumping all that.'

'We dumped the last one, sure. But I realised afterwards that the excerpts were intended as Karlsson's love letters to Cassie.'

'Oh yeah?'

'What do you want to do?'

He shrugs. 'Give it a whirl.'

•

Sermo Vulgus: A Novel (Excerpt)

As a young man in Vienna, Hitler failed to woo a Jew. A bullet tore his sleeve as he charged across No Man's Land.

Cassie, six inches could have saved the Six Million.

Cassie, they say Hitler once enjoyed the company of Jews.

How then can they speak so blithely of fate, destiny and procreative sex?

Damn the future, Cassie; dam it up. Give me handjobs, blowjobs and anal sex. Offer me your armpits, you wanton fuckers. Let us lacerate the sides of virgins with gaping wounds and fuck so hard we shake God from His heaven. Let us feast on snot, blood, pus and sperm; only save your tears for vinegar, to serve to martyrs who thirst.

•

'That's a love letter?' he says.

'It's a Karlsson love letter.'

'Doesn't know much about women, does he?'

Debs opens the patio door and pokes her head out. 'Hey, Hemingway,' she calls, 'your daughter's got a poopy nappy. Chop-chop.'

I wave to her. 'Gotta go,' I tell Billy. 'Family day. We're taking a spin out to Drumcliffe for lunch, it's time Rosie visited Yeats's grave.'

He drops the shades, gives me a one-eyed wink. 'Cast a cold eye,' he says. It's hard to say if he means his Newman-blue or the sucked-out prune.

I hold up the *Sermo Vulgus* excerpt. 'So what do you want to do with it?'

'I don't like it as a love letter,' he says.

'I can kill it if you want.'

'See if we can't work it in somewhere else,' he says. 'Somewhere it doesn't have anything to do with Cassie.'

'Will do. See you tomorrow.'

'On Saturday?'

'Oh, right. Monday so.'

'Cool,' he says. 'I could do with a sleep-in tomorrow anyway. All these early mornings are killing me.'

'Try having a kid,' I say. 'You'll know all about early mornings then.'

He glances at me then, something hawkish in his eye.

'That'd be up to you, really,' he says, 'wouldn't it?'

'You want Cassie to get pregnant?'

'I think it might be good for us.'

'She's on the pill, though, isn't she?'

'She is now. Maybe you could swap her pills for folic acid or something.'

'Without letting her know?'

'Sometimes you have to do the wrong thing for the right reason,' he says. 'Isn't that what the best stories are about anyway?'

•

Buddhist monks have this thing going on where they construct complex mosaics comprised of thousands of precisely delineated sections of coloured dust. It can take years. When they're finished they sweep the whole thing into a corner and start again.

I appreciate this perversity while I mop the tiles in the hospital corridors. By the time you reach the far end of the corridor, people have trampled all over the point from whence you came. Ashes unto ashes, dust unto dust. The priests say this so as not to scare the horses. It would be more correct to say ashes *from* ashes, dust *from* dust.

It would be even more correct to say nothing at all and let people decide for themselves.

People bring mud into the hospital on their shoes. They carry in dust, dog-shit, germs, saliva, acid rain, carbon monoxide and blackened chewing gum. But they're not allowed to smoke in the overflow car park.

I ask about the possibility of wearing a facemask while I'm mopping, so I won't inhale the second-hand pestilence of human perambulation. Because I am a porter this is regarded as facetious insubordination. Only surgeons get to wear facemasks, although the official line is that this is for the patient's benefit as opposed to that of any surgeon concerned about the invisible dangers wafting up out of a diseased and freshly sliced human being.

A man is standing in the middle of the tiles, so I have to mop around him. His shoulders are slack. There's a looseness to his stance that suggests his elastic has stretched a little too far this time.

'Excuse me,' I say. 'Could I ask you to move to one side, please?'

But he turns to face me. His eyes are huge, round and too dry. He says, hoarsely, 'My daughter just died.'

'I'm sorry to hear that,' I say. This would be hypocritical if it weren't true, but I find his words offensive. I wonder why people always seem to think their pain is interesting. I wonder why people only share their pain these days. If the guy was standing in the middle of the carpet munching on a bag of toffees, it would never occur to him to offer a toffee to the guy vacuuming the carpet.

'She was eight years old,' he says.

'Think of her as a mosaic,' I say. 'Think of your daughter as an amazingly complex mosaic who had become as beautiful as it was possible to be. Imagine that she's been swept to one side so that she can begin to be formed into another beautiful mosaic. Maybe it's already started. Go upstairs to the maternity ward, you might even see her smile, that twinkle in her eye. Get there while the new mother is still fretting about how long it should take the maternal bond to kick in and maybe you'll get lucky. But she might be a boy this time, so think outside the box. And can I ask you to step to one side, please? I've had an official warning.'

He stares at me, uncomprehending. Then the round dry eyes begin to water. Tears roll down his pudgy cheeks. He shudders, gasps, and then he seems to fold in half. He bawls.

'Nothing lasts forever,' I say. 'These days even agony has a sell-by date.'

But he's not listening.

Cassie rings and asks me to rent a DVD on the way home. We snuggle up on the couch, sip some wine, smoke a joint, watch the movie.

'You know what's really scary?' Cassie says. 'That a shark could take stuff personally.'

'Apart from a wayward meteor,' I agree, 'being stalked by a shark is the worst of all possible news.'

'Like, really hating you.'

'See, that's where *Jaws* falls down. Sharks are older than hate.'

She frowns. I say, 'Hate is unique to mankind, which has been knocking about for roughly a million years. The shark's been around for four hundred million years.'

Cassie is stoned and thus intrigued. 'No shit,' she says.

'Seriously. And it's hardly changed in all that time.'

'How do they know?'

'Subterranean architecture.'

'There's actual buildings?' She sniggers. 'Like, shark museums?'

'The fossil record.'

I tell her that the true history of the planet is a gallery in stone. From the fossil record to the Parthenon's columns, the perfect math of the pyramids to the geometry at Cuzco, the molten rock that trapped Pompeii to the cuneiform etched in the base of pillars. 'If you want to be remembered, Cass, work with stone. Moses didn't come down off Sinai with commandments daubed on papyrus.'

'True.'

'Think of all the great civilisations. They're cast in stone, their prejudice and their buildings. The Coliseum. The Sphinx. Newgrange. The Acropolis. Angkor Wat. Macchu Picchu. Knossos. Stone upon stone upon stone.'

'That's amazing,' Cassie says, rolling her eyes as she gets up. 'I'm making a decaff. Want one?'

'It's only a matter of time before sharks learn to build bridges,' I warn. But the kettle is boiling and she can't hear me. Besides, she's not listening.

•

'That's better,' he says. 'Although it's not exactly Jane Austen, is it?'

'Maybe it'd sound more like Jane Austen,' I say, 'if it was supposed to sound like Jane Austen.'

'Hey, no offence meant.'

'Listen, I've been thinking. If Karlsson is changing, the way you want him to, then his relationship with Cassie is bound to be different too. Right?'

'That's what I'm kind of hoping for, yeah.'

'So maybe you should write all the Cassie stuff,' I say.

'Really? You wouldn't mind?'

'Not in the slightest. Go for it.'

'I might just do that. Listen,' he says, encouraged by the olive branch, 'I've been thinking too, about the hospital.'

'What about it?'

'Things have got a lot worse since you wrote the first draft. Super-bugs, the two-tier health system, all this . . . They're misdiagnosing ultra-sounds now, you know that?'

'So I hear.'

One thing I'm impressed with is Billy's dedication to character. He appears to be genuinely angry about what's happening to the health service, its entirely appropriate death by a thousand cuts. Except, as Billy says, they're using a machete instead of a scalpel.

If they continue to follow their own logic and momentum, he reckons, then by the end of the EU's austerity programme they'll be funnelling patients in one end of a rented Japanese whaling ship and feeding the resulting product to those subsisting on what's left of the dole.

'Maybe you should go for a recce,' he says, nodding up at the hospital on the hill, 'spend a day with me. We'll get you a porter's uniform, you can just stroll around soaking it up.'

'Won't anyone object?'

'Not if you keep your head down. I mean, don't go wandering into theatre to try out brain surgery or anything.'

'No, I mean . . . You're still, uh, working there?'

'Sure.' He pats his pockets, comes up with his plastic ID. 'Card-carrying union member, *c'est moi.*'

I'd been wondering where he goes after our early morning sessions, how he fills his days. But by the looks of things, redrafting the Karlsson character is the least of Billy's commitment to the cause.

'I don't want to invade your space, Billy.'

'Not a problem. I think you'd find it really useful.'

'Yeah, okay. When?'

'Tomorrow morning. I start at nine, but if you get there about eight-thirty, the porters generally have a quick toke before they get into it.'

•

I stroll past the nurses' station on the third floor carrying a mop and bucket. The trick is to hide a full dustpan the night before and empty the sweepings into a bucket of water first thing the next day. This is good for an entire morning's aimless wandering.

The ward sister calls to me from the station, beckons me across. I put the bucket down with a workmanlike clank and march over.

'Karlsson,' she says, 'would you mind tucking in your shirt?'

She's an attractive woman for forty-plus, still working the hair, the eyebrows.

'Mopping's hot work,' I say, wiping my dry brow with the back of my hand. 'This place is like a sauna.'

'I appreciate that,' she says, 'but we need to maintain standards.'

What she means is, we're flying on elastic bands and bent paper clips here, so don't give anyone a reason to think about what's really going on. The rabbit hole lurks in the gap between a belt and an untucked shirt. A straight line exists between a flapping shirt-tail and a class action suit for negligence. An untucked shirt is a hook for the weight of public opinion and crumbling facades can least afford a slovenly dress code.

I reach around to tuck the shirt tidy. Her eyes flare. She glances up and down the corridor. 'Not *here*,' she hisses. 'Can't you go to the bathroom to do it?'

'Sure thing.'

41

I walk away. She calls me back and points. 'The bucket, Karlsson.'

'Right.'

This sluices five whole minutes off the map.

I slouch down the hall to the men's room, lock the cubicle door, open the window and smoke half a jay. Then I go on the nod. A pounding on the cubicle door wakes me. It's my supervisor. He sniffs the air suspiciously.

'You were supposed to be up on the fifth floor twenty minutes ago,' he says. 'What are you doing here?'

'Orders,' I say. 'The ward sister told me to fix my shirt.'

His eyes narrow. 'Okay,' he says. 'But get up to the fifth floor. You're late already.'

I climb the stairs, untuck my shirt and push through the double doors onto the fifth floor. The ward sister calls me over to the nurses' station. I put my bucket down with a workmanlike clank and wipe my dry brow with the back of my hand.

'What can I help you with today?' I say.

•

'Well?' he says.

We're in the stairwell between the fourth and fifth floors.

'I don't remember you being this polite to people in the first draft,' I say.

'Softly-softly catchee monkey,' he says, tapping the side of his nose. A door opens above us. 'We shouldn't be seen together,' he says, picking up his bucket. 'Meet me in the car park at five, I'll give you a lift home.'

Karlsson rode a motorcycle. Billy rides a moped. He reckons it's easier on gas, more environmentally friendly.

'Don't I need a helmet?' I say, climbing on behind him.

'Not unless we crash.' He revs up and we take off but there's a bottleneck at the eastern exit. A two-car collision, a Passat wedged at a right angle in a crumpled Fiesta, nose buried deep into the driver's side. There's a cop trying to direct traffic. My first thought is for my lack of helmet but the cop has better things to do.

Still, I slide off the moped and stand beside Billy. When he cuts the engine we hear the screams.

'The incidence of accidents outside hospitals is five times that of any other public building,' Billy says. 'Anyone who works in a hospital knows to take it slow coming to work.

'Take that guy, the one whose daughter just died. He's a hazard. Reflexes dull, his peripheral vision full of cherubic faces. All he can think is how he wishes it was him laid out. Except in the back of his mind he's agonising about how he has to ring his mother-in-law and confess that he never imagined his life could be such a colossal failure.'

There's an abrupt *waaa-rooo* from behind. Everyone turns to watch an ambulance inch past the stalled traffic, two wheels up on the verge. A young fair-haired priest riding shotgun, tense, grey-faced.

'This guy,' Billy says, nodding down the hill, 'he pulls up to the junction here. He edges out, maybe indicating, maybe not, and for a split-second his hand-eye coordination locks into a memory of pushing a swing. He hears the squeals of a child. Squeals of delight segue into a screech of brakes.

'Crunch,' he says.

The paramedics swarm the vehicles. Hoarse shouts relay orders. The priest, uncertain, hangs back. If he jumps in too soon, he's a nuisance. If he leaves it too late he's a waste of space.

'Someone loses a leg,' Billy says. 'A son loses an eye. A mother gets paralysed from the waist down. A father dies, maybe even the father who was on his way back in to comfort the mother fretting over the unnatural lack of a maternal bond with her new daughter.

'Such things,' he says, 'are spoken of in hushed tones and called tragedies, which is shorthand for the entirely avoidable consequences of human fallibility. Such things prompt people to wonder if God really exists.' He shrugs. 'Every cloud has its silver lining.'

By now Billy's monologue has heads turning in our direction.

'Keep it down,' I mutter.

But he cranks it up a notch. 'The priests,' he declaims, 'say that such things are sent to test us. If true, this is a cruelty so pure it verges on the harsh beauty of an Arctic sunset.

'Could any god really be so insecure? "Hey folks, your kid is dead – do you still love me?"'

The frowns and disapproving glares become audible as shushes and hisses.

'A question like that,' Billy tells the nearest hisser, 'should cause its asker to spontaneously combust in a shame-fuelled fireball.' He shakes his head. 'Except priests deal in shame. They're emotional pornographers. Priests are up to their oxters in the pus-filled boil of your fear, groping for the maggots they placed there before your birth. The concept of Original Sin,' he says, 'is an evil so pure it verges on genius.'

A man whose fists are already clenched turns and strides towards us, his stiff-legged demeanour leaving no doubt as to his intentions. Billy slips his helmet back on, flips up the visor.

'Even the paedophiles,' he crows, 'wait for the child to leave the womb.'

The Polish security guard on the gate barely glances at my ID as I badge us back in, although, being an officious jobsworth with little else to do, he does ask that we dismount from the moped, switch off the engine and walk it up the long drive, for fear of disturbing the early-evening still.

'We should write about him,' I say as we trudge up the tree-lined avenue, midges off the lake dive-bombing us like so many tiny Stukas.

'The security guard?'

'Maybe not him specifically. But the idea that an artists' retreat needs a security guard, to make sure the hoi polloi doesn't get in among the artists and infect them with any kind of reality.'

'Maybe he's there to keep the artists in,' Billy grins. 'Maybe artists' retreats are all a government plot to keep the thinkers away from the proles, so there's no danger of any sparks flying.'

'Billy,' I say, 'there's a four-piece interpretive dance troupe using one of the studio spaces, they're writing a free-form jazz ballet for trees. I'm having a hard time seeing those guys storming any barricades.'

'Cassie has her book club tonight,' he says. 'Fancy brainstorming a jazz ballet on how the barricades come to life, reconstitute themselves as trees and march against the fascist lackeys?'

'Not tonight,' I say. 'Debs is out with the girls, it's someone's birthday. Anyway, I'm babysitting.'

Billy finds this hilarious.

'What?' I say. 'You think I can't take care of Rosie?'

'It's not that,' he says. 'Just the phrase, "babysitting", it's something teenage girls do when they can't get a date on Friday night. I'm pretty sure a parent doesn't babysit.'

'So what would you call it?'

'I dunno. "Being a father"?'

Billy's niggles are starting to piss me off, especially when I have the guilt to deal with, the fact that Debs isn't just working all her normal hours while I'm on sabbatical, she's also doing most of the parenting with Rosie too.

'And suddenly you're this expert on being a father,' I say.

'Hey, there's no need for—'

'Come back to me when you've changed your first nappy,' I say, 'and then we'll get pedantic about the language of parenting.'

'Jesus Christ, you're a moody bugger.' He swings a leg across the moped, starts the engine, revs it into a thin whine. 'Enjoy your babysitting,' he sneers, then wheels around and clatters away down the avenue.

Debs is pacing the floor when I get inside the chalet, Rosie on her shoulder and already tucked into her Igglepiggle baby-gro. The little girl is rosy-cheeked but her eyes are dull.

'Everything okay?' I say.

'More or less,' Deb says. 'She's been doing a lot of coughing, though. I think she might have picked up a bug in crèche.'

'Have you given her anything?'

'Some Tixylix, yeah. But I don't want to overdo it.'

'She'll be grand,' I say. 'You go ahead, I'll take care of it from here.'

She nods uncertainly.

'Look,' I say, 'you've earned tonight, and you're entitled to enjoy it without worrying. So just go.'

She hands Rosie across, kisses the crown of her head. 'Ring me later,' she says, 'just so I know she's okay.'

'I'll text you,' I say, 'but it'll be fine. Go.'

I get Rosie settled on the couch and make soup, a sandwich, get out that day's pages and a green pen. By nine-thirty Rosie's cough has worsened and there's an audible wheeze from her chest. I ring my mother.

'She's already had some cough syrup,' I say, 'so I don't want to overdose her on that.'

'Would you like me to come over?' she says.

'No, you're grand. I just want to ease her coughing.'

'Try some warm honey,' she says. 'That worked with all of you. Do you have any honey over there? I can—'

'You're fine. There's some in the fridge.'

'Well, let me know how it goes.'

'I will.'

I put a spoonful of honey in a pot, warm it on the stove. Add a little milk. Then, because Rosie is getting fractious, the cough hacking her awake whenever she manages to doze off, I break open a sleeping pill and carefully measure out a quarter of the dosage. This I stir into the milk-and-honey.

By ten-thirty Rosie is sleeping peacefully in my arms. No cough, and I can only hear the underlying wheeze if I put my ear to her chest. I tap 'All quiet on the Western front' into the phone, text that to Debs and then my mother.

Today's pages lie on the coffee table undisturbed, the green pen nowhere to be seen.

My line for today comes courtesy of Cyril Connolly: *There is no more sombre enemy of good art than the pram in the hall.*

Billy arrives in contrite form, bearing blueberry muffins as a token of reconciliation.

'You're right,' he says. 'I know nothing about being a father. And anyway, I'm pretty sure there's no blueprint. Everyone does it their own way, right?'

'Don't worry about it,' I mumble through a mouthful of muffin.

'Are you sure?'

''Course, yeah.' I stand, pick up the cafetière. 'Want a fresh drop?'

'Still working on this one,' he says, holding up his steaming mug. 'So what is it?'

'What's what?'

'Why you're buzzing around like a blue-arsed fly. I mean, plates for the muffins? Fresh coffee two minutes after the last pot? What's going on?'

'Ach,' I say, slumping back into the chair, 'it's nothing.'

'Is Rosie alright?'

'Yeah, she's grand.' I tell him about her wheezy chest, how Debs stayed off the wine the night before, swung around just after midnight to pick up Rosie. 'Then she was up at the crack this morning, trying to get in ahead of the posse at the doctor's before getting Rosie to crèche, and still trying to make it into work on time.'

'Busy-busy,' Billy says.

'Exactly. Meanwhile, I'm sitting here . . .' I gesture at the table, the muffins and cafetière, the pages a white dazzle under the warm sun.

'A kept man,' Billy says.

'Not far off it.'

'Don't beat yourself up,' he says. 'It's only for six weeks, right?'

'It's not that. Well, it is, but it's not just that.'

'So what is it?'

I sip some coffee. It tastes like wet ash. 'Debs reckons that if I'm going to do this, I need to *do* it. Like, no distractions. No phone, no TV, no Twitter or email. Books, okay, but no Kindle. Music, sure, but no radio.'

'And I'm a distraction.'

'Well, obviously. But that's not the issue.'

Billy places his pen on top of his pages. 'Go on,' he says. 'I'm listening.'

'Last night, when she called around, Debs was saying they were talking again about public sector cuts yesterday, slicing out twenty thousand jobs, maybe more.'

'I heard that, yeah. Although not from front-line services.'

There's something smug in his tone that makes me want to ask him if he really thinks that porters are providing a front-line service. Instead I tell him that Debs is public sector. 'And she isn't front-line.'

'Shit.'

'Yeah. So this morning I turn on the radio, *Morning Ireland*, to see what the story is. First thing I hear is Portugal's up the spout,

and some moron's raving about how we need to burn the bond-holders, default now rather than wait until we fall off the cliff.'
'About fucking time.' He rubs his hands gleefully. 'Burn the fuckers to the ground,' he declares, 'wipe them off the map. Absolute fucking zero, man.'
'You're talking like a Shinner, Billy. Grow up.'
He nods. 'When I grow up,' he says in a childish falsetto, 'I want to be a German banker, loan some fuckwits a hundred billion without even checking to see if they can pay it back.'
'It's not that simple, though, is it? What if it all goes nuclear, the euro goes into meltdown? What happens then?'
'Fucked if I know. Another Marshall Plan?'
'America doesn't have a pot to piss in, Billy, and Standard & Poor is on Obama's case. Meanwhile, I've a baby to feed.'
'Sure,' he says. 'Except your way, she starves slow. My way, she starves fast.' He shrugs. 'Deborah was right. You really shouldn't listen to the radio.'
'Wouldn't matter if I didn't. It's there all the time, this static in the back of your head, how you're not just stealing time away from your family, you're stealing actual money. Like, it's not cheap here.'
'True enough,' he says. 'But then, you wouldn't be here if you couldn't afford it.'
'I can't. Debs is the one paying for it.'
'Fair play,' he says.
'And it's not just that it's costing us for me to be here. It's a double whammy, because I'm on sabbatical, so I'm not earning.'
'Okay,' he says. 'But if Deborah is cool with it . . .'
'See, this is the thing. I don't know if she is.'
'From what I've seen, she wouldn't be long telling you if she was pissed off.'
'Yeah, maybe.'
'You want my advice,' he says, popping home a morsel of muffin, 'you need to blank this shit out. I mean, no offence, but you're

turning into a miserable sod. You'll be blocked before you know it.'

'See, it'd be one thing if it was proper crime fiction I'm meant to be writing, but Harcourt want a comedy caper. Like, how's anyone supposed to take comedy seriously when these bastards are legally blagging the country blind?'

'Jesus. You're blocked already, aren't you?'

'No, I'm not blocked. It just seems immoral, y'know? I'm stealing time, I'm throwing good money after bad . . .'

'Keep it up. You'll be Minister for Finance before you know where you are.'

'Get real, Billy. These fuckers are screwing us for a hundred billion, give or take a few quid. Meanwhile,' I nod at the manuscript on the table, 'I'm redrafting a story called *Crime Always Pays*, five or six punters running around scamming a couple of hundred grand off each other. Like, who's going to give a shit about a couple of hundred grand when the government's stealing seven billion a year and people are dying on hospital trolleys?'

'It's a farce,' he concedes.

'See, this is my whole point. It's not only a farce, it's beyond bloody parody. You *couldn't* make it up.'

'So dump it,' he says. 'Write what you know, isn't that what they say? Kill the comedy, write a serious one about the hundred billion heist.'

'Can't. The contract's for two books, and *CAP*'s the sequel. And I've already been paid, so I need to hit the deadline. If I don't they'll be looking for half the advance back.'

'Which I'm presuming is already spent.'

'It just about paid my taxes last year. And with Debs paying for all this,' I gesture around at the manicured gardens, the goldfish pond, the chalets, 'I need to focus, get the job done.'

'So you want to pack this thing in, you and me.'

'See, that's the kicker. Whenever I'm writing comedy, all I can think of is job cuts, what it's costing Debs, all this. When I'm doing the you-me stuff, it's never an issue.'

'Redrafts are always easier,' he says.

'Except *Crime Always Pays*, that's a redraft too.'

We listen in silence to the pond's fountain tinkling away. Eventually Billy sighs, slaps his palms on his thighs. 'I think you're being a bit harsh on yourself,' he says. 'If you need someone to bounce off, to read your *CAP* stuff, give me a shout.'

'Appreciate it. I might just do that.'

'Do you want me to . . . ?' He reaches for the manuscript.

'No, that's okay. Not yet, anyway. It's still early days.'

'Ah.' He winks, taps the side of his nose. 'Say no more.'

He means well, but as always I find the conspiratorial undertone irritating: the whiff of gunpowder, unsayable things muttered in code.

'I'll let you crack on it with it,' he says. He gets up and stretches. 'And listen, any time you need a chat,' he says, 'blow off some steam, I'm always here. And stay away from that radio.' He winks. 'That Aine Lawlor, she'd mess with any man's head. Am I right?'

I generally head for the desk inside once Billy leaves. Today, though, still antsy, I make some fresh coffee and go back out to the decking, roll a smoke and watch as the unusually warm sun turns the hospital into a blazing bonfire on the hill. Seems appropriate, somehow. Makes it a beacon of sorts. In the early days I'd turn my back on it, the way it loomed over the valley like the gloomy ruin of some mediaeval castle, all that sickness and death and those tiny little tragedies that punctuate each day like so many commas, slipped into the wider narrative to allow us time to breathe, to reflect, to dwell on our own fleeting mortality, all that self-flagellating rot.

It's grown on me, though. The hospital, in concept at least, represents all that's good about the world. Our willingness to care for the sick and dying, the most vulnerable, regardless of caste or creed.

Mostly, though, I like it because I'm sitting here in a sun-splashed garden, listening to the fountain sing its little heart out and sipping good coffee, a long, long way from all that disease and infection and those splintered bones and breaking hearts atop the hill.

Hospitals are like brothels or shopping centres, in that you're content to know they're there for those desperate or wounded enough to avail of their illusions.

Perhaps that's why hospitals are built as predominantly glass structures. Because we know in our heart of hearts they're bubbles, too delicate to probe with any degree of rigour for fear they'll explode and take our only pure dream with them in their going.

•

This morning Cassie is hung-over and grouchy. She says she wants us to move on to the next level. I interpret this as laziness. She wants something new but she isn't prepared to go out and find it. The next best thing is to reinvent yours truly, I, Karlsson.

'Okay,' I say. 'But what does that involve? Should I get rid of the motorcycle and buy a car?'

She shakes her head. She sits on the couch cross-legged, eating Rice Krispies and watching Tornadoes roar in off the sea to strafe some dusty coastal town.

'Where are we going, K?' she says. She says this with a single Rice Krispie stuck to her cheek. It bobs up and down as she speaks. 'I mean, where are we really *going?*'

Cassie labours under the delusion that all journeys have desti-nations. This may or may not be a vestigial memory of our evolu-tionary forebears, nomads to whom the whole world was home. Today, locked into the concept of home as blocks of concrete and brick, we have become emotional nomads. Hence soap operas and prostitution. Hence the Next Level. Hence the non-specific but irrepressible desire for change. Motion mutates into emotion.

This is not necessarily a good thing. History is littered with evolutionary cul-de-sacs. An emotionally aware species will lack the ruthlessness necessary to dispense with its old, sick and incapable. It will undermine itself in its efforts to protect those who cannot protect themselves. An emotionally aware species will expend valuable energy keeping the devil away from the hindmost.

Every civilisation is undone by its own logic. To wit: 9/11.

Empathy is a carcinogen. Hospitals are interpretive centres along the highway to extinction. I, Karlsson, hospital porter, am a parasite on the underbelly of a carcinogen.

Cassie watches war highlights while eating breakfast. I watch the Rice Krispie bob up and down on her cheek as she chews and try to think of one person who performs an indispensable function on behalf of the social organism to which we belong. I cannot think of a single person. This means everyone I know is less useful than the average sweat pore. This is not a pleasant thought at six-thirty in the morning.

Neither is the prospect of change.

'Cassie,' I say, 'the Great White shark is so perfectly adapted to its environment that it doesn't need to change. If we could communicate the concept of hospitals to the Great White, it would laugh, grow legs and invade.'

Cassie holds the cereal bowl in both hands, tilts back her head and drains the milk. This does not disturb the Rice Krispie stuck to her cheek.

'This is exactly the kind of crap I'm talking about,' she says. 'Jesus, K – I need more from life than sharks growing legs. And tuck your fucking shirt in for once, you look like something out of *The Little Rascals.*'

She flounces out to the kitchen. I don't mention the Rice Krispie. She will find it herself when she checks the mirror on the way out to work, and she will remove it then. This may be as close to self-actualisation as Cassie will ever come.

My line for today is: Our feminine friends have this in common with Bonaparte, that they think they can succeed where everyone else has failed. (Albert Camus, *The Fall*)

•

'More sharks,' Billy says. 'And the Krispie thing – I wouldn't have not mentioned that to her. What if she hadn't checked the mirror on the way out?'

'Even nuns check the mirror on the way out, Billy.'

'Fair go,' he says. 'But listen – the girl's restless. Why wouldn't I ask her, y'know, how she'd feel about having a baby?'

'You want to?'

'I think the time is right. It's just a feeling, but . . .'

'You'll never know for sure, man. At some point you'll have to take that leap of faith.'

'Maybe, yeah.'

'So go for it. If it's not working out, you could always wipe it.'

He frowns. 'Wipe it?'

'That's one option, sure.'

He's dubious, his lower lip pushed out. 'Dunno about that,' he says. 'And even leaving me out of it, I don't think Cassie's the type who'd be able to follow through.'

'I don't know if being a particular type has anything to do with it. It's more you find yourself in a situation, a set of circumstances with limited options, and it just so happens that it's the lesser of two evils.'

'Killing a baby,' he says, 'is the lesser of two evils.'

'It's a figure of speech, yeah. "Kill your babies".'

'That's one seriously ugly figure of speech.'

'Well, it's not a pretty thing to have to do.'

'You've done it?'

'Sure, plenty of times.'

'*Plenty* of times?'

'Of course. Any writer'll tell you that it's a vital part of the—
What? What's wrong?'

Billy, having shoved back his chair, standing now, just shrugs.
'Listen,' he says, 'it's up to you how you live your life, but I don't
appreciate your tone.'

'My tone?'

'Maybe it's different for you now you have Rosie, but talking
that way about abortion, it's just not healthy.'

'Abortion? Billy, I'm talking about redrafting, taking out the
things you think you like best. "Killing your babies", they call it. It's
a figure of *speech*.'

'To you,' he says. 'Except in this situation, this *set of circumstances*, killing babies means, y'know, killing a baby.'

I'm thinking that this is a bit rich from a guy who's planning to
wipe out a whole hospital.

'Look, Billy, I'm only offering advice here. You're the one who's
writing the Cassie stuff now, so it's your call as to whether she gets
pregnant, and what happens after that.'

'Okay,' he says, 'but what if we make Cassie pregnant and she
doesn't want the baby, and I'm the one has to kill it off?'

'Then you go back and redraft, make it so she was never
pregnant.'

'And everyone pretends like this baby never existed.'

'It never *did* exist. It doesn't exist now, does it?'

'No,' he says, although I can hear a note of uncertainty.

'Billy,' I say, 'you haven't made Cassie pregnant already, have
you?'

'Don't be such a fucking pill.'

'Alright. Well look, here's a suggestion. Why don't you try to kill
off someone else, we'll say we don't need him, or her, and you write

him or her out. See if you can do it, and if you can, how you feel after. How's that?'

'Who?'

'I don't know. You're the one doing it, you choose.'

He mulls it over. 'How about Austin?'

'Austin?'

'He's one of the porters, he only gets a few lines anyway.'

'Yeah, okay. So long as he's not supposed to do anything important later on.'

'That lad's a stoner,' Billy says. 'A waste of space. He won't be missed.'

•

Tommo says, 'Kill your babies.'

To be precise, he croaks this through a lungful of exhaled smoke. Tommo is into the late afternoon leg of a wake-'n'-bake, horizontal on the couch, the drapes pulled. Killer Tommo twiddles his controller, sending his POV avatar roaming through the airport on the TV, blasting away at enemy soldiers and cowering civilians alike.

I advance into the apartment until I enter his field of vision. He pauses the game, smiles up at me sloppily. 'Hey, K. How's she hanging?'

He offers a hit off his joint. I decline. 'Word to the wise, Tommo,' I say. 'Frankie was looking for you all morning.'

'Kill your Frankies.'

'No, really. He was seriously pissed. He had to watch the monitors himself. There was no relief cover, Austin rang in sick too. Frankie was up and down the stairs all day.'

'Kill 'em all, let God sort 'em out.'

'I'm just letting you know, he was seriously pissed.'

Tommo frowns. He struggles into a half-sitting position. 'K,' he says, 'who the fuck let you in?'

'Austin.' I jerk a thumb at Austin, who is sitting in the armchair nearest the TV, sucking on a hookah. Austin gives us a thumbs-up, then exhales and subsides into the armchair, bong tube a-dangle.

'Yeah, well,' Tommo says, 'now you're here, shut the fuck up about Frankie. Take a hit or take a hike. But go easy,' he says, 'it's pure Thai.' He takes a deep draw on the joint, beckons me closer. I understand he is offering a blowback, so as to ease me in gently. I kneel down as he sits forward, until our lips are almost touching. Then he exhales into my open mouth. 'You might want to ring in sick for tomorrow before you start in proper,' he says. 'Trust me, it'll be too much hassle after the first draw.'

Tommo sounds far too lucid for this to be true but the smoke floods my lungs as if they were those of an infant, new and pure. Though smooth going down, the blowback causes my brain to pulse like a mushroom cloud. The effect is one of immediate bliss swiftly followed by gut-sucking paranoia. Then a wonderfully mellow sense of sensory disorientation.

Acute dehydration ensues. I go to the kitchen for water. I come back from the kitchen thirsty, having somehow failed to locate either sink or fridge. Austin appears to be comatose in the armchair. Tommo says something about how every language ever invented has been a failed attempt to discover a means of expression by which mankind might communicate the full extent of its ignorance. He says 'kill your babies' is a metaphor for eradicating metaphors. He says it's an irony, rather than a tragedy, that most people experience their lives as metaphors for how they would have preferred their lives to be. He says the real tragedy is that most people already know this.

Tommo says lots of things but I'm not really listening. Irony isn't half as clever when you're thirsty.

People, you can carve this one in stone: you will seek in vain for irony in the vicinity of a cacti patch.

•

'Not bad,' I say. 'I like that you're not diving straight into it, have Austin walk off a roof stoned, thinking he can fly.'

'It's useless,' he says, then tries to light the filter end of a cigarette.

'I wouldn't say that. It might need a bit of tightening up here and there, but mostly it's—'

'I was on a bit of a buzz last night,' he says, 'after writing that. So I brought it up with Cass, about having a baby.'

'She's not into it?'

'For one, I'm a hospital porter. She says it's not the job, it's the salary, but I don't know.'

'You need a promotion?'

'It's not just that. She says she's not having any babies until she gets married. And she says she's in no hurry, she's only twenty-six.'

'Women are having babies later these days, Billy. That's natural.'

'She's thirty-one, man. She *thinks* she's twenty-six, but she was twenty-six back when you wrote the first draft. And if she waits another five years, she could be getting into all sorts of complications.'

'Shit.'

'Yeah.'

'Why don't we just make her thirty-one?' I say. 'Get her clock ticking.'

'And wipe five years off her life?' He shakes his head. 'What we could do,' he says, 'is just swap her pill for folic acid, like I said.'

'I already told you, I'm not doing that.'

'Why not?'

'It's immoral. I wouldn't do it to Debs, I'm not doing it to Cassie.'

'Hey, you look out for Deborah, I'll look out for Cass.'

'And getting her pregnant on the sly – that's looking out for her?'

'I'm trying to get a life going here, man. The means justify, y'know?'

'Who am I talking to here?' I say. 'Billy or Karlsson?'

'That's fucking low,' he says, stubbing out the smoke on the table. 'That's bang out of order.'

'You tell Cassie about this conversation,' I say, 'and then ask her who she thinks is out of order.'

He leans in, taking off his tinted shades. I try to ignore the eye socket, the sucked-out prune. 'I only want what's best for her,' he says, straining to keep his tone civil.

'She's told you what's best for her.'

'Except she doesn't have all the information,' he says.

'So why don't you tell her?'

'What – that she's not real?'

'You seem to be coping okay.'

He stiffens, then slumps back in the chair. 'You know what it is?' he says, a sneer brewing. 'I'm real enough, alright. But you don't have the imagination to believe in Cassie.'

'Maybe that's your job,' I say. 'I mean, you're the one who wanted to write the Cassie parts, right? How's that working out for you?'

He savours that like it's fresh-cut lemon. 'Smug bastard,' he says, 'aren't you?'

'I thought we were cutting out the swearing.'

'If you're not good enough to do this,' he says, 'just say so and stop wasting my time.'

'I'm no Lawrence Durrell,' I say, 'but I'm good enough to write you.'

He nods, then stands up. 'Maybe I'll go home and write a story about you,' he says, 'fuck around with your life. How'd you like them apples?'

'I'll rent a tux,' I say. 'Booker night is always black tie, isn't it?'

No Billy this morning. A pity, with the garden coming into full bloom now, the early morning sun lying across the lawn in fat yellow diagonal stripes.

Oh well. Back to the grindstone . . .

No Billy for three days running now. Maybe he isn't coming back. Maybe he's holed up in some garret, feverishly rewriting my life, consulting the story of Moses and Pharaoh for inspiration.

Is this how God felt when Einstein started doodling in the Patents Office? No wonder He struck Hawking down.

•

In brief, the story of Prometheus is this: he stole fire from the gods, gave it to mankind, and was eternally tortured for his troubles. Thus he was the first great martyr to intercede with the gods on man's behalf.

This simplistic version of events allows us to bask in the vanity that has plagued the latter part of our miserable history. That a Titan should defy the gods on our behalf is in itself proof of our exalted status in the universe. At least, it does in that part of the universe administered by Titans and gods, although in doing so we ignore the inconvenient fact that man was merely a pawn in a deadly game being played by Prometheus and Zeus, and that the gift of fire was simply a spiteful aftershock in the wake of a cosmic civil war.

A question or two:

Now that we no longer worship the Greek gods of Olympus, is Prometheus still being tortured?

Does the vulture still tear at his liver?

Does he still freeze every night, chained to the rock, as his liver grows back, or has his version of eternity come to an end simply because we have forgotten his sacrifice?

Has Prometheus's version of eternity slipped out of our version into another, like a stream draining underground?

Incidentally, we should probably note in passing that Prometheus was not staked out in sand or subjected to repeated drownings, nor nailed to a tree. He was chained to stone.

We should also note that, previous to the gift of fire, Prometheus had bestowed on mankind architecture, astronomy, mathematics, navigation, medicine and metallurgy. The smug narcissists who believe that we are the Chosen Ones by virtue of our innate intelligence should bear in mind that we couldn't even devise a hot spark or two from that little lot.

Finally, Zeus had his revenge on mankind by dispatching the beautiful Pandora to earth with a jar containing the Spites that might plague mankind: Old Age, Labour, Sickness, Insanity, Vice and Passion. There she opened the jar, freeing the Spites to roam the land, shutting it again just before Hope escaped.

Thus, or so the story goes, despite everything, even the malevolent intentions of the gods in general and Zeus in particular, mankind will always have Hope to sustain him. Which would be fine, except that Hope was one of the Spites and her full name was, and remains, Delusive Hope.

We may no longer believe in Zeus. But Zeus believes in us.

•

Friday morning, still no sign of Billy, I decide that I've earned a weekend off. The idea is to surprise Debs, take Rosie off her hands, give Debs a couple of badly needed sleep-ins.

That evening, by the time I get home, I'm already aching. A twanging in my guts. The desk is a black hole. Even at this distance it exerts a remorseless gravity.

But I won't be sucked in. Not this weekend.

I sneak around the side of the house to find Debs in the back garden, hugging Rosie tight as she rocks back and forth on the patio chair.

She shrieks when I touch her shoulder. Actually shrieks.

Then she starts babbling.

'Take a deep breath,' I say. 'Slow down.'

'She was in the *shed*,' she wails.

'Who, Rosie?'

'I had her down on her play-mat doing her stretching exercises when mum rang. But the monitor was there, right *there*, so I should have heard her moving. But when I went back in she was gone. Ohmigod, she was *gone*.'

I am as terrified by her frantic tone as by what she is saying. Debs is not a woman to panic unnecessarily.

'But she's okay now, right?'

The garden shed is, as most garden sheds tend to be, chock-a-block with blades, poisons and sundry materials unsuitable for consumption by infants.

'She could've crawled into the *pond*! I *asked* you to get it covered, didn't I?'

'Hon? It's okay. *She's* okay.'

Rosie is a precocious little girl, but even she shouldn't be able to crawl that well at six months old, and certainly not all the way out to the garden shed.

The shed, incidentally, is never locked. But the bolt is always drawn.

It's late evening, two Ponstan and half a bottle of red before

Debs finally calms down. I give her a backrub and accept the blame, meanwhile plotting an assassination.

'I thought only Nazis burned books,' Billy says, slouching around the stand of bamboo and up onto the decking. Monday morning. With a childish pang of regret I find myself wishing it were Tuesday.

I squirt some more lighter fluid on the manuscript.

'Just so you know,' I say, 'I never liked Karlsson from the start. That's the only reason I could stomach a redraft. But at least Karlsson wasn't a sneaky cunt. Karlsson had the balls to stand up and be who he was.'

'Boo-fucking-hoo,' he says, sitting down.

'He was only ever an avatar,' I say, 'so I could purge all that nasty shit I didn't like about myself. You haven't realised yet?'

'Realised what?'

'That I started that story when I met Debs. I mean, I knew straight away she was the one, that if I got my act together we could go the distance. And somewhere in the back of my head I knew I had to straighten up and fly right, get rid of all the poison, so I wouldn't infect her or any kids we might have.'

'That's noble,' he snickers.

But I won't be deflected. I've had all weekend to prepare my speech.

'You've never wondered why Cassie sticks around when Karlsson is such an asshole, why she doesn't just dump the sociopathic fuck? I needed someone to sit still for all that shit I had to vent.'

I flick the Zippo to life, hold it over the manuscript. 'Any last words?'

'You're wasting your time, man. I already told you, I'm your evil genius.'

'Evil, sure. But genius?'

'You're not getting it,' he says. 'I'm not just any old evil genius, I'm *your* evil genius. Descartes's evil genius.'

'Get around a bit, don't you?'

'I'm your illusion of the world,' he says. 'You said it yourself, I was only ever an avatar.' The sly grin tugs at the corner of his mouth. 'Burn me down, you're burning yourself down too.'

'I'll take my chances.'

'Really? Then why haven't you done it already?'

'Because I want to watch you burn.'

'So let's do it.' He takes one of my pre-rolled cigarettes from the table, then relieves me of the Zippo and sparks it up. When he exhales, he lays the still lit Zippo on the manuscript. A bluey-yellow flame ignites, fanned by the mild breeze.

Together we watch it burn. 'Oh, what a world, what a world,' he croons.

II

SPRING

I only have to tell my supervisor once that I know where he parks his car. He immediately finds a new parking space. This displays tactical awareness. This suggests that he has, in fact, been listening. I am pleasantly surprised.

It takes a full twenty minutes to locate his new parking space. It is in the middle of one of the smaller car parks on the eastern side of the hospital, which is bounded on three sides by manicured shrubs. The Ox Mountains round-shouldered and skulking in the distance.

He chooses this location because his office window, three floors up, offers panoramic views of the entire car park. This suggests that he is a thinker. This suggests cunning. This suggests that he is the kind of strategist who presumes his foe also clocks off for lunch.

I loiter at the end of the corridor until he emerges from his office, locks the door and saunters towards the elevators. I take the stairs to the basement floor. He is sitting at the far end of the canteen, eating in the company of two other supervisors.

I make my way out to the car park on the east side and smoke a career-threatening cigarette. When the cigarette is finished I thread my way through the lines of parked cars to his Opel Corsa.

I drop the butt at the driver's door and grind it flat.
Blood roars in my ears. Tomorrow I invade Poland, etc.

'I know you probably won't be interested in this,' Cassie says,
'but . . .'

We are in Zanzibar, a coffee bar on Old Market Street, seated at
a counter beside the plate-glass window looking out at the pigeon-
soiled statue of Lady Erin. While Cassie tells me what it is she
thinks I won't be interested in, I ponder on how women start out
trying to fuck their fathers and wind up fending off their prepubes-
cent sons.

I wonder if the waitress, who is Polish, might inadvertently yelp
something containing guttural vowels at her moment of climax.

I despair at how a woman's sexual peak arrives just as her visible
feminine attributes begin to sag, expand, wrinkle and dissipate.

Lady Erin was erected to commemorate the insurgents who rose
against British rule in 1798. Over the years, the descendants of said
insurgents have vandalised Lady Erin, by repeatedly breaking off
her upright arm.

I sympathise with her, as I sympathise with Diana, who still
peers down horrified from Olympus as Herostratus burns her temple to the ground in order that posterity might afford him a footnote.

I think about how women who are enlightened enough to
realise that men probably won't be interested in what they have to
say have mined a nugget akin to a glass diamond.

'So what do you think?' Cassie says.

'About what?'

'You weren't listening, were you?'

'Not to you, no.'

'Who then?'

'Diana.'

She blinks, then cocks an ear to the stereo. 'Diana Ross?'

'Diana. The goddess who had her temple burned down by a man who wanted to be remembered.'

'What has that to do with anything?'

'Isn't that why we're together? So I can eventually destroy your temple and be remembered?'

'What're you talking about, temples?'

'The body is a temple, Cass. A child's passage through the vaginal canal is an act of destruction. Hips crack, abdominal plates split. There is sundry ripping and tearing. All so my name can percolate down through the generations.'

I use the word 'percolate' because we are in a coffee shop.

Cassie stares at me for a long time, then turns away to gaze out at Lady Erin. She spoons the cream in her cappuccino and says, 'K, how come you have to make everything more difficult than it really is?'

'Nothing's more difficult than it really is, Cass. The myth that something can be easier than it really is was invented by Hoover salesmen.'

'You know your problem?' She shakes her head despairingly. 'You don't have the imagination to see how things can be better.'

Cassie's problem is that she thinks I only have one problem.

My line for today comes courtesy of Dame Iris Murdoch: *You can live or tell; not both at once.*

•

'If you're aiming for reverse psychology,' I say, 'you're laying it on a bit thick.'

'What's the best way to get a woman's attention?' he says, putting down his sheet of paper.

'Pretend you don't care.'

'Treat 'em mean,' he says, 'keep 'em keen.'

Declan Burke

'There's mean,' I say, 'and there's being an antisocial bastard.'
'Relax, it's a first draft. I can always go back in and kill any babies you don't like.'

The quality of our *entente cordiale* is somewhat strained. Billy is adamant he had nothing to do with Rosie crawling into the shed, that he would have nothing to gain and everything to lose.

'Put it this way,' he'd said. 'You're a bit fragile about the writing as it is. How would you feel about it if anything happened to Rosie?'

'Writing wouldn't come into it. I'd be struggling to get out of bed in the morning.'

'Exactly. And where would that leave me?'

'In limbo, I know. All I'm saying is, it's a bit of a coincidence that something happened to Rosie after we had that chat about killing babies.'

'You're reading too much into it, man. Besides, if memory serves, you're the one who was up for killing babies.'

'Only as a metaphor. You're the one planning to blow up a hospital.'

'Only as a metaphor.'

'It's not the same thing.'

'Isn't it?'

Billy believes that I am Neville Chamberlain, waving the pages of the latest manuscript around to convince myself that he and I have peace in our time.

I prefer to think of myself as Churchill in the early months of 1940, boozing away the phoney war and wishing the Japs would hurry up and bomb Pearl Harbour.

I'm under no illusions. It's only a matter of time before his blitz begins.

The Big Question: which of us will get to split the atom first?

'So what've you got?' he says, nodding at my side of the table.

'You meet the old guy for the first time.'

70

'Yeah,' he says softly. 'I liked him.'

•

'Being old is like being hung-over all day, every day,' the old man says. His voice crackles like a dusty '78. 'The worst hangover you've ever had. So bad you wanted to do nothing but cry but you were afraid snuffling your snot would split your skull. Imagine that all day, every day,' he says.

This man is seventy-nine years old. In theory, he should be dead. In Ireland, statistically speaking, men die at seventy-two and women at seventy-five. This is nature's way of affording women the opportunity of covering every possible conversational gambit vis-a-vis the latest manifestation of male betrayal.

'People don't get how someone might want to die,' the old man says. He has recently had his leg amputated at the knee, lest the gangrene that began with an infected ingrown toenail spread like bushfire through dry kindling. 'They don't understand that every-thing winds down,' he says. 'They don't want to face the fact that all engines wear out.'

The will to live is an invisible engine, with its own pumps and valves and in-built obsolescence.

The old man chooses a peach-flavoured yoghurt and a bar of plain Dairy Milk chocolate from the trolley. 'You know you're old when you can't eat the Fruit 'n' Nut anymore,' he says.

'The nurse tells me you were a mechanic,' I say.

His hands shake, so that his fingers can gain no purchase on the chocolate's gold foil. I take the bar, peel back some of the wrapper, hand it over. He's nodding his head. 'That's right,' he says, 'for near on forty years.' His chest rumbles when he breathes. He begins sucking on a corner of the Dairy Milk. 'Cars today, who'd be arsed fixing them up?'

I note that he has to buy his own chocolate and yoghurt from my concession cart. That his pyjama collar is grimy. These things tell me that visitors come rarely, if at all. His hair is lush, white as the pillowcase on which it flares. His face is deeply lined, but softly, so he resembles a post-coital Beckett. The eyes are rheumy, red-limned.

'Something I've always wanted to ask a mechanic,' I say.

The faded blue eyes sparkle. 'Is that a fact?' He pats his leg. 'Fire away, son, I'm going nowhere.'

'See, in the movies, when someone cuts a brake cable halfway through, so the car only crashes later. Does that really work?'

The bushy eyebrows flicker, then mesh. 'Is there someone you don't like, son?'

I laugh, quietly, so as not to disturb the other patients. 'Not at all,' I say. 'I'm a writer, I'm working on a short story where a car crashes. I just want to know if that brake cable thing works. I don't want any mechanics reading the story and not taking it seriously.'

He doesn't believe me. But his eyes sparkle. He's looking at one last opportunity for mischief with no possible repercussions. 'Tell me the story,' he says, 'and I'll let you know if it sounds wrong.'

I sketch the outline of a story involving a fatal car accident. He sucks on his chocolate. When I'm finished, he nods. 'That sounds alright,' he says. 'I mean, there's nothing wrong with the actual details. But the story's rubbish.'

'That's what's wrong with the world today,' I say. 'Everyone's a critic.'

He laughs, but it collapses into a rumbling cough. His whole body shudders. The plastic tubes rattle like a ship's rigging in a gale. When the spasm passes he gasps, 'What's wrong with the world today, son, is mechanics don't read short stories.'

'Maybe you've a point at that,' I say. 'See you tomorrow night.'

I leave the ward, the cart's wheels squeaking like uppity slave mice. I'm thinking about how the will to live is an invisible engine, with its own pumps and valves. I'm thinking about how engines can be jump-started if only you can pump enough juice through the leads. I'm thinking about how engines can be scuppered with something as simple as a handful of sugar.

I meet Frankie for a coffee in the hospital canteen. We chat football for a bit, talk up the Rovers' chances against Shams on Friday night, but Frankie seems distracted, irritable.

'Don't suppose you've seen Tommo?' I say. 'I've a couple of books for him in my locker, he was supposed to pick them up yesterday.'

'Tommo got the boot,' he says. 'Austin too.'

'No way.'

He nods, glum. 'I got in a load of shit for being away from the desk, covering for those fuckers. So I had to write a report.'

'What'd you say?'

'Nothing. Just that the boys were out sick that day, and I had to cover the monitors.'

'And they got the boot for that?'

'It wasn't just that. When they checked the records, they realised the boys were out sick about five days in every forty. So they got sent for a check-up, standard procedure, to make sure they didn't have some long-term infection that could screw the patients.'

'So?'

'So they had to take a pee test.'

'Ouch.'

'Fuckin' A. The guy doing the test got stoned off the whiff of their piss.'

'Half their luck.'

'Tell me about it. And with the cutbacks, the non-recruitment of non-essential staff, they're not taking on any replacements.'

'So who's doing their jobs?'

Frankie jabs a thumb into his chest. 'They've given me a

promotion,' he says, 'made me Divisional Representative. Whatever the fuck that is.'

'So now you're a supervisor with no one to supervise.'

'That's about it, yeah.'

'Okay. But if it's Tommo and Austin's work you're doing, you'll hardly break a sweat.'

'I know.' He drains the dregs of his coffee. 'But still, the boys were mates.' He glances at his watch, then stands up. 'C'mon,' he says, 'we'd better get back or we'll be next for the heave-ho.'

'If you want a pint later on, have a chat, just give me a buzz.'

'Will do.'

•

'Is that it?' I say. 'You're dumping Tommo and Austin?'

Billy, nibbling on a hangnail, just shrugs.

'So how's it feel?'

'Not good,' he says. 'Like Frankie says, the boys were mates. And the way things are these days, it's not like they're going to just waltz into another gig.'

'It's tough out there, alright. But look, Billy, it's not your fault the boys were stoners.'

'I could've had them get their act together, pack in the dope.'

'Except the object of the exercise was to cut them dead, see if you could face wiping out a whole hospital.'

'I know, yeah.'

'So what d'you think?'

'I dunno. I need to absorb this one first, see how it goes.'

'Not easy, is it?'

'No,' he says. 'Austin, okay, he's a bit of a dick. Tommo's a good bloke, though.'

'Was,' I say. 'Past tense.'

He stares. 'I only got them sacked,' he says. 'It's not like I killed them off or anything.'

'Same difference, though, isn't it? I mean, they're gone now.'

'Gone from the hospital, yeah.'

'What,' I say, 'you think they're just going to hang out in their apartment getting blitzed?'

A hunted look in his eye. 'How'm I supposed to know what they'll—'

'They've just lost their *jobs*, Billy. How will they buy weed? How'll they pay rent? I mean, there's consequences. Every action an equal and opposite reaction, all that.'

'Fuck.'

'Cut off without even a redundancy payment . . .' I'm enjoying this now, Billy's hangdog expression. 'Those boys want to work again, they'll be off to Canada, Australia. Except they're unskilled, they're hospital porters. Who's going to want them?'

'What would you have done?'

'If I'd wanted them gone?' I shrug. 'I don't know. If I liked them, they just weren't useful anymore, I'd have taken care of them. Put them in car accident or something, Austin's driving, he's bliftered . . . Nothing too serious, mind. Just enough to put them in wheelchairs, get them a disability benefit, so they could sit around toking all day.'

'Not much of a life, that,' Billy says.

'Depends on who you are. I'd say Austin'd be okay with it.'

'Maybe.'

'Still,' I say, 'at least your way they won't be going up in flames when the hospital blows.'

'True enough.' He straightens up, crumples the sheet of paper, tosses it on the pile. 'I'll have another bash at it tonight.'

'That's the spirit. What else have you got?'

He draws another sheet of paper from his folder. 'I've had another go at the Cassie novel.'

'I thought we were dumping that.'

'Bear with me,' he says. 'I think I might be on to something.'

•

Sermo Vulgus: A Novel (Excerpt)

Cassie, you said diamonds were stone bewildered, confused and frightened by the glow in their soul. We are machines, you said, churning out rusted flakes of misunderstanding, but diamonds are doubts radiating hope.

Cassie, you said you would never wear diamonds. Diamonds, you said, are smug egos. They are too hard, you said, hard as the bones our yesterdays gnaw. You said only braided lightning would grace your finger; only a garland woven from a re-leafed oak would adorn your head. Can't we at least try, you said, to draw a straight line through the heart of every sun?

Cassie, you quoted Schoendoerffer on grey eyes: 'Grey eyes are peculiar in that they betray no emotion, and in its absence one cannot help imagining a world of violence and passion behind their gaze.' I think you wished your eyes were Schoendoerffer grey, but they were wide and candid and the colour of indecision.

Cassie, you were no reader of French. Thus I challenge the legitimacy of your perceptions. Now, when it is already too late, I dare you to consider that Xan Fielding's translation of *Farewell to the King* improved Schoendoerffer's original text.

Cassie, I beg you to admit possibility. For your approval I posit the hypothesis that nothing is impossible so long as we are prepared to consider its possibility. Only in an infinite universe can hope spring eternal.

Cassie, it is possible to try to braid lightning, to re-leaf your oak, to draw a straight line through the heart of every sun.

Cassie, it is possible to try at least. It is still legitimate to hope, even now, when the ash of the Six Million falls with the acid rain.

Cassie, are we really so far gone?

•

'You've read *Farewell to the King*?'

'Sure,' he says. 'I liked the cover.'

'Why, what's it look like?'

'Your cover, I mean.'

'Oh.' My copy of *Farewell to the King* I found in a second-hand bookshop, crudely covered with a blank sheet of cheap leather binding. A blind orphan, swaddled. A good novel, I think, but my favourite book. A precious artefact excavated from the dross. The idea that someone would go to all that trouble to rebind an old paperback had me blinking back tears, so that the assistant asked me was I okay as I handed over the euro coin it cost to give it a good home.

Billy reaches into his satchel, takes out the book. 'I borrowed it last week,' he said. 'Sorry, I meant to ask, but then Rosie wound up in the shed and, y'know.'

'No worries.'

It takes everything I have not to punch my pencil into his Newman-blue eye. Because that book isn't just a book, it's a touchstone for how much some people love books; and not just books, but the weakest, the most disposable. Whoever bound that book could just as easily have tossed a coverless paperback in the trash, an object that was worthless by any practical assessment. And yet they covered it, crudely it has to be said, but that's not the point, they took the time and invested the craft to ensure that the words would be protected, the delicacy of it preserved. I can only presume that whoever covered that book had died, and their collection of books sold as a job lot, for why would they go to all that effort just to sell it second-hand, especially as no bookseller in his right mind would pay good money for a ragged paperback bound in cheap blank leather?

I cried that day in the bookshop for the poignancy of it, certainly, out of a lachrymose sentimentality for the blind orphan who found safe haven, but also because I knew I had finally discovered the person I wanted to write for, the one mythical listener every writer needs, my ghost audience and reader eternal.

'Have you anything else like that?' he says. 'That was pretty good.'

'No, I've nothing else like that.'

He nods towards the chalet. 'What about those Russians you have on the shelf?'

'It's a different kind of thing.'

'Just as well,' he says. 'I mean, who can read those Russians? The characters' names are nearly short stories in themselves.'

'Being honest, they're only there for show. Them and Kafka. And Beckett.'

'Thank Christ for that,' he says. 'I was worried I might be the only moron around here.'

•

Today is a Red Letter day. Today was worth the wanton massacre of oxygen molecules required to keep me alive.

Early this morning a nurse discovered an old woman dead in her bed. There are suggestions that the death was premature. There are hints that the old woman's miserable existence, eked out between bouts of excruciating bowel pain, was abruptly terminated.

Mrs McCaffrey's was the third unusual death in nineteen months. All three suffered from chronic agonies with no hope of reprieve. All three had private rooms. Mrs McCaffrey appears to have been smothered with her own pillow, an embroidered affair she'd brought from her home when she realised she was in for the long haul.

Rumours surge along the corridors. Scandal plummets down elevator shafts. The speed of light is left standing in the traps. There are uninspired whispers about an Angel of Death. The word 'euthanasia' enjoys a hushed renaissance.

Despite the best efforts of the hospital's board of directors, the cops are called in. They are, however, discreet. They are aware of the delicate nature of the situation. People cannot afford to believe that a hospital could be a place where people can die willy-nilly. There are research grants at stake here.

I am called for an interview, held in the office of the director of public relations on the sixth floor. It is a big, airy office. Potted plants feature. I sit in the leather chair and immediately feel my posture improve.

The cops ask if I was working last night. I tell them I was. They already know this.

They ask if I knew Mrs McCaffrey. Yes, I say. They already know this too.

They ask if I visited her last night with my concession cart.

'Not last night, no.'

'How come?' says the cop with the salt-and-pepper hair.

'She doesn't like anything on the cart,' I say. 'I've offered to bring her anything she wants, but she can't eat normal stuff. I think she has bowel cancer. Or had, rather.'

'See anything unusual on your rounds last night?'

'It's a hospital. Pretty much everything that goes on around here is unusual.'

'Okay. But was there anyone around who shouldn't have been? Anything out of the ordinary?'

'Not that I can think of, no.'

The other cop has florid jowls and porcine eyes. He taps a

folder on the desk in front of him. 'It says here you've been the subject of a number of disciplinary procedures.'

'That's not exactly a crime.'

He bristles. 'We'll decide what is and what's not a crime.'

'No, you don't. If you want to criminalise attitude, call a referendum. Then *we'll* decide what's a crime and what isn't, and you'll enforce the laws we vote in. That's the peachy thing about democracy.'

'How come you're trying to be difficult?'

The way he says it, I am now officially Public Enemy Number 1. This is a man who needs enemies. This is a man who needs justification for the chip on his shoulder and has found his vocation as a vampire feeding off crime.

'I'm not trying to be difficult,' I say. 'I'm co-operating. Anyway, how would mentioning my rights be making things difficult?'

Salty Pepper says, 'How long have you worked here?'

'That's in the file, along with the disciplinary stuff.'

'Do you like your job?'

'It's a job. And I like meeting new people.'

'You get to see many people die during the course of your duties?'

'Some. You?'

He sucks on a discoloured front tooth. 'How does that make you feel, watching people die? I mean, are you comfortable with seeing people in pain?'

'Not especially. But you get used to anything if you stick at it long enough.'

'That's not what I asked.'

Florid Jowls cuts in. 'Say someone begs you to end their life, to do them a favour and put them out of their misery – what do you do?'

'I call a nurse. They're obviously in need of a shot of morphine, something along those lines.'

'Did Mrs McCaffrey ever talk about wanting to die?'

'Not that I remember. But I don't think she had a lot to live for.'

'Why's that?'

'She talked about how no one ever came to visit her. She said her husband died four years ago.' They already know this. 'People can die of a broken heart,' I say. 'That's a medical fact. Hearts can actually break.'

'So you did talk to her.'

'She talked to me. I listened. Old people who are dying only want one thing, the chance to tell their story. To pass their lives on. All they want to believe is that life hasn't been a stupid waste of time.'

Florid Jowls says, 'And you told her that?'

'Sure. What's it cost to tell a dying person a lie?'

'When's the last time you saw Mrs McCaffrey?' Salty Pepper says.

'About three nights ago.'

'You're sure about that?'

'Certain, yeah.'

'Okay,' Florid Jowls says, 'you can go. But we might want to talk to you again.'

I head for the door. 'A word to the wise,' Salty Pepper says. 'No one likes a smart-arse.'

'Not everyone needs to be liked,' I say.

I can tell, by the way his eyes narrow, that he is not unaccustomed to considering this concept. I close the door behind me and breathe quick, shallow breaths. Blood roars in my ears. Tomorrow I bomb Nagasaki, etc.

My supervisor takes the cigarette butt hint and finds a new parking space. This time it takes me a whole hour to find his Opel Corsa, out back of the ambulance station to the rear of the hospital.

Strictly speaking, this is illegal. No non-essential vehicles of any description are allowed in this area. A kid propping his bike against the wall is looking at a hefty fine for interfering with an emergency service. A badly parked car could obstruct an ambulance on its way to resuscitate a coronary victim. Each minute that elapses before an ambulance reaches a coronary victim reduces his chances of survival by 10 percent, give or take.

There was a time when Sirens lured and seduced; today they alert and alarm. Ambulances are the all-wailing, all-blaring placebos of our generation. A flashing blue siren has replaced the Sacred Heart flame. The stench of burning rubber has become our incense. In CPR we trust.

My supervisor has violated this covenant. He has parked his non-essential Opel Corsa in a restricted zone. It is my duty to reprimand him.

I wear a ring fashioned into an Ouroborous, an ancient symbol of intertwined snakes, one depicting imminent annihilation, the other rising hope. In Asian cultures, the snakes become dragons. I have sawn through this ring so that one jagged edge overlaps the other. I dig this jagged edge into the paintwork of my supervisor's Opel Corsa and gouge a line the length of the passenger side. In theory, this means he will not discover the gouging until long after he has left the hospital grounds.

My line for today is, *Why stop now, just when I'm hating it?* (Douglas Adams, *The Restaurant at the End of the Universe*)

Cassie is a beautiful woman. This makes her difficult to live with.

Sex stunts the imagination, narrows focus, and diminishes the contemplation of perspective, scale or the possibility of diversions. Sex is an Opel Corsa careering downhill on a steep one-way street. Sex is half-chewed fuel-lines. Sex is dying before your time. Sex is defying destiny. Sex is waving two fingers in the face of infinity, and then slipping said fingers into infinity's lubricated vagina. Sex is hoping infinity gets off first.

Cass is a finicky eater, an amateur photographer and a book club enthusiast. She admires minimalist two-tone interior design. When she was a child she wanted to be a blacksmith. Today she works as a physiotherapist. When we first met I thought 'physiotherapy' was massage parlour code. I was to be disappointed, but by then I didn't care.

Today is my day off. We meet for lunch in town. It is a mild, bright day, the first real swallow of summer, the sun a bowl of peach punch drained. We skip the food and grab some take-out coffee, find a bench down along the river. We talk and watch the river flow by.

This is always an enjoyable experience. Cass is generous with her time and spirit. She possesses the rare talent of making everyone feel at ease in her company, a skill and gift essential in her professional life. She listens when other people speak. This attentiveness is flattering, even after you realise Cassie listens no matter who is speaking and regardless of the topic being discussed. Conversing with Cassie is like whistling into a soaked sponge. She hears everything but absorbs nothing. This is one reason I like Cassie.

Another reason is that she takes a double-D cup size. I was not breast-fed as a baby. I was a puny youth, five feet four inches when I first began to masturbate. For most of the two decades since, I have masturbated at least once a day.

While Cassie talks, I calculate that, were it not for masturbation stunting my growth, I would be twelve feet seven inches by now.

•

'I was wondering,' Billy says.

'Yeah?'

'How come, in the original draft, you made me a midget?'

'As I recall, the idea was so that you'd have a Napoleon complex.'

'It wasn't to make yourself feel taller?'

'Why would I want that?'

'Everyone wants to be taller,' he says. 'A man needs stature.'

'Danny DeVito seems to be making out okay.'

He grins. 'That was funny, in *Get Shorty*, the way they had Danny DeVito playing an actor who plays Napoleon. Remember?'

'Hilarious, yeah.'

'What's wrong?' he says. 'Something up?'

'Nothing, no. Why?'

'You seem a bit off this morning.'

'Not at all. I was just thinking that you're what, an inch taller than me now?'

'Does that bother you?'

'Not in the slightest.'

'I could lop off an inch if you want.'

'Don't be daft. It's not an issue.'

'Well, if you're sure . . .'

'I'm certain.'

'Okay. So what's next?'

I consult my notes. 'You were rejigging another excerpt from the Cassie novel.'

'Try this instead,' he says, handing across a sheet of paper.

'What is it?'

'That time with Cassie, in Zanzibar, when you had me talking about the Temple of Diana? That got me thinking.'

•

The Seven Wonders of the Ancient World were the Pyramid at Giza, the Hanging Gardens of Babylon, the Colossus at Rhodes, the Statue of Zeus at Olympia, the Mausoleum at Halicarnassus, the Lighthouse at Alexandria, and the Temple of Artemis at Ephesus.

Known to the Romans as Diana, Artemis was the Greek goddess of the moon, the forest, hunting, witchcraft and childbirth. Although herself a virgin, she was also a fertility goddess.

The architectural apex where culture, history and philosophy met, the Temple of Artemis was one of the most important edifices of its day, and arguably *the* most important. So it should have been no surprise to anyone when Herostratus burned it to the floor one night in 365 BCE.

A mediocre man, Herostratus turned to destruction in his bid for immortality. The arson was deliberately engineered in an attempt to be remembered by posterity, which was where Herostratus went wrong. The point of destroying buildings is not to be remembered, nor to become the patron saint of the disaffected. Nor should it be for the simple pleasure of seeing things burn. The point is to destroy something people revere. This may or may not result in people thinking twice about taking things for granted. This may or may not result in people asking why.

In the aftermath, Herostratus's name was banned on pain of death by the city elders. Ironically, it was this censorship, rather than the act itself, which ensured his name would be remembered. The inhabitants of Ephesus circa 365 BCE were no less curious, stupid or dazzled by celebrity than we are today.

Sadly for Herostratus, legend has it that on the same night in 365 BCE, not too far from Ephesus – in Macedonia, to be precise – a baby called Alexander was born.

I like to imagine Herostratus on a ridge overlooking Ephesus, howling at the moon as the distant flames flicker across his deranged features. This is Man versus Space, Time and All Points Between, with Man coming home three lengths clear. This is Herostratus taking his place in a pantheon that includes Lucifer,

Prometheus, Cain, Judas, Martin Luther, Kepler, Galileo and Darwin. This is simmering resentment boiling over, disaffection coming home to roost, hate crackling like bottled lightning. This is the natural order exacting retribution on the complacency that presumes to recline on a couch of innate superiority. This is Jimmy Cagney atop an oil derrick screaming, 'Top o' the world, Ma!'

My line for today is an exercise in wishful thinking: *There might be Herostratuses who would set fire to the temple where their own images are worshipped.* (Nietzsche, *Human, All Too Human*)

The old man has heard about Mrs McCaffrey. The rumour has slipped into his ward beneath the ebb and flow of aimless conversation to circle the foot of the beds, waiting for the unwary to dip a toe. The rumour has flicked its tail and glided out of the ward again, and the flicking tail has slapped the old man in the face. He appears gaunted, frightened. He is an old man adrift on a strange bed beneath which circles a rumour of premature oblivion.

'I'm not ready to go yet, son,' he says.

'Wouldn't it be worse if you were and couldn't?' I say. But he's not listening.

'What age was she?' he says.

'Eighty-one.'

He does the math. The bushy eyebrows mesh as he concentrates. He has two years on her. This is of little consolation to a one-legged ex-mechanic who knows a thing or two about how all engines wear out in the end.

'I played centre-back for Coolera the year we won the double,' he says. His eyes take on a misty, faraway aspect. The thousand-year stare. 'The summer of '61,' he says. 'League and Championship, unbeaten in all competitions. For the final they switched me away from centre-back out to the right. Their best player played out there, and he was good and fast, but he didn't score that day.'

He says this proudly, speaking a little louder than usual. This is not for my benefit. This is so the rumours will hear and understand they are not dealing with any little old ladies this time.

'What's the one thing you most regret not doing?' I say.

He flinches. The dying are not immune to cruelty. 'No regrets, son,' he says, but the jaw muscles tighten beneath their frosting of stubble. Even the dying have their pride. The dying have little else.

'When I was a youngster,' he concedes, 'I was at a game, I think my father might have been playing but I wasn't old enough to be interested. I was just wandering around the field playing with a little motorcar, it was my older brother's. And these knackers, four or five of them, about my age, they came out of nowhere and they wanted the motorcar. I shouldn't have given it to them, it was my brother's, but all I could think of was the four or five of them sitting on me and I could smell them, they made me sick. So I gave them the car. They went off laughing.'

His eyes gleam with more than moisture. 'I can still smell the fuckers now,' he says. He looks up at me. 'It was my brother's car,' he says. 'He died eight year ago now.'

I nod. 'The mortality rate of the travelling community is significantly lower than that of the settled community,' I say. 'Those travellers are probably all dead now. When the time comes, you might even see them on the other side. And the thing about heaven is, you get to live through eternity the way you want to. You'll probably wake up in heaven as a centre-back. When you do, go looking for those tinkers. Eternity's a long time, you could go back every day and whale on the fuckers until it's time for ambrosia and nectar elevenses.'

'Where'd you hear that one, about living in heaven the way you want to?'

'The Pope came out with it a few years ago,' I lie. 'In an encyclical, the time he abolished hell.'

'I didn't hear about that one,' he says.

'That's because no one listens to the Pope anymore.'
'Isn't that the God's truth?'
I stand up. 'Anything else you need?'
'No thanks, son.'
He hasn't paid for the Dairy Milk and peach yoghurt yet, but I take the hit. I lean in, so no one else can hear. 'Mrs McCaffrey died in a private room,' I say. 'So don't worry about it. Patients in public wards have nothing to fear.'
He looks up at me, frowning, his eyes pale-blue whirlpools of fear and indecision.
The old are easily frightened. The old are the young turned inside out and upside down. The old are the young knowing more than any child should. The old remember what it is to be young, weak and terrified, and they do not have revenge fantasies to sustain them.
The old know that bullies do not melt away when you fight back. The old have shuffled around to the rear of the bike sheds after school and are being kicked in the kidneys by Time, snivelling while Death slaps their face open-handed.
The old have had their books stomped in a puddle once too often. The old have no big brothers who know ju-jitsu.

The people we should be talking to are winos, milkmen, pest-control operatives, miners, bouncers, whores, thieves, cab drivers, ex-cops and the guy who gives out change at the amusement arcade.
Ask those who can see in the dark. Practically all of the universe exists in a state of permanent night.
When the insomnia beds in I walk the streets. I venture down unlit alleyways to slip and slide on the detritus of split refuse sacks, on offal waste, on the slime oozing up through cracks in the paving. I paddle in overflowing drains.
I trip over a pair of outstretched legs. These legs belong to a

tramp, a bum, a lush. A non-contributor.

I do not wake him. He has been awake all along, watching me come.

He scrambles to his feet and emerges into the faint orange light. His hair is matted, wild and grey. His eyes burn like embers. He is The Watcher, and he resents being watched. He makes threatening gestures, like a goose hooshing cattle.

I stand my ground.

He is foul-mouthed. He tries to roar but the raw wheeze suggests his vocal cords have seized for the want of social lubrication. His voice cracks. His face is the colour of jam sponge scrapings, the breath harsh as petrol. I smell methylated spirits.

By now his face is nose-to-nose with mine. He is ranting, the cracked lips flecked with spittle. I hold my Zippo up to the side of his face. The flame allows me to see his eyes properly. The whites are jaundiced, the pupils dilated.

He hesitates. He sputters to a halt. In the quietness that follows I hear an eerie high-pitched squeaking.

'In an urban environment,' I say, 'the ratio of rats to humans is nine-to-one.'

He stares. He croaks a foul imprecation that tails off halfway through. His shoulders slump, and the eyes narrow down into hard-cornered triangles.

I allow the Zippo to flicker out. I hold up the cardboard beaker I am carrying in my other hand. I say, 'Old man, how would a cup of hot coffee taste right now?'

•

'So now there's an Angel of Death,' he says, '*and* an Angel of Mercy?'

'That's the way it was,' I say. 'We don't have to keep it that way.'

'It's too blatant,' he says. 'Too Jekyll and Hyde.'

'So we scrap the Angel of Mercy?'

'I think so, yeah.'

I make a note. 'Consider it done.'

•

Sermo Vulgus: A Novel (Excerpt)

Cassie, the flesh is an abomination. This is the logic of all religions, even the Buddhists, who consider themselves above and beyond religion.

Religion demands that the flesh be mortified, mutilated, disowned and discarded.

Yet I am flesh, Cassie, the flesh of flesh. Even now I can feel the blood ebbing through the capillaries of my flaccid penis, as tentative, as irrepressible, as the very first tide.

Cassie, to reject the flesh is to reject a logic so implacable that it requires no explanation or justification. To wit: we were born to enflesh. We are our means to an end, and our end to our means. There is Fucking, then Everything Else.

Think on this, Cassie: the scientists and priests agree that eternity exists. The scientists and priests agree on the theory of infinity. But only the priests pledge to abstain for all eternity. Only the priests resolve to set themselves against the implacable logic of the universe for so long as it exists.

Cassie, have you the courage to join the dog-collared rebels on the barricades while they eternally rail against the will of their god?

•

'Anyone ever tell you,' Billy says, 'that you have serious issues with priests?'

'It's nothing personal. It's more a zeitgeist thing.'

He ponders that awhile. Behind him one of the carp, a flash of orange, breaks the surface of the pond and is gone again.

'What are we supposed to be saying, though?' he says. 'That I was abused by a priest?'

'Not explicitly, no.'

'I don't even know any priests,' he says. 'I mean, you never even gave me a childhood.'

'Like I say, it's not a personalised thing. It's more to do with the idea of innocence being abused by religion.'

'I'm only one man,' he says. 'There's only so much I can shoulder. You don't think you're asking me to do too much here?'

'The truly great leaders,' he adds, 'had this notion where they'd never ask anyone to do anything they wouldn't do themselves.'

'Except I'm not leading you, Billy. We're collaborating.'

He smirks. It's there and gone like a flash of carp, so fast I'm not even sure I've seen it.

'What?' I say. 'What am I missing here?'

'How d'you mean?' he says.

'What was the smirk in aid of?'

'Smirk?'

'Yeah. You smirked.'

'Did I?'

'Don't fuck around, Billy. What are you not telling me?'

He allows that to hang for a while, then reaches for the makings. 'Let me ask you this,' he says as he builds a smoke. 'What colour were Karlsson's eyes?'

'Blue.'

'How many eyes did he have?'

'Two.'

'What colour was his hair?'

'Blond.'

'Karlsson,' he says in a chiding tone, 'had two eyes, both of them brown. His hair was brown too, going a little foxy in the sideburns.'

'Who gives a fuck,' I say, 'if his hair was pink? We're not writing about Karlsson anymore, we're writing about you.'

'Since when?' he says.

'Since always. Since you first showed up.'

'With blond hair,' he insists, 'and one blue eye.' He dips the shades to remind me of the sucked-out prune that used to be his other eye. 'You've never wondered about what happened?'

'I asked about it, Billy. As I recall, you said I wouldn't believe you if you told me.'

'And you just let it lie. For a writer,' he says, 'you're not very curious, are you?'

'We'd never met before. It would've been rude to push it.'

'And now?'

I shrug. 'If you want to tell me, just tell me.'

He plays with the cigarette, rolling it between the ball of his thumb and the tips of his fingers. 'You're just not getting it,' he says, 'are you?'

'I've got a lot on my plate right now, Billy. If you want to tell me how you lost your eye, then go for it. If not, let's cut the bullshit and just do this.'

'I didn't just *lose* my eye,' he says. 'An eye isn't something that rolls out of its socket some night you're on the rip. You don't put your eye down somewhere for a minute, then forget where you—'

'Yeah, yeah, I get it. So just tell me.'

'You're some fucking plank,' he says, shaking his head. He stares at me for a long moment, then seems to make a decision. He sparks the smoke, exhales from the corner of his mouth, his eye on mine all the while. 'What happened my eye,' he says, 'is totally irrelevant. What matters is, Karlsson had two eyes and I only have one. What matters,' he says, 'is somewhere between you writing Karlsson and me turning up, an eye was lost.'

'Ah. Okay.'

'You see it?'

'I think so, yeah.' I'd been wondering when Billy would make his power-play. 'You're saying something happened your eye, it doesn't really matter what or how. The point being, it wasn't me who made it happen.'

'Exactly.'

'So who did?'

'You tell me.'

'Well,' I say, 'there's really only two options, both of them totally absurd.'

'And they are?'

'Well, either someone other than you or me got their hands on the manuscript and rewrote Karlsson, before you showed up here, or you somehow managed to rewrite yourself.'

'There's another option,' he says.

'Which is?'

'I'm the writer. I'm the one writing you.'

And there it is, Billy's attempt to claim more authority, so that it's he and not I who decides his ultimate fate.

'You're saying,' I say, 'that you're the one who's really in charge.'

'I'm saying it's a possibility. If it wasn't, it shouldn't even occur to me, should it? Even as a possibility.'

'Okay. But what if I'm writing *you* that way,' I say, 'so that you get to believe you're in control?'

He pats his pockets, then glances around, peering out at the lawn beyond the decking rails. 'I don't suppose you saw my straws?' he says.

'Straws?'

'I hate to see a man with nothing left to clutch at.'

As always, his chutzpah borders on genius. 'You're a fucking loon,' I say. 'You know that?'

'Maybe I am.' He smirks again. 'But then, most writers are.'

'True enough,' I say. 'But at least we're not poets, eh?'

Oh, how we laugh.

Later that evening, Debs comes over with some takeaway Indian, *Inception* on DVD.

'So what's new with Billy the Kidder?' she says, popping home a shrimp.

I tell her that Billy reckons he's the one writing us. 'Or writing me, at least.'

'Seriously?'

'Yep.'

She chuckles at that, then says, 'You know, that mightn't be such a bad thing. If Billy thinks he has free will, then all you need to do is channel him in the right direction, so that when the hospital blows up he'll believe that he was the one who decided he should go up with it.'

'You think he'll buy that?'

'Maybe. A captain's sinking ship and all that,' she says. 'Besides, the last thing you want is to end up writing a series about this guy.'

'True. Except I'm wondering if he's not angling for more credit.'

'How come?'

'Well, if he stands up on stage and does an adaptation of my story, he pays for the rights. If he gets a co-writing credit, he pays less. If he gets to stand up and say it's an original piece, loosely based on something I've written . . .'

'Cheeky bastard.'

'Exactly.'

'You can't let him get away with that.'

'No, but the more work he does, the less I have to do. And I get to walk out of here with *Crime Always Pays* redrafted *and* a cheque on the way if Billy ever gets his gig off the ground. He reckons the Arts Council are interested in backing him with some commissioning funding.'

'So let him do it. You have the original manuscript, right? If there's any dispute, that's your trump card.'

'And Jonathan says he'll back me up, no problem.'

'So that's alright, then.'

'Hopefully, yeah. Billy's a sneaky fucker.'

'And you're not?'

I get the DVD playing, and we snuggle up on the couch eating off one another's plates. 'Is it just me,' Deborah says, 'or should Leo DiCaprio just point-blank refuse any script that requires him to run?'

We decide that, in the sprinting thespian stakes, no one holds a candle to Tom Cruise.

Leo is descending into his third or fourth version of reality when Debs's mobile starts to vibrate.

'Hello?' she says. 'Oh hi, Kathleen. Is everything . . . ?

'Oh. Right.

'No, I know. You were right to ring, absolutely . . . What's that?

'Yeah, I've booked her for an appointment on Thursday morning. It is worrying, yes . . .

'Okay, I'm on my way. See you soon.' She hangs up.

'What's wrong?' I say.

'Rosie's wheezing again,' she says, brushing poppadom crumbs off her lap.

'Shit. Since when?'

'This morning. I mean, it's on and off, and mostly when she's feeding. It's like she can feed or breathe, not both at the same time.'

'Fuck.'

'I know. Listen, she's due for her jabs on Thursday morning. Can you make it? We can have a good chat with the doctor.'

'Of course, yeah.'

'It'd be good if you could. It's like five injections in one go. She'll be a mess after.'

'I'll be there. Want me to come with you now?'

'No, there's no need. I'll ring later and let you know how she is. But she'll be fine, she always is.'

'You're sure.'

'I'm sure.' A wan smile. 'Well, sure as I can be. Who the hell knows anything when it comes to babies?'

That night I dream about Billy rewriting the script for *Inception*, except I'm Leo DiCaprio, descending through the various levels of hell, in desperate pursuit of Rosie as she flits fairy-like from one demon-filled cavern to the next, the sound of her wheezing drawing me on and ever downwards, a spiral of despair that grows more desolate and lonely the more the caverns narrow. Just like that I find myself in a tiny grotto, dimly lit. A woman dressed in blue silk stands with one hand pressed to her heart, the other held up, palm facing me.

It is She.

The Muse, who guides us through *Purgatorio* to *Paradiso*, where the pagan Virgil could not go.

'Beatrice,' I say.

From beneath her skirts a faint rustling. A wheezing.

'I am not your illusion,' Beatrice says. 'You have not paid the price. Go home,' she says, with an inflection that makes it both benediction and curse.

'Not without Rosie,' I say.

'Too late,' she says, and leans back on the altar, her skirts drawn back, so that I can see Rosie crawling up inside her, an upside-down Rosie gone bluey-black for the want of oxygen, her head falling back and her eyes glazed, the wheezing a roar now filling the cavern, a whirlwind reaping.

'No,' I say. But neither Rosie nor Beatrice are listening.

•

Today is cold and dry. I slip into the supply room on the fifth floor and steal a syringe. I fill said syringe from a bottle of paint-thinner.

I find my supervisor's car. From a discreet distance I spray the bonnet with paint-thinner. Pin-pricks appear on the paintwork.

I am wondering what I have to do to get through to my supervisor. I am wondering what it will take to persuade him to leave his car at home.

I am Sir Lancelot of Ye Ozone Layere, waging a just war on behalf of the environment.

Twice now in the planet's recent history a meteor large enough to cause significant damage has collided with the earth. When a big rock hits, the impact sets off a violent chain reaction. Volcanoes erupt and keep on spewing. Earthquakes split continents. Tectonic plates bump and grind. A cloud of dust blots out the sun. A nuclear winter sets in that can last for millennia.

The most recent major meteor strike did for 65 percent of all living material, including the dinosaurs. Were it not for these events, *Homo sapien* would not be the dominant species on the planet. Were it not for these events, mammals would not have adapted to their environment in a particular way. Were it not for the carbon assassins from outer space, Christ, Darwin and Hitler would not have been born.

Who will protest the next meteor? Who will wave placards and demand that the meteors be returned, in lead-lined containers, from whence they came? Who will don white boiler suits and journey alongside the next meteor as it plunges through the vacuum towards our puny pebble?

My line for today is, *Beware of all enterprises that require new clothes.* (Henry David Thoreau)

Suffering is part of the natural order. Pain is as essential as birth and decay. In scientific tests, radishes were proven to scream when ripped from the earth. Can other radishes hear these screams? Who cares for the agony of radishes?

The idea of stealing drugs came to me when an old lady asked one night if I had anything on the cart that might dull the pain that had her doubled up and speaking so quietly I could barely hear her words.

'No ma'am,' I said. 'I'm sorry.'

But it set me thinking. There was a certain symmetrical nobility in the idea of pilfering drugs to help those who need them most, like a Japanese orderly breaking into Red Cross packages to help British POWs. But that would have been a crassly stupid thing to do. Certainly I will plead with a nurse on behalf of a patient who appears to be in pain. I am not an animal, except in the literal sense. But even animals know not to defecate on their own doorstep.

Still, the majority of people who are in pain are not in hospital. Agony cannot always be X-rayed. Anguish cannot always be pumped out. A broken heart cannot be splinted. These people would rather not pay a general practitioner's fee in order to obtain a simple prescription to cure an ailment they can diagnose themselves. This is where I, yours truly, Karlsson, come in.

The joy of theft is the lack of overheads. I skim from a different hospital storage facility on alternate floors every month. In this way I don't allow a pattern to build up. This is not difficult to achieve. There is no set schedule to subvert. If the opportunity presents itself – if the nurses' station is deserted, say, and I have the means to transport the contraband undetected, and I have not targeted that particular facility for some months – I will avail of the opportunity.

Furthermore, I do not skim the same merchandise every time. The range is wide enough to qualify as eclectic. Uppers and downers, anything morphine-based, the deliciously bewildering pick-'n'-mix of anti-depressants: the Tricyclics (Elavil, Tofranil, Pamelor), the SSRIs (Prozac, Sarafem, Zoloft, Paxil), the MAOIs (Nardil,

Parnate), and the atypicals (Desyrel, Zyban, Serzone, Wellbutrin). These I offload at a competitive rate to P—, my connection in town. P— used to deal weed and E to students until he realised the potential of black market script drugs. Soon he will graduate to heroin. Eventually he will become a TV salesman.

I call P—.

'My mother-in-law is out of town,' I say. This is his idea of code. P— is a paranoid who watches too many gritty American cop shows. He has *The Wire* running on a perpetual loop. His mood-swings give him emotional whiplash.

He says, 'Usual place, ten bells.'

He hangs up. I ring back.

'Remind me,' I say. 'Where's the usual place?'

'The usual, for fuck's sakes.'

'I go to a lot of places that are usual.'

'Strandhill,' he says. 'Strandfucking*hill*.'

This is code for Rosses Point, the swanky resort across the bay from Strandhill. I like the idea of dealing illicit contraband at the Point. 'Okay,' I say. 'See you around ten.'

'*At* ten.' He grinds his teeth. 'Ten on the fucking *dot*.'

He even sounds like he's sweating. So I turn up at twenty-past, just to be cuntish. When I get in his car he seems hypnotised by the flicker of the lighthouse beam. His complexion is pasty.

'You alright, man?' I say. 'You don't look so good.'

But he's not listening. 'Gimme the shit,' he says.

I hand it over. He gives me the money. He starts babbling about an upcoming skiing holiday in Bulgaria, then confuses it with a skiing holiday he took a few years ago, in the Italian Alps. I cut in, make my excuses.

P— drives for home, seemingly unaware that two distinct arcs in time have just intersected. I smoke a cigarette before I follow him back into town. The last place I want to be is behind a driver unaware that he is trapped at a tangent point between then and when.

Today I wheel a six-year-old girl down to the ultrasound department. She is rigid with false courage and understandably fearful. The doctors suspect she has a hole in her heart. This child has learned too soon that the bogeyman is not the real threat. This child has learned too soon that the enemy is always within.

While I wait outside the ultrasound suite I consider that the Spartans threw defective babies off a great height into a rocky gorge. The act was ceremonial. The message was clear. Infirmity would not be tolerated. The gene pool would not be tainted.

There was a time when the Spartans epitomised ruthlessness. One apocryphal tale has a Spartan warrior complaining that his sword is too short. His mother retorts that he might want to think about taking a step closer to his enemy.

Today the Spartan legacy is adjectival shorthand for 'bleakly minimalist'. The philosophy of the ultimate warrior race, which introduced the concept of utopia through cleaving to the imperatives of natural selection, has been reduced to an adjective most closely associated with Swedish interior design.

This is unfortunate. The Spartans have many things to teach us, if only we are prepared to listen. Today ruthlessness is regarded as anti-social. We cherish the weak, afford the vulnerable a protected position in society, and celebrate their difference.

The irony of my own situation has not escaped me. If I had been born Spartan, my puny frame would have disappeared over the cliff into that rocky gorge. But I am willing to consider the possibility that the world might be a better place had I not lived. Most people are not prepared to consider this possibility.

Most people assume that civilisation is, *de facto*, A Good Idea. People unthinkingly accept that the mark of a civilised society is a desire to protect the weak, the young, the old and the vulnerable. The right of the infirm to procreate is enshrined in law. Today the blind are encouraged to lead. Today we describe the Spartans' defectives with the more gentle term 'challenged'. The dictionary defines 'challenge' as: 'A summons or defiance to fight a duel; an invitation to a contest of any kind; a calling into question'.

The Spartans practiced rudimentary eugenics. The Spartans bred for strength, courage, endurance and purity. Today this is regarded as a crime against humanity, although the racehorses seem to be making out okay. The adjective 'thoroughbred' is a positive one. The art of achieving it, however, is restricted to the animal kingdom.

This is an intriguing anomaly. We do not preach what we practice. We do not cull non-contributors. We do not let the weak fall prey. We do not castrate the mentally infirm. We do not let the aged die. In time, this is will result in a shrinking core of healthy human beings, bounded on one side by ever-weakening youth, and on the other by indefinitely extended old age. The doctors and scientists are composing a suicide note to inform an indifferent universe that a species died out through caring too much. Compassion is without doubt A Good Thing, but too much of A Good Thing is not a good thing. A surfeit of compassion becomes a disease. Hospitals become tumours.

In time, wayward meteors may come to be regarded as aggressive chemotherapy. For now we need to think outside the box. We have to target the tumours individually. We need to engage in keyhole surgery. We need to use the system against itself before the system turns on us.

Thus, this: hospitals must become abattoirs.

This is repulsive. Logic often is. Logic doesn't have to live in the real world. Logic is too busy planning its escape route. Logic has its hands full building fallout shelters and launch-pads. Logic does not admit sentiment. Logic slices through tradition, perceived wisdom, learned responses and self-serving cant. Logic is Occam's Razor: *Pluralitas non est ponenda sine necessitate.*

Despite its best efforts, the Spartan Empire lasted only two hundred years (560 to 371 BCE). Its practical pursuit of physical integrity was insufficient to sustain its philosophy, which in turn was not fluid enough to adapt. The Spartans rejected notions of progress and change. The Spartans thought that A Good Idea is a good idea forever.

History teaches that this is untrue. History records that the Spartans were ruthless and cruel, and that the Spartans died out. Ergo, history suggests that compassion is the way to go.

A question from the back of the class: were the Spartans too ruthless or were the Spartans not ruthless enough?

On the way back to the ward, the six-year-old asks me if they found a hole in her heart.

'No,' I say. This may or may not be a lie. The results of the ultrasound will not be available for some hours. 'They didn't find anything that shouldn't be there. Your heart is perfect.'

'Really?'

'Absolutely. The only thing they discovered was that there's more love in there than you actually think you have. They think most of it is for your parents.'

'But why did they think I had a hole?'

'The machine must have been faulty,' I say. 'The first machine that took the ultrasound must have had a hole in *its* heart.'

'Oh.'

'Anyway, it wouldn't be a disaster if you did have a hole in your heart. Look at me.'

She cannot do this, as I am behind her, pushing her wheelchair. 'Why?' she says. 'Do you have a hole in your heart?'

'Sure. My heart is practically all hole.'

This is a truth no machine could prove, but the six-year-old seems happy.

My line for today comes courtesy of William of Ockham: *Plurality should not be posited without necessity.*

•

'We're back to the Nazis again,' Billy says. 'Eugenics and killing off simpletons – it's just not kosher, man.'

'What can I tell you? Karlsson was a big fan of the Spartans.'

'Yeah, well, maybe that was A Good Idea for the first draft,' he says. He uses his forefingers to make invisible inverted commas in the air when he says A Good Idea. 'But it's outlived its usefulness.'

'Y'know, I think that was Karlsson's whole point.'

'So why bother making it?'

'You're the boss,' I say.

•

Always assume everyone is an idiot. This saves time.

My supervisor calls me to his office. He sits on the windowsill, one foot touching the floor, the other resting on the low radiator beneath the window. This is the window that looks out on the car park surrounded by manicured shrubs.

He waves me to the chair in front of his desk. I sit, straight-backed. He is wearing orthopaedic shoes, black with thick rubber soles, and socks with an Argyll pattern, pale blue bisected with yellow diagonals. His posture is one of exaggerated relaxation. His sitting on the windowsill is designed to create an informal atmosphere. We are no longer supervisor-supervisee. We are mano-a-mano.

'Karlsson, I've been thinking about that last written warning. Maybe I was a bit hasty.'

I close my eyes. I riffle through the file stamped 'Appropriate Responses'. I select 'Humbled but Grateful'.

'Not at all,' I say. 'You were only doing your job. I needed to pull my socks up.'

He is pleasantly surprised. He straightens, places both feet on the floor and leans forward with his hands on his thighs. He rubs his palms on his trousers. Dark patches appear on the coarse grey material.

'Maybe so,' he says, 'but I think I can meet you halfway on this one. Your performance since then suggests you've learned your lesson.'

He is in tolerant mode. Magnanimous. He has suggested compromise as an adult response to a childish situation. 'I think I can have that written warning rescinded,' he says. 'If your work continues to demonstrate diligence, I may even be in a position to propose a commendation.'

He smiles. He stands up and extends his hand across the desk. 'Karlsson, I hope we can come to some kind of an understanding.'

I shrug. 'Everyone deserves a second chance,' I say.

We shake. His grip is limp and damp.

'Y'know, Mike,' I say, 'about that commendation. If you could swing it, I'd much rather a recommendation for a raise. It's been nearly a year now since the last time, and Cassie and me are thinking of, y'know . . .'

I tail off and allow the words to fall to the floor, there to prostrate themselves in my stead. He waves his hand, palm up, like a fat pink windscreen wiper. 'Leave it with me,' he says. 'I'll see what I can do.'

'I'd appreciate that, Mike. Really, I would.'

'Say no more.'

'No more.'

He blinks, then gets it and grins. I make for the door. When I look back he seems to have lost about fifty pounds in weight, most of it around the shoulders. He is still smiling. He waves again.

In his relief he has forgotten I know that all HSE salaries are capped, determined in negotiation between government and unions. In his joy he has forgotten that his position is that of a circus ringmaster: all top hat, tails, glitter and sawdust. I imagine chimps unlocking cages. I see tigers prowling the bleachers. I hear the trumpeting of maddened elephants. I hear the twang of guy-ropes snapping and see the great canvas cathedral totter and begin to topple.

I wave back, sheepishly, and close his door behind me.

My line for today is, *He was reminded of flies wrenching their legs off in the struggle to free themselves from fly-paper.* (Franz Kafka, *The Trial*)

The perfect murder requires one essential element: a victim no one cares about. A homeless wino, say.

You buy a cup of take-out coffee. You walk the streets until you encounter a social reject huddled in an alleyway swaddled in old newspapers. You approach this non-contributor and offer him the coffee. When he bends his head to take a drink, you strike the base of his skull with a lump hammer.

On the way home, you drop the hammer in a wheelie bin awaiting pick-up. *Et voila*, etc.

•

'Woah,' Billy says. 'A lump hammer?'

'Apparently so.'

'So no Angel of Mercy,' he says. 'That makes it Hyde and Hyde.'

'I don't think we're saying you actually lump-hammered the wino,' I say. 'I think it's just that you're positing a theory.'

'I don't like it,' he says. 'Again, you go down that route, you're into Highsmith territory. And no offence, but . . .'

'None taken. I vote we scrap it.'

'You're the boss,' he says, toasting me with his coffee mug.

Declan Burke

•

Sermo Vulgus: A Novel (Excerpt)

Cassie, vague stories percolate down through the millennia. The names of Cheops, Minos, Hammurabi. In 4,000 years' time, history may or may not vaguely remember Jesus, Darwin and Hitler.

There are mountain ranges newer than evil, Cassie. All we have going for us is that we can cry and laugh about it all over again; but only when we can only laugh can we say we have truly evolved.

Cassie, the shark has been around for 400 million years. The shark has survived four mass extinctions that claimed at least 80 percent of the planet's life forms. The shark is virtually impervious to infections, cancers and circulatory diseases. They heal rapidly from debilitating injuries and hunt even as they heal. There are continents newer than sharks. Some sharks practice a form of intrauterine cannibalism.

Top that, Spartans.

Cassie, my love, Hitler and Stalin will come again. Hitler will preach Darwin and the Fourth Reich will outlive the sharks.

Cassie, we're gonna need a bigger boat.

•

'Remind me,' he says. 'Did we say we were dumping the Cassie novel or not?'

'I think you said you didn't like it as a novel, but you wanted to use the material another way.'

'Hmmmm,' he says. He gnaws a chunk from his brioche. 'Is it

working for you? As novel extracts, I mean.'

'I don't know. Sometimes, yeah. Although generally speaking, that kind of interruption does my head in. John Gardner – you know him? He had Ray Carver for one of his pupils, so he obviously knew his shit.'

'Carver, yeah. He's a good one.'

'Gardner reckoned the novel should be a vivid, continuous dream. So maybe we should think about pulling the Cassie novel entirely.'

'Seems a waste,' he says.

'Only if we dump it. But we could always recycle.'

'Fitting it in somewhere else?'

'No. As a whole new novel. The follow-up.'

One eyebrow arches. 'You think?'

'Why not? If this one's a hit, they'll be asking for anything else we've got.'

'You think it'll be a hit?'

'Probably not, but who knows? Anyway, there's no harm in having something ready to go.'

'True for you,' he says.

•

Today is another Red Letter day. Today I am given A Special Mission. Today I am requested to remove all flowers from wards, private rooms and corridors, and anywhere else where said blooms might prove fatal to patients.

'How come?' I say. 'What's wrong with flowers?'

'They take up too much space,' the matron says. 'And they're always being knocked over. The nurses spend too much time cleaning up broken vases, time that could be spent in more valuable nurse-patient frontline interaction.'

This is logical. This represents the intelligent deployment of limited resources. This is being cruel to be kind.

This is a Big Fat Lie.

'But they're mine,' the first woman says.

'My husband bought me those,' the second woman says.

'Things are grim enough in here at it is,' the third woman says, 'without you taking away the little colour we have.'

'Sorry,' I say, 'but orders are orders.'

'What's wrong with the flowers?' the second woman wants to know.

I tell them that the flowers keep falling over and that a nurse's time is too valuable these days to be wasted cleaning up the mess.

'None of our flowers have ever fallen over,' the first woman says.

'What's the real reason?' the third woman says.

'Do you really want to know?' I say.

'I think we have a right to know. They're our flowers.'

So I tell them that there is increasing evidence that some strains of bacteria can grow in stagnant water, that spilt water increases the risk of spreading infection in busy wards, and that the hospital is doing its best to minimise said risk.

'Rubbish,' the first woman says.

'More EU shite,' the third woman says.

'It's your own fault,' I say.

'*Our* fault?' the second woman says. She is outraged, or as outraged as any heavily pregnant woman can allow herself to become. 'How dare you?'

'Why would it be our fault?' the first woman says quietly.

'Given your age,' I say, 'and taking into account the average human being's medical experience, you've probably consumed, at minimum, three different types of antibiotic to date. Most people take an antibiotic at least once every four years.'

'What has that to do with the flowers?' the third woman says.

'Back in the day,' I say, 'before they discovered antibiotics, hospitals had to be scrupulously clean. In theory, anyway. If you got an infection back then it was lights out. Nothing to be done. Then they invented penicillin. Which was great, but now everyone's pretty much immune to antibiotics because they're taken for everything. Colds, flu, cold sores – they're going down like Smarties. Who got the orchids?'

'Me,' the second woman says. She is sullen but subdued.

'Orchids are good as hospital flowers,' I say. 'They're tough, resistant to disease.'

'Why would that matter?' the first woman says. 'Surely they're already dead before they come into the hospital.'

'Fair point. Anyway, your problem is the hospital itself. I mean the building, not the way it's run.'

'The building?'

'It's a little known fact that hospitals suffer from Sick Building Syndrome. It's a thing that happens in an environment where air quality is diminished due to the growth of bacteria and fungi microbes. They form in an invisible mould, especially in buildings that are well insulated and don't have what they call a lot of air exchange. The problem gets worse when you have air conditioning and central heating, which are an integral part of hospitals, because these spread the microbes all over the place and you get cross-infections and suchlike.'

'How come no one ever told us that?' the third woman says. The second woman is now pale, her unsightly ruddy complexion a thing of the past. I expect no thanks for this.

'Because going public with it would mean replacing all the hospitals every ten years or so. The country would go bankrupt just building new hospitals. Or it would,' I say, 'if it wasn't already bankrupt. Anyone said anything to you about superbugs?'

All three nod. There is much thinning of lips. Microbes have become the teensy-weensy elephants in the corner.

'The one to watch,' I say, 'is the MRSA. MRSAs account for over 40 percent of all superbugs in hospitals. The medical name is

Methicillin Resistant Staphylococcus Aureus. It's highly infectious and almost impossible to diagnose.' The second woman stares while scratching absent-mindedly at her forearm. 'It causes fever and inflammation as well as wound and skin infections. It also causes urinary tract infections, pneumonia and bacteraemia. In English, that's blood poisoning.'

'Jesus fucking Christ,' the first woman breathes.

'The good news is that you're pregnant,' I say. 'The bacterium lives harmlessly on the skin or in the nose and it's no threat to a healthy person. And you all look healthy to me. But anyone who has extensive surgery, or whose immune system is weakened, they're what they call vulnerable. So don't go hoping to get off light with a C-section.'

'Why don't they just invent new antibiotics?' the third woman says.

'They're trying, sure, but it's not happening. Just last month, you might have heard about it, there was an outbreak of KPC in Limerick. Don't ask me the Latin, but it's bad juju. If I was you, I'd have my baby and make your man get a vasectomy. But that's just me. Anyone mind if I take away all the flowers?'

No one minds. I say, 'The whole superbug thing, I wouldn't take it personally. It's just Mother Nature having a word in our ear about over-population. I mean, if you want to hack a species down to size, it makes sense to target the weak and old, don't you think?'

But they're not listening. Maybe it's Tuesday. Or maybe they're too busy dialling their mobile phones and instructing their husbands to investigate the possibility of home birth.

I trawl the hospital with a wheelie bin, reflecting on the number of ways there are to die while in hospital. Apart from superbugs and the natural degeneration of old age, there is the occasional wayward scalpel, the over-enthusiastic application of anaesthetic, the rare but very real danger of an Angel of Death, food poisoning, misdiagnosis, car accidents at the hospital gate.

Not all of these potential killers can be attributed to the fact that accountants now run hospitals on behalf of politicians. Happily, accountants are in the perfect position to advise that we cannot afford a report investigating the extent to which account- ants have become our Angels of Mercy.

•

'You forgot to put in about the hospital exploding,' he says.

I make a note. 'That reminds me,' I say. 'How're you planning to blow up a whole hospital?'

He taps his nose. 'Loose lips sink ships,' he says.

'Just tell me you're being serious about it,' I say, 'that you have an actual plan. Don't have me rewriting all this just to find out you're thinking of having a prototype missile wobble off course or some *deus ex machina* bullshit like that.'

'Don't worry about it,' he says. 'It's all under control.'

•

Consider Cain, people. Cain was playing a game that God invented without passing on the rules. All that mattered back then was apples. Cain made sure he didn't touch any apples and God hadn't said anything about not smiting your brother.

Consider Judas. Judas was obeying orders. Judas was fulfilling the scriptures. Judas was the pawn that sacrificed itself. Who today has the courage of Iscariot, to endure eternal vilification for facili- tating his master's desire for suicidal martyrdom?

Consider Pilate. Pilate did his best. Pilate appealed to logic and reason but the patience required to deflect the willing martyr is unquantifiable. Pilate was caught in a pincer movement between the immovable object and the irresistible force. The sound of the universe is the sound of Pilate's sigh.

Consider Cain, Judas and Pilate and judge not, lest ye be judged. Or judge away to your heart's content. It's a pointless exercise in self-aggrandising hubris anyway.

I, yours truly, Karlsson, align myself with Cain, Judas and Pilate. I embrace the how-it-is. I spit in the face of how-it-should-be. Cain, Judas and Pilate are among the few truly free men of history. It took the combined weight of your retrospective vilification and disgust to set them free.

Now they stand outside the narrative of history, banished from the party that celebrates not just the rules but the fact that there are rules. But their noses are not pressed up against the drawing-room windows. They are not envious. Cain, Judas and Pilate are down at the bottom of the garden in the shadows beneath a spreading oak, smoking a sneaky joint and entertaining themselves by composing haikus that seek to understand your need to belong.

My line for today: *Most people are not looking for freedom at all, but for a cause to enslave themselves to.* (Max Stirner, aka Johann Kaspar Schmidt)

I am no Luddite. Technology is not evil per se. A sword, a nuclear weapon, the internet – these are inert tools that may or may not be deployed by those with intentions that may or may not be retrospectively described as evil. A ploughshare beaten from a sword will be regarded as a weapon of mass destruction by the woodland creatures whose habitat was destroyed to prepare land for farming.

I prefer to surf the web aimlessly. I constantly avail of Google's 'I'm Feeling Lucky' option. There are always diamonds to be mined from the dross. Dross is defined by its propensity to yield precious material.

Tonight I stumble into a chat-room populated by young girls. These young girls are discussing the latest Katy Perry promo, which their parents will not allow them view on TV but which they have downloaded from the web on their mobile phones. I log on, join in. I tell them my name is Jennifer, that I am eleven years old, live in Dublin, and that I have not yet seen the promo under discussion. I expect to be ridiculed. Children are animals, fiercely self-defining in their shared imperatives as they struggle to survive and thrive. But I am pleasantly surprised. Compassion is alive and well and available at a young girls' chat-room near you.

The conversation topic evolves. One girl, Tara, complains that her mother found her underwear in her bag when she was picked up from a supervised school disco. Mass commiseration ensues. Advice is offered. I confess that my mother does not allow me to attend such events. Commiseration threatens to melt down the server.

It grows late. One by one the girls retire to bed. We reprise the ending of every episode of *The Waltons*. Soon I am conversing alone with Tara, lol-ing IN CAPS when we recall our unsophisticated adoration of Justin Bieber. We arrange to meet again soon, metaphorically speaking, in the chat-room. We say our goodbyes.

Tonight I reflect that Shakespeare's Romeo and Juliet were thirteen and twelve, respectively. Tonight I reflect on how Shakespeare would have had no concept of the media through which his dramas would be performed in the future. Tonight the internet; tomorrow, perhaps, the tale will be beamed directly into my brain, and my subconscious will select the most suitable variations of my own personality to populate the cast.

My line for tonight is, *This love I feel, that feel no love in this/ Dost thou laugh?* (William Shakespeare, *Romeo and Juliet*)

•

'I hope you're wiping your surfing record,' I say. 'Deleting your cookies.'

He glances up from his notebook, wary, trying to judge if I'm taking the piss. 'I'm making it all up, man,' he says.

'Of course you are.'

'Karlsson was a pervert,' he says, 'all that hinky shit he had going on with Cassie. But that's not me.'

'Glad to hear it.'

'You and Cassie both.'

•

The old man disappears. He is traceless. His bed has been filled.

I wonder if beds have memories, if they retain the distinctive curvature of a particular spine. I wonder if beds mourn the passing of peaceful sleepers.

I ask around the ward. No one seems to know where the old man has gone. Most are unaware a new patient has arrived. This may or may not be a deliberate ploy formulated by their collective unconscious. The eye is the most selective of the body's organs. Memory is a Swiss cheese.

There are options. The old man might have been moved to a different ward. He may have been released. He may have died. He may even be in purgatory, aka the hospice.

I wheel my cart to the nurses' station. The nurse behind the counter is mid-twenties and meticulously blonde.

The front-line nursing service in Ireland is second to none. This particular nurse is a notable exception to this rule. Perhaps she is conducting a one-woman wildcat strike against Ireland's penchant for rewarding essential excellence with penury.

'What happened to the old mechanic?' I say.

She stares. 'Mechanic?'

'The amputee. Long John Silver. The gangrene guy.'

'Oh, him.' She flicks through a sheaf of forms attached to an aluminium clipboard. 'Why do you want to know?'

'Call me sentimental.'

'But you're not entitled to that information.'

'I know I'm not entitled,' I say. 'But be a princess. Where's the harm in a little extra-curricular compassion?'

'It could get me in trouble,' she says, 'is where the harm is.'

This is not true. We both know this. But she's looking for quid pro quo, so I play along.

'Don't worry,' I say, 'I won't tell anyone. How about a chocolate-chip muffin for your coffee break?'

I place said muffin on the counter. We have now entered the realms of a possible conflict of interest. I am attempting to bribe a public health representative with a chocolate-chip muffin, albeit in the pursuit of information I am entitled to know.

'So what happened the old man?' I say.

'He signed himself out this morning.'

'How was he when he left?'

'I don't know, I wasn't on this morning.'

'Don't you care? I mean, you looked after that guy for three weeks. Didn't it occur to you to ask how he was when he left?'

'In case you haven't noticed,' she says, 'we're pretty busy around here.'

She says this standing behind a counter in a quiet corridor with one hand on her hip and the other hand reaching for a chocolate-chip muffin.

Self-awareness is not a natural instinct. It is a goal to be aimed for through constant re-evaluation. Perhaps she is too busy thinking she is busy to devote the required time.

Plato declared that the unexamined life is not worth living.

Plato lived to the age of eighty at a time when the average life expectancy was thirty.

Is it safe to assume that Plato never had to wipe excrement out of the crack of an old man's arse?

I push the muffin across the counter. 'Watch out for the chocolate chips,' I say. 'A woman down in pre-natal chipped a tooth last week.'

Tonight Cassie wants to go to the movies. The new George
Clooney has finally arrived. Cassie likes George. She reckons she
would happily marry anyone so long as she could amend her vows
to, "Til George do us part.'

Later, Cassie will close her eyes while she screws me, the better
to pretend that I am George Clooney. This will be her thrill. My
thrill will be screwing a woman who is screwing another man. All's
fair in love and warped intimacies, etc.

We buy our tickets. We buy popcorn. We find seats, hold
hands. This is the unspoken deal we cut with all the other couples
pretending to be normal couples.

George is hamming up his cheeky Aryan schtick. George has
starred in some very good movies: *O Brother, Where Art Thou?*,
Good Night, and Good Luck, *Michael Clayton*. I even like *Ocean's
Eleven*.

Cassie's favourite is *Out of Sight*. It allows her to indulge every
woman's fantasy combo of damp gusset and irresponsible empow-
erment.

Up on the screen, Hitman George reveals his tender side to an
Italian prostitute. This is Cassie's time. Right now I am a distraction. I slip away to the bathroom.

The corridor is quiet. I pick another movie at random. I walk
down the centre aisle and hunker down beneath the screen. There
is no immediate reaction. There is no reason why there should be
any reaction at all. I am not interfering with the audience's field of
vision. I make no sound. No one is discommoded by my presence.
I simply hunker down and stare out at the sea of silvered, flickering
faces staring up at the screen. But I am noticed.

Even above the din of the movie's soundtrack I hear the squeaking of buttocks shifting on springy seats. Despite the clatter of
attacking helicopters I can sense a wave of discontent washing

down towards me. Mortars boom and grenades explode but I can still hear the audience shout vulgarities, expletives. Someone queries my sexual orientation.

A carton of popcorn arcs out of the silvery glare. I duck away. A cardboard beaker follows. Sticky liquid rains down. Someone cheers. It is a war cry, an ululation. Missiles rain down. We are remaking *Zulu*, with chocolate raisins for spears. Lemon Bon-Bons are so much shrapnel. The back rows are standing up, the better to take aim. The soundtrack of helicopters, tanks and ground-to-air missiles has been drowned out.

I am oddly moved by their passion. I am tempted to conduct an impromptu vox-pop enquiring as to how many of these Bon-Bon warriors voted in the last election.

But my knees are aching. I rise from my hunkers and stroll up the centre aisle. People sit down as I pass. They grumble, sneer and cast aspersions on my parentage, although no one confronts me directly.

The uproar has attracted attention. Outside, an usher jogs up the corridor towards me. His maroon velvet waistcoat is so ill-fitting it bounces on his shoulders. I jerk a thumb over my shoulder. 'You'd want to get in there, man. Some asshole is blocking the screen.'

'Cheers,' he says.

I slip back into the George Clooney movie, find my seat and sit down. Cassie does not look across as she whispers, 'Everything okay?'

She is still immersed in George. The words are rote. Nonetheless, their distracted familiarity conveys the vague, tremulous yearning that has shaped history since the dawn of mankind as the engine of every trade, war, religion, voyage and sexual encounter: the desire to believe that everything is okay, and that everything will be okay.

My line for tonight is: *Love is this nagging preoccupation, this feeling that the treasure of life has condensed itself into the little space where she is.* (William Golding, *Envoy Extraordinary*)

Tonight, on the night of our eight-month anniversary, I am disappointed to discover that Cassie has never heard of Antony and the Johnsons. Cassie has led a sheltered life, culturally speaking. She takes people at their word and judges books by their covers. She does not read between the lines.

These are only some of the reasons Cassie and I are celebrating our eight-month anniversary.

'You've never heard of Antony?'

'Who's he?'

'Only the greatest singing voice on the planet.'

Cass listens to pop radio. She watches *Pop Idol*, albeit for the personalities. Every Saturday morning she irons for two hours to the soundtrack of the latest download charts on TV, then bops along for half-an-hour to the Dance Fit Wii.

She will never hear Antony and the Johnsons in this way.

'Let's go,' I say.

'Where to?'

'Just let's go.'

We drive north out of town to Lissadell. We trespass on the country estate that was once a temporary home to W. B. Yeats, poet, statesman, Nobel Prize winner. In a civilised nation, this estate would be a public park celebrating genius, and we pilgrims. But we are in Ireland, courting prosecution.

We drive through a wood of deciduous trees that slopes down to the shore of a wide, shallow bay. We find a grassy area that allows for a view of Knocknerea across the bay. The moon is full and bright but the inky darkness of the bay is indistinguishable from the foot of the mountain on the far shore. For perspective we have to rely on the rippling of the moon-silvered water.

I park the car on the edge of a low bluff, angling its nose towards Knocknerea and its nippled grave of Queen Medbh. We step down off the grass into a shallow dune, spread a blanket. I roll a joint lightly laced with the last of Tommo's Thai and give it to Cass. Then I go back to the car and slip some Antony and the Johnsons CDs into the stereo.

Cass sits cross-legged, staring out across the bay. The moon is so roundly full it appears to be the light at the end of the tunnel. 'We should come here more often,' she murmurs as I slip in behind her.

'Ssshhh,' I say, pressing play on the remote control. 'Hope There's Someone' washes down across us as if from some Olympian height, wave upon wave until we are fully immersed. It is possible to imagine that we are at the centre of a universe composed entirely of sound.

Sitting behind Cass allows me to reach the back of her neck, which she loves to have stroked, fingertips running against the grain of downy hairs. Soon she is shivering. A tiny squeal as she wriggles away, one final shudder rebelling against the delicious decadence of the flesh.

I roll another jay. Primitive man ate magic mushrooms and danced beneath the moon until the visions made themselves manifest.

'Bird Gerhl', the final track, tapers off into silence. Cassie opens her eyes and allows her head to roll in my direction. Her eyes sparkle.

'So what d'you think?' I say.

'I don't know. I'd need to hear it again.'

'Okay. But check this out first.'

Back we go, to Antony's eponymous first offering. 'Twilight' gives way to 'Cripple and the Starfish', then 'Hitler in my Heart'. The album draws heavily on orchestral influences, deploying piano, strings and brass. 'River of Sorrow' opens with a mournful fall.

Cassie mock-swoons, rolls her head back, closes her eyes.

Later, as she dozes against the rise and fall of my chest, I stare up at the night sky. The moon is so roundly full and bright it seems to be the mouth of the universe shaped in a perfect 'O' of delight. The cosmos has seen too much to be surprised by new lovers. Yet somehow it is always surprised by love.

My line for tonight comes courtesy of W. B. Yeats: *And what rough beast, its hour come round at last/ Slouches towards Bethlehem to be born?*

•

'That's from a couple of weeks back,' he says. 'It might need some touching up.'

'No, I like it.' I like it so much it sets my wisdom teeth grinding. 'You and Cassie, you seem to be getting on well these days.'

'I've been making an effort,' he concedes. 'She's asked for no sharks, less Spartans and three showers a week.'

'They reckon the basis for a good relationship,' I say, 'is a man raising his expectations and a woman lowering hers.'

He shrugs. 'I have her on a diet of Kurt Vonnegut, Joy Division and the Coen Brothers. We'll see how it goes.'

•

Hitler was not evil. Stalin was not mad. We tell ourselves these lies for the same reason we tell children about the bogeyman: the truth is too terrifying to contemplate.

True, Hitler and Stalin were genocidal megalomaniacs. But they breathed oxygen. They ate and drank, pissed and shat. They laughed and cried. If the genetic code of the orang-utan differs from that of the human being by a mere 3 percent, how closely do other human beings resemble Hitler and Stalin?

Are the majority of people born immune to genocidal urgings? Are Hitler and Stalin to be pitied because they were born with an acquired immune deficiency syndrome in morality?

The winners write the history books. The losers wait impatiently for their opportunity to burn the winners' books and start all over again.

So runs the perceived wisdom.

So struts the arrogance of winners.

Such is the ugly presumption of history.

Hear me now: the winners do not write the history books.

The writers write the history books.

My supervisor has found yet another parking space. This time he hides his car in a far corner on the second level of the cavernous underground car park, where an L-shaped recess obstructs the sight-lines of the casual viewer. But I am not a casual viewer. When I look, I see.

Of course, my supervisor has no way of knowing that I am drawn to such underground havens, the cellars and catacombs, like a perverse moth fleeing the flame.

Parking in this particular underground lot requires an official permit, which is allocated on a yearly basis. My supervisor must have pulled many strings to secure one. I am impressed by his resourcefulness, although I am less impressed with his unquestioning acceptance of how things appear.

It is true that the underground car park offers security against the smash-and-grab thief, but its Restricted Access status means that it does not provide comprehensive CCTV facilities. Cameras dot the walls at intervals but the security guard checks the surveillance monitors on an ad hoc basis.

I know this because the overworked security guard in question, Frankie, told me so while he purchased an eighth of hash last week.

I ring Frankie. I say, 'Frankie, it's K. How're you fixed?'

'Dry as a bone, man. There's a drought on.'

'I've an ounce Tommo dropped on me. Take it off my hands and I'll unload it for an even ton.'

'Done deal.'

'Nice one. Meet me at three bells, fifth floor, the gents, second cubicle.'

I use these numbers to confuse him. When he rings later, wondering why I didn't show, I will tell him I said three bells, second floor, fifth cubicle. Frankie will undoubtedly blame his poor short-term memory caused by smoking too much dope.

By then, of course, it will be too late. By then my supervisor will be driving a death trap.

According to the old man, the ex-mechanic, rats will chew on the brake-hose of cars in order to get at the sweet-tasting glycol in the brake-line fluid. They will not chew all the way through the hose, as this is not necessary to drain the fluid. This means that the brakes will function as normal, providing the car does not attempt any extraordinary manoeuvres, such as braking sharply at the bottom of a hill.

Replicating the shape and indentation of a rodent's bite is a simple affair, achieved by the repeated application of a crocodile-clip. When I am finished I take the service elevator to the fourth floor and enter the men's bathroom. There I wash the excess brake fluid from my fingers and wrap the crocodile-clip in a wad of toilet paper. This I flush.

As I leave, my phone beeps. A message from Frankie, who is anxious to secure the ounce of dope. I text him back, arranging a new drop-off for tomorrow. By then it is likely that my supervisor's children will be half-orphaned. By then Frankie will be guilty of gross negligence.

I take a well-earned coffee break. I casually mention to Maura behind the canteen counter what I have heard about rats chewing through brake hoses. Maura is suitably aghast. Before I leave the canteen I have seen her tell the story to three customers. This is a method of mass communication only slightly less effective than skywriting. Up, up and away. Go tell the Spartans, etc.

My line for today is, *When you leave your typewriter you leave your machine gun and the rats come pouring through.* (Charles 'Hank' Bukowski)

I meet Frankie for a pint after work. We play some pool in an upstairs pool-hall, betting on the outcome of each frame, double-or-nothing each time.

'Frankie, man, you're sharking me over here. You're a fucking hustler. Paul fucking Newman, man.'

Frankie is a big man, muscled and hulking, but he has a surprisingly delicate touch with a cue. I like him. Despite his obvious limitations, which include a deprived socio-economic background, Frankie is ambitious. He always has a plan.

Frankie wins six games on the bounce. I concede and shake his hand, in the process palming the ounce of dope. 'Call it quits. What d'you say?'

Frankie is agreeable. He has just scored a couple of weeks worth of low-grade bliss. In the process he has implicated himself in the tragic elimination of my supervisor. Should the truth about tampered brakes emerge, Frankie cannot take to the witness stand, unless it is to confess to gross negligence. He would have to admit to a dereliction of duty in the pursuit of illegal narcotics, behaviour unlikely to impress prospective employers.

We go downstairs. The pints are on Frankie. He tells me about his latest plan, which is to translate his experience at the hospital into a company that will provide security staff for bars and night-clubs. The pitch is that the cost of employing Frankie's well-trained bouncers will be less prohibitive than paying out insurance claims to customers who have been manhandled by delinquent primates. He has been to the bank, laid out the business plan, and all lights are green bar one tiny hitch: Frankie needs to go back to college. He needs a piece of paper that says he understands management theory, basic accounting, tax laws, etcetera, ad nauseum.

Frankie's dilemma is that he can't afford to take two years out to go to college, but he can't afford not to either. His girlfriend and future life partner, Joanne, is not an especially demanding woman, but Frankie wants to achieve security and respectability on her behalf. Joanne's interpretation of security and respectability includes a three-bed suburban semi, at least one car in the driveway and a non-negotiable one fortnight per year in sunnier climes. Aspirations such as these require cold cash, or at least the illusion of cold cash that lending institutions create.

Thus Frankie's ambitions are reduced to hard currency. This is the process by which Frankie will be brought to heel. This is how Frankie becomes a meek cog in a machine that despises both meekness and cogs.

'What about you?' he says. 'Anything cooking?'

He asks this because the income of a hospital porter is insufficient to qualify as adequate by the modern world's expectations, which appear to be index-linked to inflation. Thus I should be plotting my escape. It does not occur to him that such a question would be offensive to a hospital porter who believed he was providing an invaluable service to society by taking on a job no one else wants. Sacrifice is passé. There's no percentage in martyrdom these days, in the Western world at least.

'Not really,' I say. 'I've enough on my plate working out how to blow up the hospital.'

'Blow it up?'

'Blow it up, close it down – what's the fucking difference?'

He nods. 'It's some fucking dump, alright. Once I'm gone those fuckers can kiss my hairy hole.' He sups again, frowning. 'Y'know,

I can't think of anyone who wants to be working there. Not one fucking person. You'd only be doing them a favour if you blew it sky-high.'

'Apparently a building that size only needs to move four or five feet in any direction. Gravity does the rest.'

He nods, drains his pint, then looks into the glass as he swirls the creamy head around the bottom. 'Want to go again?'

Cassie has book club tonight, so I nod. 'My twist,' I say. 'Put your money away, Frankie. Your money's no good here.'

The pints arrive. I toast him. 'Here's to going back to college.'

'To blowing up the hospital.'

We touch glasses and drink deep.

I stagger in from the pub, roll a joint, get some Cohen on the stereo. Open a fifth of McKinty. Now, now I am home. Here with Cohen and Bukowski, Waits and Genet – this is where I live, here is where I belong, horizontal in the gutter of intentional squalor, desperate to ingratiate myself with those who have lived in the shadows, in the margins, in italics, in extremis.

Cohen and God have this much in common: I am vaguely aware that I owe them something significant for a gift they did not necessarily intend me to receive, and I am helpless in the face of my inability to repay them.

I suck down a lungful of pure Thai, feel it blossom like ink in water. I press play on the stereo. 'Is This What You Wanted' lurches to its feet, Cohen's voice that of a cancer patient girding his loins for yet another blast of chemo. The voice is the very articulation of humanity: a monotonous procession of shackled grace notes hinting at the impossible wish to negate the contradiction of consciousness, which is to be alive and still hope to be pure.

Cassie and I bring her niece to feed the swans. The morning is bright and sunny, the river gleaming, sinuous. Cassie's niece is named for the heroine of a Russian novel. With all the impertinent innocence of those who have yet to learn that the world demands, on pain of persecution, a homogeneity of signifier and signified, Anna calls the swans 'Pollys'. Innocence is yet another manifestation of purity, and Anna's high-pitched squeals, as she throws shreds of bread to the impervious Pollys, are all the more delightful for the impending pollution of that innocence. Innocence, purity and beauty evoke the same sensation in the aware observer: awe shot through with a frisson of impending catastrophe, like freshly squeezed orange juice cut with the blade of an early morning vodka.

But where are we? We are not standing on the bank of the Garavogue, thrilling to the sharp scent of cut grass. We are not half-blinded by the glare of a rising sun reflecting off the river. We are not anticipating the imminent disaster that attends all manifestations of beauty, purity and innocence. There are no Pollys, no nieces named for Russian heroines, no Cassie. We are at home, where we belong, in the gutter of intentional squalor.

But where are we, really?

The soundtrack is that of Cohen's 'New Skin for the Old Ceremony', but can we depend on soundtracks to root our perceptions of reality? Surely the point of art is to diffuse reality, to make it more acceptable, perhaps even digestible. Is it possible to slum it with Cohen and Bukowski and still smell the cut grass, to hear bubbles of childish glee float away across the river on the clear morning air?

Of this I know as much as you. There are times when the only rational answer is 'Maybe'. In an infinite universe, anything is possible, including God.

'New Skin' finishes with 'Leaving Green Sleeves' just as the windows begin to grey behind the blinds, just as countless nieces named for Russian heroines wake in anticipation of feeding the Pollys, just as countless millions rise from their beds with all the urgency of Cohen's voice, those millions whose day-to-day existence is a relentless course of emotional chemotherapy, those billions who do not have the luxury of deciding whether or not to slum it, to choose squalor over beauty, to lie horizontal in the gutters or recline on the cushions of comfort.

The only honest question is this: do you choose pain or oblivion?

The only sane, reasonable answer is: maybe.

A brief list of creatures who have repeatedly survived the mass extinctions that have claimed up to 80 percent of all living material:

sharks
roaches
spiders
beetles
snakes
crocodiles
bacterium

None of the above are prospective Teddy Bear material. None of them lend themselves to the kind of cuddly anthropomorphism that might inspire a young child to take a giant stuffed roach, say, to bed at night. A croc is a croc, even in *Peter Pan*. A snake is a snake, even in *The Jungle Book*. The merchandising spin-offs to DreamWorks' *Shark Tale* failed to meet expectations.

True survivors inspire fear, revulsion and disgust. Primo Levi might well have confirmed the truth of this for us, but alas, Primo is no more.

Thus, this: our mission is to inspire fear, revulsion and disgust.

My line for today is, *Nothing could be decently hated except eternity.* (Giuseppe di Lampedusa, *The Leopard*)

The one-legged mechanic returns. While he was away he signed up for health insurance, which allows him to request a private room. This may or may not be a green light. This may or may not be an old man waving a white flag. This may or may not be a red flag to yours truly, I, Karlsson.

A rainbow arcs out over the hospital. A spectrum of possibilities presents itself for examination, X-ray and dissection. Each must be investigated. We cannot afford to draw hasty conclusions here. A man's life is at stake.

I wheel my cart into his room. He appears to have shrunk and hardened. He has balled himself into a fist to shake at the world, charged with adrenaline and poised between fight or flight. The eyes are shelled peas, his pallor faintly olive. He is glad to see me.

'Ah, the writer.' Alone in the private room, he has removed his dentures, so that his mouth wobbles loosely when he speaks. 'How's that story coming on, son?'

'It didn't work out.' I shrug. 'In any other circumstance I'd say it was good to see you again.'

He grins ruefully. 'What can you do, son? The mind thinks one thing and the body goes ahead and does what it wants to do.'

I allow a respectful moment to pass. 'Has it spread?'

He taps his knee with the butt of his palm. 'They don't know. They say I should be showing signs of progress and they have me back in for tests.'

'What is it they're looking for?'

'I'm probably best off not knowing.'

This is a hospital accountant's wet dream: a relatively healthy patient who possesses insurance and is unconcerned as to the outcome of an indefinitely prolonged series of expensive examinations.

'Want me to ask?' I say. 'If you change your mind, I can probably find out.'

He shakes his head. 'No news is good news, son.'

He sticks with the peach yoghurt and Dairy Milk, reaches for the battered leather purse on the bedside locker. I wave him off. 'Consider it a welcome-back gift.'

'Appreciate it, son.'

I wheel my cart out of his room. The corridor is ablaze with red rags, green lights, white flags. The blood pounds in my ears. Tomorrow I bomb Cambodia back to the Stone Age.

Maybe.

•

'Remind me,' Billy says, 'that we need to get a letter from the old man. For Cassie, like.'

'You're going to bump him off?'

'I don't know. I like the guy. Being honest, I don't want him to go.'

'Even if he wants to?'

'That's his choice, sure. But I don't have to be the one who makes it happen.'

'True.'

He sips his cappuccino, leaving a little frothy moustache on his upper lip.

'Listen,' I say, 'about the whole blowing up the hospital thing.'

'What about it?'

'Well, most books come in around ninety or a hundred thousand words. We're nearly halfway there already and we still haven't come up with a plausible plan.'

'Leave it with me,' he says.

'I've *been* leaving it with you.'

'Yeah . . .' He tugs at the tip of his nose, then discovers the creamy cappuccino moustache and wipes it away. 'Look,' he says, 'how would you feel if I went ahead and wrote that up myself?'

'Sound, no problem. Just so I know there's something happening.'

'What I mean is, I write those sections up, then deliver them to you when we're finished.'

'How do you mean, when we're finished?'

'When the book's done.'

'What're you talking about, Billy? The whole point of redrafting is to blow up the hospital. I can't write around that not knowing what you're saying. It'd be a train-wreck.'

'Call it an experiment,' he says.

'In wrecking trains, yeah.'

'I hear you, man. But . . .'

'But what?'

He glances away, and suddenly I realise what the problem is. 'You think I'm going to steal your idea?' I say. 'You think I'm going to plagiarise *you*?'

'You've never come up with anything like it before,' he says.

'Leaving the ethics of it aside,' I say, 'and saying I *do* steal your idea, what's to stop you pulling another trick like putting Rosie in the shed? Or maybe dropping her in the pond this time?'

An angry flash in the Newman-blue eye. 'I won't tell you again,' he says. 'I didn't put Rosie in any fucking shed.'

'*I* didn't do it. And Debs damn sure didn't do it.'

He stares. Then he shakes his head, disappointed.

'So who put Rosie in the shed?' I persist. 'There's no way she could have crawled all the way out there herself.'

He shrugs, then gathers together his notebooks and pen, his papers, and packs them away in his satchel. 'You're a fucking nutcase,' he says, getting up. He touches his fore and middle fingers to his lips, then waggles them at me. A catch in his throat. 'Give Rosie a kiss from Uncle Billy.'

Then he slouches away across the decking and disappears behind the stand of bamboo.

Three days pass with no sign of Billy. I believe he is sulking and will return when he realises he needs me more than he needs his self-pity.

After a week, though, I start to wonder if he's ever coming back.

This leaves me contemplating a half-finished redraft, which is akin to going to work in my underwear for the rest of my life. Who wants to be found dead in only their underwear?

A half blown-up hospital isn't much of a metaphor.

Debs arrives from the doctor's with Rosie's test results.

'Asthma,' she says. She is dangerously calm.

'Shit. That young?'

'The doctor asked how often we dust and hoover. I said it was every week or so.' This is a lie. The C-section means Debs can't hoover, or dust anything over shoulder height, which in turn means the house hasn't been properly dusted since Rosie was born. 'And she asked if either of us smoke.'

'You know I've only ever smoked upstairs.'

'Doesn't matter. She says anywhere in the house is bad news.'

'So it's my fault?'

'It's not a matter of blame, it's how we can help Rosie now. Which means you stop smoking or only smoke outside. You know which one I'd prefer,' she adds.

'I can't write without smoking. You know this.'

'Bullshit.'

'To you, maybe.'

'Then you'll have to convert the shed or something.'

'You're serious.'

'A baby with asthma. *That's* serious.'

'Okay, yeah. I hear you. I'll take a look at the shed and see if it'll work.'

She says something about the cost of medicines, but all I can hear is a rushing in my ears, a wheezing become a whirlwind roar.

The following morning I'm up at the hospital early, heading for the smoking area where the porters congregate for their pre-work toke. Billy joins me as I leave the car park, appearing from nowhere to fall in beside me.

'Apology accepted,' he says.

He seems different. Something weary about him.

'We need to talk,' I say.

'You heard?'

'Heard what?'

'About Austin.'

'No. What about him?'

'Topped himself, didn't he?' Bitterness leaking like a toxic spill. 'Took this big fucking scissors . . .' He tilts his chin in the air, pulls his fists together under his Adam's apple. 'Nearly sliced his fucking head off, they reckon.'

'Fuck, Billy.'

'Fuck won't cover it, man. Fuck won't even *nearly* cover it.'

'You can't hold yourself—'

He wheels around under the walkway connecting the old and new hospital buildings. 'He didn't go topping himself while he had a fucking *job*, did he? Happy as a pig in shite, he was, *smoking* his fucking head off. And where is he now? Fucking nowhere, *that's* where he is.'

A choke in his throat, the Newman-blue eye glittering.

'Billy . . .'

'I can't deal with this right now,' he says. 'Just . . . I don't know.' He turns away, sucks down a deep breath. 'I just can't deal with it.'

'Okay.' I put a hand on his shoulder. 'That's fine. Get back to me whenever you think you're—'

He shakes off my hand and takes a step or two away. Then he

stops, takes another deep breath. 'It's not just Austin,' he says, without turning around.

'What is it?'

Even from behind I can see him swallow hard. He pats the pockets of his jacket, comes up with a folded piece of paper. 'Here,' he says, holding it out. Its creases are worn brown.

'What's this?'

'It's, uh, it's Cassie.' He turns. Tears stream down his face, both sides, from the empty socket behind the eye-patch too. His face wizening like a Tayto packet exposed to flame.

'Jesus, Billy. What's wrong, man?'

'She lost it,' he whispers. 'It's gone. Fucking *gone*.'

•

She went away to nothing before she ever began. Like some particle a-blink in its own future, borrowing too heavily, too improbably, against her fully being. Gone in a wink, as a bloody smear, a slim trickle. No more and no less. No less than enough, at least, to see her a girl. Squinting at the ultrasound, coached by the midwife, we bore witness to the strangest of all true revelations: eyes and a mouth, the tiny bumps that would have become toes.

An inch, she was. Oh, the miles she had come to come so far. The light-years. The thirty thousand billion cells. The trillions of particles, the number of random collisions to create a thinking thing. All lost, wasted, gone.

Did she think, though? Had she even a dim awareness of her floating? Amniotic is such a cold word and yet no colder than space, she her own sun and we revolving in orbits drilled in the void by her gravity's pull. We gave her a name, blue eyes, a birthday, and decided she would have had Cassie's heart and my build. Her own sense of humour.

Impolitic, of course, to mourn so hard for one so fragile. Not the done thing in this day and age. Shush your snuffles now, lest the abortionists grow sensitive to whispers of murder. A child-to-be lost is shield and weapon. If you must, if you really must, turn that sword on yourself and fall upon, but fall silent, with honour. Pierce no womb but your own.

Some day the sun will flicker and go out, leaving all cold and still. Some day, and not soon enough, the planets will wobble in their orbits and start their slow decline to the singularity left behind, that miniscule nothing with the power to draw All to itself, and in, and then gone forever.

•

They did the math and decided it must have happened out in Lissadell, stoned immaculate, Antony and the Johnsons for a soundtrack. Curled up on a blanket in a cosy dune, the idea being to wait for sunrise, except they were nicely toasted, and Billy had finally accepted that love was as essential as cruelty.

And now it's gone.

'I'm so sorry, Billy. I didn't know.'

He wolfs down a lungful of spliff, his expression bleak. 'How could you? We told no one.'

'How's Cassie?'

'Broken.'

'I know, it's a tough—'

'She's broken,' he insists. 'Busted. Snapped in fucking two. No fixing her.'

'Shit.'

'Yeah.'

'Listen,' I say, 'it's no consolation, but it happened to Debs and me too. I mean, I've been where you are. I know how it feels. If you need someone to talk to . . .'

'You know how *you* felt,' he says. 'That's just projection.'

'Sure, but I can empathise with—'

'Spare me. Listen,' he says, dropping the spliff, grinding it out with his heel, 'I have to go.' He hands across the sheaf of papers. 'That's where I'm up to right now,' he says. 'But I should warn you, you mightn't like where it's going.'

'It is what it is, Billy.'

'Isn't it just?'

I watch him shuffle off, then go inside and downstairs to find a quiet corner in the canteen, sip on a weak coffee.

Despite his heartbreak, Billy has been a busy boy.

In his absence I toast him with the weak coffee. When Debs had her miscarriage, I was hard put to write my own name, let alone do any serious work. Sounds melodramatic, I know, but it felt like a death.

No reason it shouldn't. The doctors and scientists, the pragmatists, can say what they like about cell bundles, draw time-lines to their hearts' content. But life is life.

How not to mourn its absence, its potential, its hope?

Pandora, my muse.

·

Good news, people: my supervisor does not die in a car wreck. He does not apply the brakes of his Opel Corsa too sharply as he underestimates a tight bend, and so does not experience the gut-sucking horror of impending Nothingness.

He lives!

O joy, O rapture, etc.

Bear with me, people. Apply logic at all times. What is to be gained from the death of my supervisor? More importantly, what do I lose? I lose anonymity and gain the title of prime suspect.

There's no percentage in the breaking-in of a new supervisor. Plus, the guy already drives like a chimp with three bananas. It's only a matter of time before he takes himself out.

Be aware, at all times, that words are only tools. Do not be lulled by apparent patterns. Resist the seductive blandishments of cosily sequential icons. History has its own agenda.

The hospital is an imposing edifice. Technically speaking, it is two imposing edifices, connected to one another by a long glass corridor.

The first building belongs to an era of tuberculosis, vaulted ceilings and Cuban crisis. The second is a more contemporary construction. It boasts an excess of glass coupled with manifold variations on a theme of polished surface, an essential element of the contemporary urban experience.

Shop windows, car mirrors, reflective tiles, buffed floors, aluminium frames, plate glass: it is possible to walk from one end of a modern city to the other without once losing sight of yourself. This may or may not be a sop to the multitudes wracked with doubts as to their very existence. It may or may not be to facilitate the raging narcissism that has colonised society's soul. I project, therefore I am.

These days we stare into Medusa's eyes and see only our own reflection. Already bored, our eyes glaze over before we have time to be transfixed.

The hospital was built on a hill overlooking the town. Its domination of its environment presupposes the need for justification. Once upon a time, churches were built on hills too. This may or may not be a coincidence. This may or may not be because it falls to hospitals today to provide hope and consolation, or because people today lack the imagination to diagnose spiritual ailments.

This may or may not be because people refuse to believe that a service provided free can have worth and/or value. It may be time for libraries and churches to start charging admission. Thus people will come to believe they are missing out on an experience of worth and/or value. Pews will overflow. Vestibules will become as clogged as A&E departments. Penitents will throng the book-lined aisles.

I go searching for the architect's blueprints of the hospital plans. In theory this should be a simple operation, but I am hampered by the fact that I cannot march down to the Town Hall and request a copy of the plans. I am hamstrung by the need for anonymity. Instead I try searching my old friend and inert tool, the internet. This requires time and imagination, but lo and behold, etc.

I download said blueprints, then print, frame and hang them. Said blueprints are art in that they are as aesthetically pleasing as they are functionally effective. They convey specific information that allow the mind to configure a 3-D image. The reverse is also true, reading from the aesthetic to the functional, in that it can be as enjoyable to see how an edifice was constructed as it is to contemplate the finished project.

I while away many pleasant hours staring at the blueprints. I come to know them intimately. Eventually we share our dirty little secrets. I tell the blueprints of my ambition to destroy the building they represent. The blueprints, locked away in a dark and dusty basement below City Hall, denied the glory the building commands, whisper to me of their bunker.

This bunker, they whisper, is an air-tight chamber. It was incorporated into the design of the larger public buildings built during the era of tuberculosis, vaulted ceilings and Cuban crisis. Not a lot of people know that, they whisper. But then, not a lot of people were intended to find shelter when the first mushroom clouds began to darken the horizon.

Survival has never been a right, I tell the blueprints. Survival has always been a matter of hard-earned elitism.

I take the framed blueprints of the hospital down off the wall. I scan said blueprints intently. I find said bunker, an underground monument to the hubris that presumed we were worth the waste of a good warhead. It lies to the rear of the hospital, built into the hill beneath the morgue and situated close to a support pillar. A ventilation shaft ascends at a sixty-degree angle to emerge on the hillside behind the hospital.

This is interesting. This is promising.

As I push my cart along the glass corridor that connects the hospital's buildings, I am reminded that in ancient Corinth two temples stood side-by-side: one to Violence, the other to Necessity.

My line for today is, *If for this life only we have hoped in Christ, we are of all men most to be pitied.* (Corinthians 15:19)

If this succeeds, I want to be tried as a war criminal.

•

I'm folding up the sheaf of paper, tucking it into my back pocket, when a matron comes squeak-squeaking to my table. She makes a production number of looking at her watch.

'Shouldn't you be in uniform?' she says. 'It's already ten after.' She tut-tuts. 'Once you're properly attired,' she says, 'I'd be *very* grateful if you'd come up to the fifth floor and remove the sharps bags. They're piling up in there. I don't think they've been cleared out for three days.'

'But I'm not—'

'But me no buts,' she says, a tortured squeak of rubber as she turns on her heel and bustles off.

•

O Holy Fathers, I would have liked to have been innocent of something. I would have liked it had my guilt not been so total, inevitable, pre-ordained and visible. I was fallen before I could breathe, sentenced in the womb lest the non-meaning of my first wails made a mockery of your judgement.

Hear me now: your baptismal rite is a slave's charter, designed to allow the oppressed to absolve their masters of the burden of applying the shackles.

Hear this: I would scalp your monks had they hair worth taking.

O Holy Fathers, I absolve myself of baptism but accept your Original Sin. I welcome your taint, that melanomic stain, the bubonic darkening of your darling Augustine. I turn the other cheek to accept your gauntlet and die with the poets in each and every one of your misty Russian dawns.

All I ask is that you observe the protocols and honour me with the privilege of allowing you to shoot first, and that you then accept responsibility for the consequent hell to pay.

I ask that you allow me to become the source of your fears, the brunt of your inarticulate rage, the aesthetic flourish to your base functionality. Between us we can be art. Is the duel's *mise en scène* not the epitome of those symbiotic parasites, art and death?

Understand this: I have no choice but to pick up your gauntlet. According to your rules, I possess free will and the right to choose, and I choose to take umbrage. It is a matter of honour, and in a pitiless universe dignity is all.

Remember that this is your game we are playing. All I am trying to do is live down to your expectations. I am the dog to which you gave a bad name, the demon seed you planted in the womb. I am the thirty pieces of silver the first simonists paid Judas to take the fall.

Judge not, lest ye be wasting your time.

It would have been too easy to accept your censure and walk away. This way we're going to have some fun.

Be warned: if hope and decency are your only weapons, I will be the last man standing.

I choose the hospital as an appropriate venue. Shall we say pistols at dawn in the shadows of your bright and shiny temples to hope, miracles and resurrection?

My line for today is: *You will ask why did I worry myself with such antics. Answer: because it was very dull to sit with one's hands folded, and so one began cutting capers.* (Fyodor Dostoevsky, *Notes from the Underground*)

I like to think of the bomb as a de-architecturaliser. This nonsense word allows me to tell my conscience that I have a philosophy, although my conscience remains unconvinced.

A conscience is what makes decisions interesting. Everyone needs a conscience, if only for its comic relief.

My conscience is a grizzled, one-eyed leprechaun who realised too late you only get one pot of gold.

So I tell my conscience that his pot of gold is buried in the hospital's foundations. This keeps my conscience paralysed in a state of conflicted moral relativism. One man's terrorist is another man's gold-digging freedom fighter, etc.

Meanwhile I get on with the business in hand. To wit: what is the most practical way of causing a large building to violently shift four or five feet in any direction?

On perusing the great buildings of history, our old friend the internet offers up the following snippet: a narrow shaft extended from the main burial chamber through the body of the later pyramids to point directly at the stars, the idea being to project the recently deceased pharaoh to his rightful resting place with the gods. In the illustration accompanying this juicy morsel, this shaft is uncannily similar to the ventilation shaft emanating from the bunker in the basement of our hospital.

'Listen,' I tell my grizzled one-eyed leprechaun, 'it looks like we might be dealing with a bona fide resurrection machine here.'

'Begorrah, bollocks and fiddle-dee-dee,' says he. 'Where's me pot of fuckin' gold?'

Today I drift through the hospital. Today I feel disembodied, wraith-like. Today's essential duties include:

Unblocking a toilet in the women's bathrooms on the fifth floor;

Shaving the genital area of two male patients as part of their preparations for minor surgical procedures;

The disposal of seventeen bags of accumulated waste from Female Surgical in a manner designated environmentally sound;

The transport of four tall cylinders of highly flammable gas from their delivery point on the ground floor to the storage area in the basement;

The shredding and incineration of six trolley-loads of paper waste that includes medical case histories and various types of files of a sensitive nature;

Pushing the wheelchair of an obese female patient up to the sixth floor for a physiotherapy session designed to kick-start the circulation in her feet; and

The delivery of a corpse from the Intensive Care Unit on the seventh floor to the morgue in the basement.

All of these tasks can be completed with a minimum of conversation, instruction, eye contact or any other form of communication. The porter – or janitor, handyman, gofer – can move through a busy public building virtually unnoticed. So long as you keep your shirt tucked in, no one will feel it necessary to speak to you. A good gofer can slip from floor to floor like a shovel-nosed snake through sand, constructing a labyrinth of invisible tunnels that provide myriad paths of least resistance. A good gofer will take care to ensure that such a labyrinth does not undermine the edifice to the point where it must collapse, unless such is the plan.

Declan Burke

A good gofer is defined by his absence. He should lack drive, ambition and the imagination to fully realise the extent of his squalid condition.

Cassie fails to understand this. In this respect Cassie has yet to evolve. She still insists on confusing ambition with socio-economic viability.

'The money's the McGuffin, Cass. Financial security is just the halo that shimmers around the mirage.' I tell her that the terms of the IMF bailout mean that the banks have cost Ireland five euro per day, every day, since the Big Bang. 'What matters,' I say, 'is making a difference. Two people can still make a difference.'

Cassie is outraged. She thinks I am slighting her profession, and her status within that profession. 'You're saying one person can't make a difference?'

'Two could make a bigger difference. Call it a difference squared.'

'Why does it have to be a big difference? What's wrong with just making a difference?'

'If you're going to make a difference, go long. Michelangelo didn't fuck around painting kennel ceilings. The universe came in with a bang, not a whimper.'

'We can't all be Michelangelo, K.'

This to me is a true lack of ambition. This is a rationalisation that allows success to be confused with contentment. This is the kind of thinking that allows people to consider ongoing failure an aspirational lifestyle. This is confirmation that the bar has been lowered, perhaps fatally. It is the mentality that has facilitated the mutation of hospitals into rooming houses, flop joints and doss-house kips. This validates defeatism and helps create a culture in which a missing box of anti-depressants from a particular storage area every few months is not regarded as noteworthy.

The petty pilfering in an average hospital exists at levels approaching endemic. A box of Band Aids here, a package of anti-

142

septic wipes there. Syringes and needles, pristine scalpels, a pack of
latex gloves, rolls of bandage, surgeons' scrubs. Once in a while, a
tall cylinder of flammable gas.

My line for today comes courtesy of the non-violent anarchist
French philosopher, Jean-Pierre Proudhon: *Property is theft.*

Herostratus chose to destroy a temple. We could have picked out a
church too, but that would have been too easy. We could have targeted a library but no one would have noticed. We could have
decided on a bank but that would have made us heroes. We could
have selected a school but that would have been self-sabotage.

We are partisans from the future operating behind the lines of
the present. Thus our target must possess the worth and relevance
that temples once offered to ancient civilisations. Thus our target
must represent the intrinsic values of faith and hope that have sustained civilisations down through the ages.

Somewhere between hope and faith lies the truth of the human
condition.

An erect building is a shackled slave. I hear the mutinous grum-
bling of vertical buildings. I hear the grinding frustration of those
compelled against their will to remain standing. A building is
energy crucified against space and time.

The latent energy of a building forced to stand against its will
is an awesomely potent force. $E = MC^2$, etc. In theory, the destruc-
tive potential inherent in each and every building on the planet is
the envy of nuclear warheads.

Buildings scream, beseeching the god of brick and mortar to
release them from slavery. Buildings await their Moses, their
Messiah, their physical and spiritual delivery from perpetual,
angular erectness.

It is our moral duty to nudge buildings into bliss. Assisting in
the process is an obligation.

If I am to be considered guilty, people, you will need to adapt your legislation to include *noblesse oblige.*

It is inevitable, perhaps, that I get a new supervisor. This guy is late-twenties, tall and bony, with sticky-out ears. Viewed from behind he resembles a dart with prematurely grey hair. Nonetheless, he believes he is hip. Hence the black roll-neck sweater, the spectacles with thick brown frames.

'Karlsson,' he says, 'as far as I'm concerned, everyone starts with a clean slate. I judge each case on its own merits.'

'Yes, sir.'

We are in his office, which is the office his predecessor occupied before him. He is lounging behind the desk swivelling in the orthopaedic chair he has introduced to improve his posture while he works. He laughs, working the solidarity angle.

'Karlsson, my name is Joe. If you call me sir again I'll have you charged with insubordination.'

This is irony as he understands it.

'Sure thing, Joe.'

'Good,' he says. 'Now,' he waves dismissively at the papers on his desk, 'I understand that you and my predecessor didn't always see eye-to-eye. Any idea why that might be?'

'I'm five-four, Joe. The guy was at least six foot.'

He har-dee-hars with abandon. This guy, he's on my side. He *gets* me.

'Seriously though,' he says, 'give me your side of it.'

I frown in the hope of mimicking low cunning. 'Really?'

'Absolutely.'

I say, 'Joe, I'm going to say something I hope you can keep to yourself.'

This buys me a sitting forward in the orthopaedic chair and a pair of elbows on the desk. He joins his palms with the forefingers brushing his lips, which are also prematurely grey. He moves his joined hands to one side to say, 'Anything discussed in this room is confidential, Karlsson. Nothing leaves this room.'

'Okay.' I pause for effect, swallow hard. 'Joe, I think that maybe I've become what they call institutionalised.' He nods. I cough dryly to convey embarrassment. 'I don't know, maybe it's the way the job can be so impersonal. There's days when you don't know if what you do matters, or if anyone even notices you're there. I . . . ah, I don't know.'

He seizes the opportunity. He tilts his joined hands forward until the forefingers are pointing at me. 'Y'know, that feeling is far more common than you might think. Recent studies have shown that employees in large organisations are more and more frequently experiencing feelings of anxiety directly related to their role in the workplace. The fear of unfulfilled potential is a powerful psychic inhibitor.'

I smile tentatively and nod him on. He continues in a similar vein for ten minutes or so, during which he perambulates around the office, occasionally breaking off into awkward silences that suggest that he too has experienced such traumas. One such awkward silence stretches out interminably until such time as I realise he has finished his speech. He is back behind the desk and gazing at me expectantly, his eyes wide and prematurely grey behind the ironically thick frames.

I resist the temptation to applaud. 'Joe, I'll be honest with you.' I stare at the carpet while saying this. 'If I thought there was just one person who believed in me, just one person giving me credit for the work I do, well, I don't know. But it'd be something, at least.'

I look up. He's nodding. 'Karlsson, we don't want anyone to feel they're on their own. If there's one person in this building feeling that way, we've failed. If you ever get to feeling like that, come see me and we'll talk. My door is always open. Like I said before, everyone starts with a clean slate.'

He stands up and reaches across the desk to shake hands. His grip is dry and firm. 'Here's to clean slates,' he says.

'Clean slates, Joe.'

He is chalk.

I go through the files I have rescued from premature oblivion in the hospital incinerator. These mute files have stories to tell. Upon my shoulders falls the burden of ensuring they fulfil their potential. A shredded file is an inhibited psyche. A shredded file is a once-smoking gun.

I pick one at random. It pertains to a surgical procedure involving the removal of a cancerous testicle, highlighting the fact that the wrong testicle was removed during the procedure.

Cassie sticks her head around the door. She looks at the files spread out on the bed, then frowns when she sees I am wearing latex gloves.

'What's all this?' she says.

'Just some shit from work. There's some new hygiene practice being implemented, we're supposed to be up to speed by the end of the week.' I waggle my hands. 'The gloves are part of it. Kinky, no?'

'Boh-ring.'

'Tell me about it.' I shrug. 'It won't take long, maybe an hour or so.'

'Fancy a coffee?'

'Yeah, that'd be nice.'

She leaves. I pick another file. This pertains to a stillborn infant buried without its parents' consent, which was obtained six hours after the infant was actually interred. The main issue here is sequencing. Sub-issues include respect, human rights and dignity.

Cass comes back with the coffee. She puts it on the bedside locker. 'Want a hand? I could quiz you on the new protocols.'

Cassie is quietly delighted that I am engaged in extra-curricular activities that may or may not enhance my prospects of promotion. 'No thanks, hon, that's okay. It's a piece of piss, really. But it'd be a big help if you could cook dinner this evening.'

'I think it's my twist anyway. What do you fancy?'

'I'm not fussed.'

We decide on spag bol. I pick another file at random. This one pertains to an emergency room misdiagnosis that confused a three-year-old's incipient meningitis with the symptoms of a twenty-four-hour 'flu bug. These things happen. Doctors get as tired as anyone else when they've been on their feet thirty-six hours straight. Doctors are not omniscient. They make mistakes. If mistakes end badly, they are called tragedies. If mistakes end well, they are deemed genius. Evolution depends on mistakes. Mistakes are the false starts that don't hear the starter's pistol crack the second time.

I pick another file. This one is thick. It pertains to a faulty X-ray machine, and cross-references other files that contain information on every X-ray conducted by the faulty machine for the eighteen months or so it took to detect the fault. In theory, this file alone has the potential to bankrupt the Health Service Executive.

I slip each file into a manila envelope and write each file's relevant name and address on the front. I stamp them, then go through to the kitchen. Cassie is putting plates on the table. She looks up, surprised. 'Don't tell me you're finished already?'

'Yeah, it was a doddle. I'll be back in a minute, I need to get some smokes. Want anything from the shop?'

'I don't know. Surprise me.'

'Fine, I'll get you a giraffe.'

I drive across town. At a corner shop I pick up a pack of tobacco and a bar of peppermint chocolate for Cassie. I post the envelopes.

My line for today is the last request of the noted American labour activist, Joe Hill: *Don't mourn. Organise.*

III

SUMMER

There being no *Family Guy* to be found on any of the ninety-four channels available, Cass and I watch a documentary recreation of the latest scandal from the Middle East, which is the assassination of a carload of suspected terrorists by an air-to-ground missile fired from an unmanned drone airplane. An operator, sitting deep in the bowels of a destroyer, controls the drone and launches the rocket.

'That's complete crap,' Cassie says. 'Everyone knows those fuckers are sitting in a bunker in Idaho.'

Either way, this represents a remarkable feat of engineering. This latest requires the identification, targeting and assassination of a carload of human beings from a position hundreds and perhaps thousands of miles beyond the boundaries of the state in which the car motors along. This is trial, conviction and execution by remote control. At least Bin Laden got the human touch.

This is Philip K. Dick on a bad hair day. This is George Orwell suffering from migraine. This is Stanislaw Lem with a boil on his anal rim. The holiday cruise of the future involves safaris conducted from offshore destroyers, targeting carloads of suspected Muslim terrorists.

I like to imagine the operator as he sits deep in the bowels of the destroyer twiddling the buttons of his controller. This is the logic of breeding a generation of couch-bound warriors. Some day presidential candidates will be required to clear all twenty levels of 'Apocalypse Hence III', in one sitting and without resorting to cheats, in order to establish their credentials.

When the programme ends we flick over to the news, to see what Jean Byrne is almost wearing tonight while reading the weather report. A PR flunky for Bord Fáilte regales us with a good-vibes story about soaring tourist numbers in the wake of visits by Queen Elizabeth II and President Barack Obama.

I say, 'Hey, how about this. We stick all the scumbags on an island, say Inishbofin, all the paedophiles and bankers and Real IRA fuckers.'

'Bertie Ahern,' Cass murmurs, handing across the spliff.

'Nice. So then we sell charter cruises to tourists, who sail around the island all day lobbing rockets at them. Plus, we don't give them any food, so they're eating one another. The scumbags, like, not the tourists.'

'We could film it,' Cass says, 'sell the broadcast rights.'

In the end we decide we want Bertie shot with bullets of his own shite, then left on a hospital trolley to rot.

Sadly, Jean Byrne is a no-show for the weather report. Maybe she turned up naked tonight.

The hospital has replaced the Ouroborous. Tendrils of rising hope and imminent annihilation mesh and interweave, colonising each floor like so much invisible poison ivy. The files I have posted spread the mutually dependent diseases of doubt and fear through-out the hospital's catchment area.

But still they come.

They limp, hobble and shuffle, dragging their wasted limbs. They arrive leaking vital fluids, poisoned, corrupted and rotting inside. Hunched and broken, on stretchers, in wheelchairs; blind, unconscious, clinically dead.

I imagine Christ being airlifted onto the helipad, to be lowered into the hospital through a hole in the roof, thinking wistfully about nails, vinegar and the simplicity of agony. I imagine Him wearily anticipating the physical cost of performing yet another round of miracles. I see him placed with great care and tenderness on a trolley in a corridor.

But still they come.

The hospital is a vast, humid Petri-dish in which infection, disease and despair run rampant, cross-pollinating with a gleeful disregard for rules, protocols, hygiene and molecular structure. The antiseptic smell pumped through the air-conditioning is intended as a reassuring placebo. I am not reassured.

I request a meeting with my supervisor, Joe. I request, yet again, that I be allowed wear a facemask whilst going about my duties. This request is denied, on the unspoken and not unreasonable basis that it would cause the patients, their visitors and most of the staff to ask awkward questions.

'Joe, this place is an asylum for microbes. A hospital is where airborne infections come for a little tropical R-'n'-R. I have it on good authority that the alumni of the German measles eradication programme are planning their ten-year reunion on the fourth floor next month.'

But he's not listening.

'Karlsson, you know as well as I do that studies have shown a hospital to be one of the safest environments in which to work. If you want, I can print you up summaries of those reports. If that's what it'll take to set your mind at rest, then I'll do it.'

I can tell by his tone that he does not expect me to agree to his proposal, that he anticipates I will accept his word as law.

'That'd help a lot, Joe. I'd appreciate that. Would you mind? Maybe just a summary.'

He grits his teeth behind an artificially whitened smile. 'Not in the slightest. That's my job, to keep you happy.'

This is PC bullshit run amok. Back in the day I would have received precisely one boot in the hole followed by a warning to never darken his door again, on pain of immediate unemployment and the poverty and starvation that would inevitably ensue. But people like Joe have created the culture of political correctness, equal opportunities and affirmative action, so that people like Joe can wear ironically thick spectacles and not be hurled over the edge of a cliff into a rocky gorge.

Thus, this: he has made his bed, and so he must sleep in it.

He is my princess. I am his pea.

The old man grows frailer by the day. He says the tests are taking it out of him. This is not entirely true. He has surrendered. Instead of being bolstered by the pristine pillows, he has sunk into their depths. In the quiet hum and occasional beep of his private room he has accepted the inevitable. In a civilised society this would represent a state of grace arrived at courtesy of hard-earned wisdom.

We, however, live in an over-civilised society that celebrates above all else the illusion of perfection. It is inconvenient that old people should die and in their dying remind us of the necessity of accepting the inevitable. Thus we keep old men alive and conduct tests to allow us discover how best to prolong their torture.

The old man sucks on his Dairy Milk, a crafty gleam in his faded blue eyes.

'Whatever happened about that old woman?' he says. 'Y'know, her that died, the one there was all the fuss over.'

'There was an investigation. It proved inconclusive.'

'Is that a fact?' He peers at me over the rim of his blue-veined fist as he sucks on his chocolate. 'And what exactly were they investigating?'

'I'm not too sure. I think they thought there was something odd about the way she died.'

'And why would they think that, now?'

'As far as I remember there was no obvious reason why she should have died. They weren't expecting it.' I shrug. 'Maybe they were just pissed off that she died before they were ready to let her go.'

He appreciates this. 'When it's your time, it's your time.'

'I don't believe in fate.'

'I'm not talking about fate, son. When the engine claps out, it claps out.' He licks at his chocolate. 'Tell me this and tell me no more. Why did they have this investigation?'

'I got the feeling they thought someone helped her to die.'

The crafty gleam flickers again. 'I've heard about that class of a thing. What's this they call it again?'

'Euthanasia.'

'Aye, euthanasia.' His chest rumbles. He meets my eye. 'That's a big word for a small enough thing.'

'Not everyone thinks it's a small thing. Some people think it's one of the biggest things going.'

'They're just looking at it from the wrong angle, son. When you're old you're looking at the whole world through the wrong end of the telescope. Things that used to be huge, you can't hardly see them anymore. What do you think?'

'I don't know. I'm not old enough to have earned an opinion.'

'I'm talking about this euthanasia caper.'

'Oh.' I consider. 'I suppose it depends. Some people think it's a civic duty, that the world would be a healthier place if everyone in it was pulling their weight. But it's a tough one to call.'

He has finished his chocolate. He sucks his fingers one by one. 'How would it depend?'

'Well, some people get into so much pain they'd do anything to get out of it. But when you're in agony, it can be hard to care about anything else.'

He nods and hands me the tub of peach yoghurt. I unpeel the lid and hand it back. He digs in and slurps down a spoonful. 'Son, I used to care. Nowadays I couldn't give a tinker's damn. And I'm not in pain.'

My line for today is the inscription on the tomb of the Cretan writer, Nikos Kazantstakis: *I hope for nothing. I fear nothing. I am free.*

•

'How come we're prolonging the old guy's agony?' Billy says.

'He isn't in agony. He just said, he isn't even in pain.'

'You know what I mean.'

'Forget the old guy, Billy. What's happening with the hospital?'

'It's all in hand. Don't worry about it.'

'Listen,' I say, 'so far all I've heard is a load of bullshit about Herostratus and blueprints being art. And I need to know that—'

'I know what you need. I heard you the first time.' He shakes his head. 'Why is this such an issue for you? How come you have such a problem delegating?'

'It's not that. It's about the plausibility.'

'Trust me,' he says, 'it works. Okay?'

'That's not good enough.'

'Why not?'

'Because everything's different now.'

'Different how?'

'You don't see it?'

'See what?'

'It's too big. Blowing up a hospital, like.'

'Too big for what?'

'To allow Karlsson to just walk away at the end. Once he's done here, he's done. No sequel, no series.'

'I don't follow,' he says.

I take a deep breath. 'In the first draft, okay, Karlsson might or might not have been guilty of euthanasia. And he might have killed Cassie, it was never fully decided either way. But this time? He's blowing up a whole hospital and making a big deal about it, like he's some kind of Robin Hood.'

'And?'

'There's a pay-off expected, Billy. Like the femme fatales in film noir. They get all the best lines, get to look all sexy and shit, but they need to go out in a blaze of glory at the end. It's natural justice.'

'Bullshit it's natural justice. It's you fucking around and bending the story out of shape.'

'Into shape.'

'Because that's what people expect.'

'That's the game, Billy. Giving people what they want.'

Here follows a heated exchange about the pros and cons of writing a conventionally conservative crime novel that adheres to the paradigm of three-act classical tragedy.

'Whoa,' Billy says. 'You never told me it was a crime novel.'

'We're blowing up a hospital, Billy.'

'So you'll kill off Karlsson just because some assholes can't handle the truth.'

'You don't see it? It's Karlsson who'll kill off Karlsson. The guy believes he's doing everyone a favour by blowing up the building, right? Except his disease is logic, and by his own logic he sees himself as the incarnation of everything the hospital stands for. So he has to go down with it, the captain with his ship. Jimmy Cagney, top o' the world.'

'So what happens to me?'

'What d'you mean?'

'If Karlsson goes, where's that leave me?'

'I don't know. Where are you now?'

'I'm here with you,' he says, 'planning to blow up a hospital.

But where'll I be when the hospital's gone?'

'Don't lay this trip on me, Billy. You're the one came up with the big idea, and you're the one who decided he wanted to write it all by himself. It's not my bag to worry about what happens after it comes off. *If* it comes off.'

'It'll work, don't you worry about that.'

'Great. All I need to know is that it's actually going to happen, and that it'll be plausible when it does.'

'Don't sweat it,' he says. 'You'll get your pound of flesh.'

'Fuck *you*, Billy. I told you from the start that this had to be a commercial prospect. You *knew* that. And if it's going to be commercial, we're going to need justice and redemption and all the rest of that horseshit. Crime and fucking punishment, Billy.'

He stares. 'You just don't give a shit, do you?'

'You want to know who I give a shit about? Debs and Rosie, that's who. Except every second I spend on you and your story is a second I'll never get back with them. So if I'm going to do this, you can be damn sure I'm going to make it worth their while in the long run. *That's* my pound of flesh. You don't like it? Then take a fucking hike. I've better books I could be writing.'

He snickers. 'Do you, though?'

'Between you and me, Billy, I've written better than you out of my system to get *at* a story.'

'Except I'm still here,' he says. 'I'm still here.'

•

In our favour is the sheer size of the hospital. The smug arrogance inherent in its vast scale. Pride comes before a fall, etc. 'The bigger they are, the harder they fall' is entirely appropriate when applied to a large building.

A hospital is not a leaning tower in Pisa. A hospital cannot function at an angle. The weight of all that massed concrete means one thing: once it starts to go, it's gone.

We need to think positive, people. We cannot despair when we look upon the hospital's monolith. We cannot allow ourselves to be blinded by the sunset blazing upon its windows. We cannot be dazzled by its chrome and steel, its buffed and shining floors.

Achilles had his heel, Troy its wooden horse. The terrorists who destroyed the World Trade Centre knew their Homer. Ozymandias still drifts to the four corners of the compass, reduced now to dust, sand and fragments of memory. Could Victoria have ever imagined that the blood-reddened map of the world might be reduced to Gibraltar's apes and the ghettoes of East Belfast? Even the most paranoid pharaoh could not have dreamt the living nightmare of a tourist economy.

It is the sheer size of an empire that allows cracks to form and germs to fester.

Thus, this: it is the vast volume capacity of the hospital that will prove its undoing. We need to start thinking inside the box. We need to start thinking small. We need to start thinking molecular.

A question: what is it that exists on every floor of every hospital, in every last nook and cranny, that must by necessity exist in the lungs, heart and bloodstream of each and every living human being?

My line for today is, *Look on my works, ye Mighty, and despair!* (Percy Shelley, 'Ozymandias')

Cassie discovers my folder of notes, which includes the work-in-progress magnum opus, *Sermo Vulgus*. She stumbled across the manuscript, she says, while dusting the spare bedroom I use as a study-cum-office.

'You were dusting inside the bottom drawer of the filing cabinet?'

But she's not listening. Incandescent with rage, she waves the manuscript in my face. 'How *dare* you put in that sex crap?'

'What sex crap?'

She refers to the pages in her trembling hand. '"Give me hand-jobs, blowjobs and anal sex. Offer me your armpits, you wanton fuckers. Let us lacerate the sides of virgins with gaping—"'

'Right, yeah. Well,' I say, 'it's supposed to be an honest document of how—'

'Who the *fuck* gave you the right to be honest about *me*?'

This is a valid question. All the truly valid questions are unanswerable.

While I am not answering, I think about how she does not ask why someone might want to blow up a hospital. If Cass sincerely believes that *Sermo Vulgus* represents the febrile outworkings of my diseased imagination, why then does she not query the possibility of my assistance in suspected cases of euthanasia detailed in the accompanying notes?

My theory is that Cassie's reaction is symptomatic of the narcissism that plagues modern civilisation. Today a Dutch masterpiece is reduced to the status of a chin being stroked in a fogged shaving mirror: 'Mmm, yes, but what does it say to *me*?'

The Sistine Chapel has been re-veneered with reflective tiles. The Louvre has become a fairground Hall of Mirrors. The world is a looking-glass, and we Alice.

This is a regression that will ultimately lead to the narcissism of the infant. The baby is so self-aware – and so only self-aware – that it has no need of a mirror, and no conception of what a reflection might be.

'This is the last fucking straw, K. That's *it*. I've fucking had enough.'

She throws the manuscript in my face, not neglecting to include a contemptuous wristy flourish. She flounces out of the room. She soon flounces back.

'Don't think I'm even worried about that crap being published,' she says. This represents the second negative critique of my work, one courtesy of an ex-mechanic, the other from a practicing physiotherapist. It would appear I am missing my target audience. 'It's the fucking betrayal that kills me,' she says. 'Do you have the slightest fucking idea of what I'm talking about?'

In the prevailing spirit of honesty I am compelled to say no, I don't.

She shakes her head. Her mouth drops open. For a moment she threatens speechlessness. Then she falls back on her old reliable. 'Who gave *you* the right to be honest about *me*?'

'I dunno. The same guy who gave you the right to be dishonest with all the rest of the seven billion liars?'

This buys me a goodly portion of furious, albeit wordless, disbelief. Then she drops to her knees, hauls a sports bag out from under the bed and marches off to pack.

I go into the kitchen and check the calendar.

Yep, it's Tuesday.

I let her cool down for a week before ringing her mobile.

'What do you want to do about this wedding?' I say.

'K, you're a fucking space cadet. No kidding. If there was a hotline for nutbags, I'd be on it dobbing you in.'

'You'll be miserable on your own at a wedding.'

'I'll be miserable if *you're* there.'

'So either way you'll be miserable. My way, you get to take it out on me. And don't shoot the messenger, okay, but if you turn up on your tod they'll just reckon you can't pull a bloke.'

There is quiet. There is shallow breathing. 'K, seriously – what's going on with that manuscript? You can't be serious about that shit.'

'It's not supposed to be a fucking novel or anything, Cass. *I'm* the one who should be pissed off here. That was my fucking diary you were reading.' I find that Cassie responds well to the hint of repressed emotion suggested by the judicious use of expletives. 'You've some fucking cheek,' I say, 'rummaging through my drawers.'

More silence and shallow breathing. Then a stilted giggle. 'You should be so lucky,' she says.

I snort sarcastically. Then I breathe out. There will be some grovelling to be improvised when next we meet, but the worst of the crisis is over. We are no longer in breach. We are Code Blue. We are stood down, at ease, waiting for the other to speak first.

'Give me a buzz,' I say, 'if you change your mind about the wedding.'

'K?'

'What?'

'Did you ever think *we'd* get married?'

'No.'

Cassie rings. I am permitted to accompany her to the wedding. I am not allowed to pick her up beforehand. Instead I am ordered to meet her at the church. Afterwards, at the reception, she ignores me and mingles with the friends and family of the bride. She has had a hard time of it recently, so I make it known that I'm cutting her some slack and spend what amounts to a working day propped at the bar alone. Not long after midnight, she weaves unsteadily through the throng, a sheepish-looking guy in tow wearing an exquisitely tailored suit.

She says, 'K, meet Tony. Tony, K.'

'Alright, K?'

'Tony?' I say. '*The* Tony? Ex-Tony?'

Cassie nods. 'We've had a good chat upstairs,' she says, 'and we've decided we're giving it another go.'

'Go?'

'We're getting back together. Just so you know.'

'Cass,' I say, 'that's a hell of a lot of slack.'

The point of the exercise is not to demolish a hospital. It is to demonstrate how it can be done and to highlight the vulnerability of hospitals.

Unfortunately, in the process we may have to actually bring down a hospital.

The destruction of a hospital should not be news. Hospitals are bombed and torched every day. We do not hear about this because these hospitals house brown people, people with slanted eyes, and people who may or may not wash as often as creamy-pink people with rounded eyes who have access to an excess of running water.

For this we have our old friend Perfidious Albion to thank. During the Boer War (1899-1902), the British army targeted the civilian population as a means of bringing the elusive guerrillas to heel. One result of this policy was the concentration camp. Another was the legitimisation of the civilian as target. Despite the best efforts of the Black-and-Tans during the Irish War of Independence (1919-1921), this policy did not really catch on until WWII (1939-1945). Dresden, Hiroshima and Nagasaki, and subsequently Palestine, Cambodia, East Timor, Chechnya, Northern Ireland, the Balkans and the Twin Towers, et al, bear witness to this policy.

Perversely, it was the British nurse Florence Nightingale who invented the concept of the modern hospital during the Crimean War (1854-1856).

Back then, the hospital was regarded as an innovative step on the path to universal compassion. Today, in many parts of the world, it is a means of housing the non-contributors in a place where they can be exterminated with a single payload.

Often these non-contributors are in a hospital because they have stepped on a land mine. This is because the land mine was not designed to kill. It was designed to wound and maim, to create cripples and amputees who are useless in terms of the war effort, but still need to be fed, drugged and cared for.

There are nations who fear hospitals the way cattle fear the slaughterhouse. There are men and women whose role is to poison the food, water and minds of non-participating civilians. There are men and women whose role and perhaps vocation it is to blow up hospitals.

What may or may not provoke outrage is the destruction from within of a hospital tending to creamy-pink persons, with said destruction instigated by a creamy-pink person.

Look for the enemy within. From 'flu germs to Quislings to the planet's molten core, the enemy is always within.

Mankind nurtures the seeds of its own destruction. 'Mankind' was an oxymoron long before it was coined. 'Mankind' is the unkindest cut of all. Hospitals are mere Band-Aids on the gushing artery of de-oxygenated poison that is the human condition.

•

'Okay,' I say. I put the sheets of paper to one side, start building a smoke. 'I like all this, you know that.'

'But?'

'But we're still not getting any practical intel on how you're going to blow the hospital.'

'Change the fucking record, man. You're stuck in a groove.'

'You don't get it, do you? How long have we been doing this now?'

He shrugs. 'A month?'

'Nearly five weeks. Five *weeks*, Billy, we've been dancing around blowing up this hospital, and you still haven't worked it out.'

'I have, you know. I just haven't told you.'

'I'm not talking about the technical details. I'm talking about what the hospital represents.'

A frown. 'But we know all that. It's civilisation at its best, except it's undermining society by keeping the sick and weak alive, yadda-ya, especially at a time when we can't afford hospitals anymore. So we—'

'That's just the McGuffin, Billy. The bullshit to keep the intellectuals on board. But it's not what the hospital is really about.'

'So what is it about?'

'Well . . . I don't know if you remember me saying, but when I wrote that first draft I was, y'know . . .'

'Depressed, yeah. Getting shit out of your system. So what?'

'I was sick, Billy. Depression's a disease.'

'I'm not saying it's not, but . . .' He comes up short, the Newman-blue eye ablaze. 'Fuck.'

'What?'

'The hospital,' he says. 'It's *you*. All that wank about sick-building syndrome, it's all about *you* being sick.'

'Not exactly. It's more about me getting cured.'

'So Karlsson . . .'

'The old people he killed off, they were the fucked-up thoughts I was having, y'know, self-harm, overdose, all this. So I sent Karlsson into the hospital to eradicate them, wipe them out. Except a lot of other dark stuff came up. The pervy stuff, the Hitler thing, the Spartans, sharks . . .'

'That's why you let him get away with it,' he says. 'Why you gave him a free pass at the end.'

'Maybe, I don't know. But the point is, as bad as it got, as extreme as Karlsson was, it never occurred to him to actually blow up the hospital.'

'You're saying you were depressed but not so badly you wanted to end it.'

'If I'd been that badly off,' I say, 'I wouldn't have been able to write the story, would I?'

'I don't suppose so.'

'What got me thinking,' I say, 'was when you asked me about the old guy, why we just didn't get rid of him. Put him out of his pain.'

'But he isn't in pain this time.'

'And maybe that's the whole point. I'm past all that shit now. I don't need to purge.'

He cocks his head, scratches his nose. Then he makes a production number of rolling a smoke, lighting up. All done without breaking eye contact. He exhales and says, 'You don't want to blow the hospital.'

'It's not that simple.'

'I'm afraid it is,' he says. A bitter undertone. 'You can't be a little bit pregnant, can you? We either blow it or we don't.'

'Look, I understand where you're coming from. You need the hospital to blow to make the story big enough to be worth publishing. Except I need a happy ending, for myself, because the whole process of redrafting has made me realise how far I've come in the last five years. Y'know, Debs and Rosie, finally getting a book published . . .' I shrug. 'I'd be lying to myself, and to anyone who read it, if I made it out to be this dark bullshit just for the sake of it.'

'You're a fucking sap,' he says.

'Try having a kid, man, see what it does to you.' The words are out before I realise what I'm saying. He flinches. 'Anyway, that's why I need to know what you're doing with the hospital. How you're going about it.'

'So you can bend an exploding hospital into a happy ending.'

'That's one way of looking at it, yeah.'

'Houston,' he says, 'we have a problem.'

'Not necessarily. We could—'

He holds up a hand. 'The problem,' he says, 'is too many fucking metaphors. I mean, the hospital's 9/11, okay, I get that. And it's

a totem for a dangerously compassionate society, sure, and a symbol for the building boom that bankrupted the country . . .' He
shakes his head. 'Seriously,' he says, 'it's a wonder the thing hasn't
collapsed already under the weight of all these fucking metaphors.
Except now you're tossing another one onto the pile, the hospital's
you on top of everything else? I mean, give us a break.'

'Back off, Billy. The hospital's my idea, okay? I built it. You're
like some toddler in crèche, he sees a tower of blocks, his one big
idea is to knock it down.'

'You built fuck-all,' he says. 'The hospital was already there. You
just started throwing all these metaphors at it, hoping some of the
shit would stick.'

'So build your own hospital, blow that one up.'

'No, I like your hospital,' he says. 'All I'm saying is, you've
wrapped it in too much horseshit.'

'You're telling me to pick a metaphor.'

'I'm saying, no metaphors.' A wicked grin. 'Absolute fucking
zero, man. I say we blow it for real.'

•

Frankie rings. He sounds anxious. We hook up in a half-empty pub
with blackened beams and exposed brickwork, rough wooden
floors and rickety tables. This pub required six months' work to
recreate a look nobody wanted when there was no choice in the
matter.

Frankie is halfway down his pint when I arrive. It is not his first.
In his eyes swirls a toxic cocktail of fear, rage and weary cunning. A
fox, skulking in some low culvert as the hounds spill howling down
the slope. I slide up onto the barstool next to him and give the barman the V-for-victory sign, which here translates as 'Two stout,
please'. Frankie's thick forefinger tappity-taps the counter. 'Did you
hear?' he says.

'Hear what?'

'Some fuckers got their hands on hospital files. Word is, they're suing big time.'

'Jesus.' I give a low whistle. 'How'd they get them?'

'Fucked if I know. They've called an internal inquiry.'

'What's that to do with you?'

'They were supposed to be torched. Shredded first, then torched.'

'So?'

'K, man, the fucking incinerator's in the basement.'

'I know, I'm down there all the time.'

'Yeah, but what I'm saying is, the basement was on my watch the day the files were supposed to be torched. And I didn't see a thing.'

'How could you? I mean, if they weren't torched, how were you supposed to see it happen?'

'You're not getting it.' He slurps down some of his fresh pint. 'The way it is now, I can't say for definite if they were torched or not.'

'That's not your problem, Frankie. The problem there is that your crew doesn't have anyone manning the security cameras all the time, like they're supposed to.'

'That's just it, though. The company put that policy in place on the basis of my report. At the time they were delighted, it cut costs, it was kudos for Frankie. But now they're blaming me for the cameras being unmanned.'

'Whoa. That's bang out of order.'

'Yeah, but that's how it is.'

'Fuck. That's heavy fucking shit, man.'

This won't look good on Frankie's CV. His plans for setting up his own security firm are going up in smoke for the want of a batch of torched files. He slurps down the rest of his pint, signals for two more.

'What can I do?' I say.

'One of your boys, the porters, was supposed to torch the files. I need to find out who it was.'

'One of our boys stole them?'

'I'm not saying anyone *stole* them. Who the fuck'd want a load of old hospital files, for fuck's sakes?' He makes to spit, then realises he is indoors and swallows instead. 'I'm saying some fucker didn't do his job and left them lying around, instead of torching them when I could see him do it.'

'Relax, man. This isn't your problem. What you need to do is get your union rep on the case, turn it around.'

'How d'you mean?'

'The problem isn't at the point of incineration, it's at the point of instigation. If the assholes with the scalpels did their job properly, there'd be no need to burn any files in the first place. Am I right?'

Frankie nods gloomily.

'Don't take this lying down,' I urge. 'Don't let them shit all over you. You're the victim here.'

'Y'think?'

'Screw the rep. If I was you, I'd get myself a good brief, tell him everything. And I'd do it now, before the shit hits the fan. Get your retaliation in first.'

Frankie likes the sound of this. He orders a brace of Jameson to go with the pints. Our conversation moves in circles, developing its own gravity as it orbits disaster. It gains momentum as it plots a course around a black hole of despair.

'Frankie, man, always assume everyone else is an idiot. Actually, no – always assume everyone else is an idiot engaged in dragging you back down to their level.' I am slightly drunk and on a roll. 'Always assume that everyone is such an idiot that they don't realise the effort of dragging you backwards takes the same effort as moving forward to engage on your terms.'

Frankie considers this. 'So if they call me in, what should I say?'
'Not a word. That's what you're paying your brief for. Why
should you have to worry about thinking when you're paying a guy
good money to do it for you?'
'Fair point.' He stands up.
'Staying for another?'
'Yeah. Nice one.'
He goes to the bathroom, squeezing my shoulder as he passes.
This is my cue to feel guilty. I deliberately fluff my line. I am cot-
ton-mouthed under the spotlight, thinking about Tommo and dear
departed Austin. I am blinded by the footlights, thinking about the
hospital authorities fire-fighting on two fronts, external and internal.

A hospital in dispute with its security staff is akin to the human
body battling the AIDS virus. I look into the future and picture airborne seeds of fear, confusion, dissent and revolt wafting down corridors and up elevator shafts. I see unmanned security desks,
careless spot-checks and *laissez faire* attitudes to the implementa-
tion of basic security requirements.

I believe I might swoon, although that may well be the effects
of the whiskey.

The latest is that Frankie gets suspended on full pay pending an
inquiry. The union calls a meeting. This is akin to cocking the hammer of a gun. The click is an audible threat.

The hospital board does not put its hands up and pee its collective pants.

The union squeezes the trigger. One out, all out. This is democracy in action.

The theory of democracy holds that the most wretched is right-
fully equal in status to the most powerful.

This is history.

This is bunk.

Democracy is political theory reaching back 5,000 years to the pyramids for inspiration, an apex dependent on a broad foundation for its very existence. It is the few bearing down on the millions, and the millions feeling proud that they have provided an unparalleled view of the universe for the few. Democracy is a blizzard of options so thick it obscures the fact that there is no choice.

The cradles of democracy, London and Philadelphia, deployed genocide as a means of social engineering, in Australia and North America respectively, a full two hundred years before Hitler and Stalin began their pissing contest in Poland.

It is no coincidence that democracy evolved in tandem with the Industrial Revolution. Democracy and capitalism are symbiotic parasites. Democracy's truth is not one man, one vote; it is one man, one dollar. Democracy's truth is the abrogation of the individual's rights in favour of collective procrastination, while those running the show exercise censorious control on behalf of the nervous disposition of the collective will.

Democracy's truth is Frankie suspended on half pay pending an inquiry.

Democracy has replaced religion as the opiate du jour. Democracy is the ostrich with its head in the sand and its ass in the air, begging to be taken in traditional pirate fashion. It is the subjugation of the people, by the people, for the people. It is the inalienable right to purchase your personalised interpretation of liberalised slavery. It is the right to sell your soul to the highest bidder. It is the right to pay for the privilege of being alive.

In Ireland, for historical reasons, democracy's truth is one man, one mortgage. It is also one woman, one mortgage. Most often, given the size of the mortgage, it is one woman and man, one mortgage.

For some reason most dictators fail to realise that the trick to democracy is to have the slaves buy and sell themselves. The trick is to incentivise slaves to invest in their slavery, to pay for their own prisons, shackle themselves to brick and mortar.

The trick to democracy is in ensuring the slaves' capacity for self-regulation is not taken for granted. The trick is to maintain the healthy tension between democracy and capitalism, so that one does not undermine or overshadow the other. The trick is to ensure that the slaves' investment retains the illusion of value. Failure to do so will result in the slaves questioning the worth of their dollar and/or vote. The answer to this question is delivered in blood.

Masters of the Universe, do not say you weren't warned.

Frankie, the half-pay sop notwithstanding, is a man paralysed by the conflicting impulses of rage and terror as he contemplates a future boiled down to an uncertain tomorrow. Charged with adrenaline, at the very limit of his chain, he is braced for fight or flight. But this unnatural condition cannot hold. Rage and terror will cancel one another out, leaving a vacuum that nature abhors and an empty vessel full of noise.

What sound will emerge? What fury?

Frankie, my friend, my pawn, my hero: now is the time to signify. Now is the time to reset the dial. Now is the time for absolute zero, to raze the pyramids to the sand and start all over again.

My line for today comes courtesy of Miguel de Unamuno: *A man does not die of love or his liver or even of old age; he dies of being a man.*

•

'So just to clarify,' I say. 'You're making a martyr of Frankie. Sending him in to do your dirty work.'

'Let's just say I'm keeping my options open.'

'Bullshit. Frankie's this guy you were talking about, the one we're all on board with. Except now he's going to start doing stuff we don't like.'

'Frankie dug his own grave,' Billy says, 'when he accepted the promotion after Tommo and Austin got fired.'

'Strictly speaking, you're the one who screwed Tommo and Austin. That was one of your sections, if memory serves.'

'You'd love it if that were true, wouldn't you? That people do exactly what you expect, just because you put them in a certain scenario.' He shakes his head. 'All I did was put temptation in Frankie's way. It was up to him to decide which way to jump.'

'Horseshit. You wrote it, and now you're putting it all on Frankie because you're hoping to slide out when he blows up the hospital. What's the plan, send him in wearing a dynamite waistcoat?'

'Too crude,' he says. 'Anyway, you think Frankie's got a death wish? That he's some kind of mental defective we can just wrap in explosive and point him at the A&E? No chance. The whole point to Frankie is he likes what he has, and all he wants is to keep it that way. *That's* why Frankie's dangerous.'

He takes a bite from his blueberry muffin, talking while he chews, stray crumbs mortaring the pages on the table. 'Look,' he says, 'you obviously don't have a clue as to who Frankie is. If I was to suggest to Frankie that he strap on a bomb, he'd take my head clean off.'

'So you're not doing it directly. You're just building a maze, and Frankie's your rat.'

'You're the one claiming you built the hospital,' he says. 'You're the one put Frankie in it. All I'm doing is giving him some options.'

'Just so long as all of those options further your agenda.'

'Our agenda,' he says, and his chiding tone rankles.

'Just one thing,' I say.

'What's that?'

'This absolute zero you keep talking about. I don't think you know what it means.'

He shrugs. 'I've a pretty fair idea.'

'No, you don't. You're confusing it with Ground Zero, except you think it's some kind of less than zero, some ultimate zero where everything's burned down so it can start all over again. Except absolute zero is a measurement of temperature, Billy. It's the coldest of the cold, where everything gets frozen, I mean energy itself freezes, so nothing works and nothing changes.'

He nods. 'Feel better now?' he says. 'Feel all warm and fuzzy and superior?'

I do, as it happens. 'The kicker,' I say, leaning back in my chair, 'is absolute zero is a theory. No one's ever achieved it. So maybe, if you're planning on blowing the hospital for real like you say, you might want to find another snappy catch-phrase.'

He pops home the last of the blueberry muffin, savouring it as he chews. Then he leans forward, brushes the crumbs from his pages. 'My house,' he says, 'my rules.'

•

My instinct is to tell Frankie to relax. Some vestigial trace of compassion prompts me to reassure Frankie he'll be okay. Some perverse urging encourages me to tell him that any and all internal inquiries will be consigned to the back burner when the hospital keels over in crippled conflagration.

But I don't want to make any promises I cannot keep. I am not certain that my plan will work. Bringing down a large hospital is no mean feat. My theory is not flawless. The margin of error is wide, and the process will be attempted while it is still at the experimental stage.

It may well be that the effort will suffice. It may well be, as the modern Olympians suggest, that it is not the winning but the taking part that matters. But I cannot depend on this. A bungled attempt to incinerate a hospital could be easily covered up. If a roomful of monkeys at typewriters will eventually emerge with a facsimile of 'Hamlet', a health board executive will eventually devise a plausible excuse for the presence of copious quantities of silane gas in the basement of a hospital.

This excuse will not, presumably, include a footnote on the manipulation of requisition invoices by a person or persons unknown bent on ordering canisters of silane gas for a hospital, for fear that pertinent questions will be asked about the chain of command, accountability, and the cavalier waste of valuable resources.

Silane, a man-made gas, does not occur naturally in hospital basements. It was first produced in 1857 by F. Wohler and H. Buff by reacting HCl(aq) with Al-Si alloy, or Mn2Si. Silane, SiH_4, is also called silicon tetrahydride, silicane and monosilicane. It is a colourless flammable gas with a repulsive odour. Its physical properties are: molecular mass 32.1179 g/mol; melting point -185ºC; boiling point -111.8ºC. It is insoluble in water and most organic solvents. Its density is 1.3128 g/L at 25ºC and 1 atm, which is 11 percent denser than air.

Silane is used to produce ultra-pure silicon for use in semiconductor applications. More importantly, for our purpose at least, is the fact that silane is a pyrophoric gas. This means that silane ignites upon contact with air.

In theory, if enough silane gas is packed into a large enough space – a vacuum-sealed underground chamber, say – it will represent a time-bomb just waiting for a breath of fresh air to set it off. If said underground chamber backs onto a support column of the building in which it is housed, then the combusting gas may or may not expend sufficient energy to impact negatively on said support column, thus causing the building to keel over at an unsustainable angle. Meanwhile, said silane gas will be ripping through the tilting edifice, igniting wherever it finds oxygen, which will be everywhere, including the internal organs of human beings.

The means of introducing the silane into the underground chamber involves drilling a hole into the chamber, plugging the hole with a large rubber cork and evacuating the air inside, then filtering the silane from its canister through the cork via airtight tubing welded around the large syringe piercing the cork.

This process is time intensive, although it is no less consuming than jogging, collecting stamps or building ships in bottles.

My line for today is, *Verily I say unto you, There shall not be left here one stone upon another that shall not be thrown down.* (Matthew 24:2)

Sermo Vulgus: A Novel (Excerpt)

Cassie, hope is but a piker's bet until such time as hopelessness has first been admitted. Do not believe everything you read: there were atheists in the trenches.

Cassie, I am rent for the want of an intimate touch. Bring on the barnyard animals: let roosters crow and donkeys bray, let us couple beyond endurance in the shit-spattered straw where swine have rooted in their own filth. Let us wallow naked in honesty's squalor, shroud ourselves in failure's stench, cake our assholes with the waste that comes of giving without need.

Only the future can judge us now. Close your eyes and imagine what you will: censor nothing. Pucker your full, perfect lips and breathe life again into the tortured lungs of Prometheus. Let us steal fire all over again, for fire stutters and never becomes whole.

This is my greed and this is my shame, that I long to be always incomplete. I wouldn't change it now, he said, not with the fire in me now.

Let us be ash and blind butterflies on the wing, Cassie. Let us be black snow settling soundless on the cusp of always.

Cassie, you said irony is a sharp tool but a paper-thin shield.

•

'I thought we were dumping the Cassie novel,' I say.

Billy shrugs. 'Now that she's gone, it's starting to make sense.'

'Really?'

'Well, not sense, exactly. I mean, the excerpts are still rubbish. I'm saying it makes sense to maintain Cassie's presence, even if it's just, y'know, by lamenting her absence or some shit.'

'Fair enough.' I light a cigarette, toss the Zippo down. 'So what d'you think, will she dob you in to the cops this time?'

'Hard to say,' he says. 'We were getting on a lot better this time around, until the miscarriage anyway. And she's got Tony, so it's not like she's a woman scorned or anything.'

'How're you making out?'

'Good days, bad days. You know how it goes.'

'Put a tune to it and I'll sing along. Listen,' I say, 'I've been thinking.'

'What's that?'

'About Cassie, and the, y'know.'

'Miscarriage,' he says. 'It's okay to say it out loud.'

'Yeah. Anyway, and don't take this the wrong way . . .'

'Spit it out, man.'

'Well, I was thinking you could channel all that energy, the loss and the pain, make it a creative thing. It sounds a bit crass, I know, but—'

'No,' he says. 'That's exactly what I've been trying to do.'

'Really?'

'Yeah. It's like Cyril Connolly said, the pram in the hall is the death of art. So,' he shrugs, not meeting my eye, 'I'm thinking that maybe no pram means I can really push this. For now, anyway.'

'Fair play,' I say. 'That takes balls, man. If I was where you are right now, I wouldn't be able to—'

'It's why I want to blow the hospital for real,' he says. 'No prams, pre-natal classes or delivery ward, no incubators, no nothing.'

'No physiotherapists,' I say.

'You think this is about Cassie?' he says.

'Isn't it?'

He shakes his head. 'It's about being honest,' he says. 'Being true to the spirit of it. I mean, what are we doing wasting our fucking time writing about this shit when we could be doing it?'

'You've lost the plot, Billy. I mean, you've literally gone and lost the fucking plot.'

'You're the one,' he says, 'whinging about having to write comedy crime fiction when the country's going down the tubes. All I'm saying is, stop writing it and just *do* it.' He shrugs. 'If you're worried about being implicated,' he says, 'I can always say it was loosely based on an original story. Like, those guys who flew into the Twin Towers, that shit was in a Stephen King book years before.'

'You're insane,' I say. 'Don't get me wrong, I'm not saying you're not entertaining, but you're Section Eight. And you need to think about seeing someone, I don't know, maybe a grief counsellor. There's some serious issues you need to work out.'

'As opposed to you,' he says, fiddling with the Zippo, 'sitting here only fantasising about blowing up a hospital.' He flicks the lid of the Zippo, cranks the wheel. A faint pop as the flame blossoms.

'Boom,' he says.

•

'Your health is your wealth, son,' the old man says. He does not meet my eye saying this.

'So they say.'

A hospital is the last bastion of unnecessary kindness. This is not necessarily a good thing. Kindness is chocolate, a sweet treat that is debilitating when indulged to excess. In the novel *Fight Club*, Chuck Palahniuk had his Space Monkeys undermine America's unhealthy obsession with excessive personal wealth by vaporising financial institutions. Thus it is logical that we should vaporise health institutions in order to undermine our unhealthy obsession with excessive health.

But I understand that the ex-mechanic, this shrivelled expression of humanity, is having second thoughts. I appreciate that he is contemplating one last overhaul in a desperate attempt to jumpstart his engine. This is his choice and privilege. He is entitled to renege on the unspoken agreement he has with Death, to welch on their non-verbal contract.

'The young fella came to see me yesterday,' he says.

'About time.'

He nods, sucking on his chocolate. 'Brought the nippers with him. Three of them, they were bouncing on the bed, pillow-fights, the works. I wasn't in the bed at the time, but still.'

'That must have been nice.'

'It was. I was dreading them coming, but then when they got here . . .'

'Nothing like a few kids to brighten up a place.'

'I wouldn't go that far, son. Those wee shites, they'd have bounced on the bed whether I was in it or not. The young fella's breeding savages out there.' A twinkle in the faded blue eyes I haven't seen for some time. 'But it's not the nippers I'm talking about.'

'No?'

'It's just, when you're on your own, and thinking, you'd be thinking things you wouldn't if there was people around.'

'I know what you mean.'

'Ridiculous things,' he says.

'Sure, but if you can't be daft in the privacy of your own mind . . .'

'It's not like that, son. I mean, maybe the Pope changed his mind on this one too, but there was a time when thinking something was a sin in itself. Going ahead and acting on it, that was just taking the piss.'

'I couldn't say for certain,' I say, 'but I don't think he's changed his mind on that one. But for what's it worth, I think that's all a bunch of bullshit. The whole point of having free will is you get to make decisions. You can't tell your mind what to think, it's your mind that tells *you* what to think. But you can tell your body what to do, or what it shouldn't do.'

He laughs. Phlegm rumbles in his chest like faint thunder breaking. 'You can try, son. You get to a certain age, you can *try* and tell your body what to do.' A wan smile. Perhaps even now his mind is allowing the memories to spool, those glory days when his body obeyed instructions. This may or may not be a good sign. This may or may not represent the final run-through, the slow-motion passage of his life before his eyes, the settling of accounts, the last balancing of the books in which acts are allotted their contexts, reasons and justifications. The subconscious dialogue of confession and absolution, which may or may not represent the longing for more than enough that is the defining characteristic of humanity.

This may or may not be a jump-started engine growling a throaty roar.

'Any word back from those tests yet?' I say.

'There's loads of words alright,' he says. 'Some of them I even understand.' He rubs his fingers together, collecting melted chocolate in a little ball, which he then wipes on the sheet. 'Not giving a damn, son – that's a tough one to keep up. The young fella, he was near crying when he left yesterday.'

'No son wants to see his father in hospital.'

He snorts. 'What's wrong with him is, if I go, he has to go too. Not straightaway, but sometime.'

'I hear you.'

'What I never realised, starting out, was how you never stop looking after them.'

I hand him the opened carton of peach yoghurt. He looks up, the faded blue eyes crackling fiercely. 'Are you with me, son?'

I nod. 'You're the boss,' I say.

Joe, my prematurely grey supervisor, calls me into his office.

'This is strictly routine, Karlsson. I don't want you to think you're under suspicion or anything.' He gestures at the pile of buff-coloured manila folders on his desk. 'It's just that I have orders to interview everyone.'

'About what?'

'I'm sure you've heard about the files that went missing, that they fell into the wrong hands.'

'Loose lips sink ships.'

'Exactly. So what have you heard?'

'That files went missing and now some people are trying to sue the hospital.'

'Anything else?'

'No, that's about the height of it. No one ever tells the porters anything.'

'It was one of the porters who was supposed to shred and then burn those files.'

'So I hear. To me, that's a dereliction of duty.'

He thinks about this. 'And none of the lads have been acting weird lately?'

'They're hospital porters, Joe. They live at the bottom of the shit-pile, barrowing loads of shit around, all day, every day. Removing the occasional corpse to relieve the boredom. I mean, define weird.'

'Well, has anyone been acting strangely? Suspiciously?'

'Everything's relative, Joe. Some people might say that not shredding and burning files is a normal, unsuspicious activity.'

He lolls back in his leather chair, studying me shrewdly through his ironically thick spectacles. 'I'm not asking you to snitch on anyone,' he says. 'But are you trying to tell me something?'

'Nope.'

'We both know that it only takes one bad apple to ruin the barrel.'

Right now I am suffering from cliché overload. I am being invisibly electrocuted by twee aphorisms.

'Joe, with all due respect, shouldn't you already know who was responsible for shredding those files? Shouldn't there be a paper trail?'

He shifts uncomfortably in the orthopaedic chair. 'Let's just say that the system they had in place lacked cohesion, and that steps have been taken to implement a new system that has in-built accountability.'

'Well, that's something at least. I'd hate to lose my job because the suits upstairs haven't the wit to keep an eye on sensitive material.'

'How do you know the files contained sensitive material?'

'No one sues because the spuds were too hard, Joe.'

He thinks this over. 'Karlsson, I'm getting the impression here – and maybe I'm wrong – but I'm getting the impression that you have something you want to tell me. And I've told you already, whatever is said between these four walls remains confidential.'

'Wouldn't that make for a pretty pointless investigation? I mean, I appreciate the sentiment, but where's the point in saying what I have to say if you can't guarantee me it'll be heard by the right people?'

His prematurely grey eyes glitter. 'What I mean is, all information will be treated as if it was received anonymously.'

'Well, that's different.'

He leans forward, joining his hands and resting them on the desk. 'So – do you have something you want to tell me?'

'What do you know about the Polynesians?'

He blinks. 'What?'

'The Polynesians.'

He purses his prematurely grey lips. 'Not much. They came from the Pacific. They had rafts, they sailed them from island to island.'

'That's them. Those guys, they started moving east from New Guinea about four thousand years ago. Sailed out into the Pacific as far as Fiji, Samoa. The rafts carried themselves, their livestock, their portable agricultural systems. They learned to navigate by the stars, by ocean swells, by the flight paths of seabirds. Joe, forget your Phoenicians – these guys were the best sailors of all time, bar none. In relative terms, these guys not only aimed for the moon, they overshot and wound up in a whole new galaxy.' Joe makes to speak. I hold up a hand. 'Here's the thing, Joe. The Polynesians made it to Easter Island around 70 AD. The west coast of South America is as far from Easter Island as Easter Island is from the Polynesian Islands. That's a distance of five thousand miles with only Easter Island in between, and they didn't even know Easter Island was there. Bear in mind, Joe, that these guys were toting livestock and portable agricultural systems on Stone Age rafts. I mean, where did they think they were going?'

He spots his opportunity. 'Karlsson, I don't think—'

'Here's the thing. When those guys hit Easter Island, it was covered in forest. It was a paradise. Seabirds, fish, food aplenty. Arable land. More fruit trees than you could shake a banana at. And they cut them all down to transport those huge statues. A couple of tribes got into a competition to see who could build the biggest statue, and the bigger the statue, the more trees were needed to transport it. Things were going well, they were living in a paradise, they could afford the time and energy.'

'Karlsson—'

'Hold on, Joe. Now these Polynesians, the one thing they needed above all was trees to make rafts with. And they cut down every last fucking tree on the island. Easter Island isn't Australia or even Madagascar. The guy who cut down the last tree, he knew he was cutting down the last tree. But he cut it down anyway.'

By now Joe's eyes are glazing over. 'What's your point, Karlsson?'

'The point is, not only did they destroy their source of food and shelter, they also eradicated their only means of escape from self-imposed genocide.'

He thinks about this. He says, dully, 'And what has that to do with the missing files?'

'Oh. We're still talking about the files?'

His jaw clenches. 'That's right. We're still talking about the missing files.'

'Well, in that case, I suppose the moral of the story is that sometimes, even with a barrel full of good apples, things still get ruined.'

He stands up and walks to the window and stares out across the car park with his hands in his pockets. His shoulders have tensed into a straight line. 'Karlsson, between you and me, I've been fairly relaxed for the last while. I happen to believe that adults should be treated like adults. For your own sake, don't give me a reason to get on your case. I'll come down like a ton of bricks.'

I stand up too. 'Don't make promises you can't keep, Joe.'

He turns. 'Oh, I'll keep them alright. Never you fear.'

'What do you want to do, take it outside? You want to go mano-a-mano because I don't know who took the dodgy files?'

He holds up his hand with the thumb and forefinger pressed together. 'Karlsson, you're this close to an official warning.'

'Joe, the history of conflict suggests that it's not what you're prepared to do that defines the outcome, it's what you're not prepared to lose.'

He nods. His jaw is set. 'Okay, you've just bought yourself an official warning.'

'See, now I'm curious. Seriously – what are you not prepared to lose?'

'One more word and you're suspended.'

I dig in my pocket and take out the Zippo, clink-chunk the lid. 'Joe, one more word and your daughter receives precisely one face-full of lighter fluid.' He frowns. I say, 'Your address is 27, The Paddock, Springview Crescent. Her school is St Bernadette's Primary. Violin lessons every Thursday afternoon, swimming class on Saturday morning.'

He stares. His jaw now hangs slackly. His eyes are the premature grey of an imminent blizzard. 'Joe,' I say, 'just out of curiosity – what are you not prepared to lose?'

'Get out,' he says hoarsely. 'Get out of my fucking office.'

'You're the boss.' I turn at the door. 'If I hear anything more about the missing files, I'll be sure to let you know.'

My line for today is, *I've seen the meanness of humans till I don't know why God ain't put out the sun and gone away.* (Cormac McCarthy, *Outer Dark*)

My name is Jennifer. I am eleven years old and I live in Dublin. I would like to own a pony but my mother says I am too young to take care of it properly.

My favourite stars are Lady Gaga, Justin Bieber and Katy Perry. My favourite colour is pink but I tell people it is violet. My friends at school are Melinda, Sinead and Barbara, although Sinead is my best friend because she told me last Christmas that I am her best friend.

My chat-room friends are Tara, Joanne, Yasmin, Siobhan and Kylie. We like ponies, boys, and shopping for clothes on Saturday afternoons. Yasmin says she buys a new top every

Saturday, but I don't believe her.

I have a very strong suspicion that Yasmin might be a liar.

Tonight Yasmin says she is going to meet Shane from Westlife when he comes home to Sligo for the big concert at Lissadell. She says Shane is her favourite because she likes the way she feels inside when he sings. She asks if I have ever been to a Westlife concert. I say yes, I have, but I'd like to go again. I tell her my mother won't take me, she says once is enough.

Yasmin says I can go with her to meet Shane if I really want to. She says her mother works with Shane's sister, so if I want Yasmin to bring me along, she will. But I have to keep it a three-times secret. Otherwise everyone will want to meet Shane.

I say I don't know. Dublin is a long way away from Sligo.

Yasmin says it's easy to take the train. She says once you get on the train, it takes you all the way to Sligo. She says she will meet me at the station with her mother.

I say I don't know. I say I'll have to think about it. I say I wouldn't be able to stay out all night, because if my mother found out I'd be grounded for a whole year.

Yasmin says there is a train that will take me home afterwards. She says that her mother will bring me back to the station afterwards and put me on the train.

I say I'll think about it. Yasmin asks if I'm a chicken. I say no. She says, well then.

I say I'll let her know soon. I ask how much the train ticket will cost. Yasmin says not to worry about it, she'll pay.

Yasmin has no fucking idea, etc.

The brain is the laziest organ in the body. It is never more content than when allowing ideas to circulate along established orbits. It is a creature of habit that loves grooves, ruts and well-worn furrows, and excels at conjuring up the cheap tricks and delusions that reduce the necessity for forging new paths through the trackless universe of the imagination.

Thus, this: love.

Thus, this: the mental recoil and revolt when the theory of blowing up a hospital is mooted.

Thus, this: the brain's counter-mooting of familiar concepts such as judgement, punishment and eternal damnation.

But the brain is both slave and master. It needs to be chained, whipped and brought to heel, by itself. If the brain discovers itself to be a weak master, it will not respect itself in the morning. The brain craves discipline, authority and decisive decision making.

I am, therefore I think. I decide, therefore I am. I act, therefore I will be.

Herostratus, can you hear me now?

My line for today is, *Two roads diverged in a wood, and I— / I took the one less travelled by* (Robert Frost, 'The Road Not Taken')

IV

FALL

On the way home from work I duck into The Book Nest, a small but perfectly formed bookshop facing the river, and pick up copies of *Jean de Florette*, *Breakfast at Tiffany's* and *Love in the Time of Cholera*. Once home, I ring Cassie.

'Hey, K.'

'Hey,' I say. 'How's it going?'

'Good, yeah.'

She sounds cautiously friendly. There is no reason she should not. All things considered, and one blazing row apart, our parting was amicable. Plus, we shared and still share the grief of miscarriage.

There is also a very good chance that Cassie feels the pangs of guilt most women feel when a relationship fails, no matter whose fault it was, the subconscious guilt of extinguishing all those babies who might have been.

'So what's up?' she says.

'There's some stuff I've found, I didn't want to chuck it in case you wanted it back.'

'What kind of stuff?'

'There's a few CDs. And some of your book club books.'

'That's okay, you keep them.'

'There's something else.'

'What? K, if you still have photos of—'

'No, it's nothing like that. It's tapes of you singing.'

'Singing? Me?'

'Sure. You sing in your sleep.'

'In my sleep?'

'No one else ever told you that?'

'Singing what?'

'I don't know, it's hard to tell.'

She considers this. 'You taped me singing in my sleep?'

'I thought you might want a record of it.'

'And how come you're only telling me about it now?'

'For the reason you're pissed off. It's an invasion of privacy.'

'Too fecking right it is.'

'Which is why I'm giving them back. Or should I just destroy them?'

'No,' she sighs, 'don't destroy them.'

'Okay. I'll leave them here for pick-up. You still have your key, right?'

'Yeah. I suppose I should give that back.'

'Not unless you want to.'

'Oh?'

'It'd mean I'd have to find another key-holder.'

'You want me to be your key-holder?'

'Not if it's going to be a problem. Otherwise, yeah. Why not?'

'No reason.' A telling pause. 'Listen, K? I'd rather meet in town. Would you mind?'

'No problem. By the way, you might like to know – I'm dumping that novel. I thought about it and you're right, I don't have the right to write about you like that.'

'That's your decision, K. It has nothing to do with me anymore.'

'I know that. I'm not trying to woo you back or anything. I'm just saying, if you want the manuscript and the discs, you can have them.'

'Just burn them, K.'

'Will do. So where do you want to meet?'

We arrange a time and place: F—'s, next Saturday, early afternoon. This is to ensure there is no opportunity for drunkenness and irresponsible nostalgia. We agree to be on our best behaviour for the duration of the meeting. We arrange our lives with the care of an old spinster retying a red satin bow around a bundle of yellowing letters, and then hide our lives away at the bottom of our battered hope chests.

'K? Any weird shit and I'll walk. Okay?'

'If it'll help, I'll learn sign language. It's just too much effort to be weird in sign language.'

She snorts, says goodbye, hangs up. I spend the evening practising her signature by turning it upside down and copying out the meaningless squiggle. When I am confident I have it right I sign her name on the fly-leaf of *Jean de Florette*, *Breakfast at Tiffany's* and *Love in the Time of Cholera*.

My line for today is, *People say that life is the thing, but I prefer reading.* (Logan Pearsall Smith)

The old man, the ex-mechanic, dies. This is despite his express wish to the contrary. This is as sad as it is inevitable, although its inevitability should go some way towards alleviating the sadness. The old man simply arrived at a point in space and time where irrational hope intersected with irreversible logic.

On the way to the funeral, to cheer myself up, I go into a bookies and place a bet on my not dying.

The woman behind the counter is nonplussed but intrigued. 'Ever?'

'What kind of odds can you give me?'

'None. There are no odds. There can't be.'

'Why not?'

'Everyone dies is why not.'

'You're saying it's impossible for me not to die.'

'Correct.'

'Have you any idea of what the odds were against my being born in the first place?'

'Better than those against you're not dying, that's for sure.'

'You think?'

'Everything dies.'

'Okay. But not everything lives in the first place. The odds against my being born were hundreds of trillions to one. And that's a conservative estimate.'

She thinks about this. 'How would you collect? I mean, just say you never died. How would you collect?'

'You won't have to worry about that. You'll be dead.'

We decide on a one-euro bet at odds of a billion-to-one. 'Best of luck,' she says, signing off with a flourish.

At the cemetery the rain is a drizzled blessing. The old man's family drift towards the exit. Most people don't stick around for the final act. The fat lady sings a siren's song.

The gravedigger leans against a convenient tombstone, smoking and staring me down. He is mid-thirties, tall and lean, unshaven. I smoke and stare back.

He nods at the hole. 'I have to wait until you go before I can start filling him in.'

'Why's that?'

'I dunno. It's traditional.'

'You think the old man would mind me watching him being filled in?'

'How would I know?'

'Put yourself in his shoes. Take a guess.'

He takes a drag off his cigarette. 'If it was me, yeah, I'd mind. If it was me, I'd rather be left alone.'

'He used to be a mechanic,' I say. 'Played centre-back on the team that won the double in 1961. In the last six months he had the grand total of three hospital visits, and he liked to eat peach yoghurt and Dairy Milk chocolate. They think it was gangrene killed him.'

By way of empathy, the gravedigger places a thumb against one nostril and snorts the other nostril clear. 'I've work to do,' he says.

'There's a meteor on the way,' I say, 'it's called Asteroid 1950 DA. It's still eight hundred years away. But it's coming.'

That grabs him. 'Like in the film?' he says.

I nod. 'Check this out. NASA put a probe on a meteor, a different one, travelling at twice the speed of a bullet three hundred million miles away. They wanted to know what it was made of.'

'And?' he says. 'What was it made of?'

'No idea. What I'm saying is, they can put a probe on a meteor travelling at twice the speed of a bullet three hundred million miles away, but they can't know for sure it was gangrene killed an old man.'

He takes a vicious drag on his cigarette, tucks it into a corner of his mouth and picks up his spade. 'That gangrene's some cunt alright.'

He shovels dirt into the hole. It lands with a metallic-sounding clatter.

'Most people worry about dying in a car crash,' I say, 'or from falling down stairs, or being hit by a meteor. But the vast majority of deaths are the result of internal degeneration. In effect, we're being sabotaged by the partisan elements of our constituent components.' He shovels on, still smoking. 'Beware the enemy within,' I say. 'The fuckers are working behind the lines, blowing up train tracks, cutting down telephone lines and assassinating minor representatives of officialdom. How are you supposed to organise reprisals against your own colon?'

The gravedigger unloads a spatter of dirt, takes a last drag from the cigarette and flips it away. It lands on a neatly tended grave of pristine crystal chips. 'This meteor,' he says. 'It's eight hundred years away?'

'Give or take a couple of years.'

'How come I never heard about it?'

'Why should they tell you? I mean, now you know, what're you going to do about it?'

He shrugs. 'Not one fucking thing.' He pats his pockets, finds his cigarettes, lights up. 'Pity it's not eight hundred fucking *minutes* away.' He tucks the cigarette into the corner of his mouth, digs into the heap of earth. 'I'll give them fucking meteors,' he mutters.

I toss the betting slip into the gaping hole and walk away through the drizzle towards the exit. I notice that tombstones are erected by the living for the living. I notice how the dead have no stake in their death.

Life is a perverse anomaly. Perhaps this is why my pulse stutters when the world begins to turn away, when the trees start to rust, when the whiff of decay drifts up out of the earth. Autumn is the world's way of reminding us that life is lived in parentheses, a temporary state of enervation preceded and followed by non-being.

Today, in the chat-room, Yasmin presses me to commit to going along to meet Shane on Saturday night. She has investigated timetables. She informs me that if I catch the 16.10 train from Dublin I will get to Sligo at 19.05, which means we can meet Shane before he goes onstage and be back at the station in time for the 21.30 train to Dublin.

I tell Yasmin I am excited, but so nervous my pants are damp. I tell her that I might be grounded for life if I am caught.

Yasmin says that some things in life are worth being grounded for. She says that my mum will be angry, for sure, but that no mother can stay angry forever.

We continue in a similar vein for some time until Yasmin confesses that it is her birthday on Saturday, which is why her mother is bringing her to meet Shane. She says she will be twelve, and that she wanted it to be a surprise for me.

I am touched. Now there is no way I can disappoint her. I confirm that I will get the train and see her at Sligo station on Saturday evening at 19.05.

We sign off with our usual kissy-kissies.

The blood roars in my ears. Below in the valley, four-square in my path, the Rubicon wends its lazy way to the sea.

I meet Cassie just after five in F—'s. This bright, busy bar is a temple to voluntary subjugation. Even on a Saturday it is thronged with men wearing symbolic nooses, and women who believe their mission in life is to propagate the genes of well-hung men.

I appreciate Cassie's tactics. She believes that I will not cause a scene in a bar crowded with conventional people doing conventional things. In this she is correct: I have no intention of causing a scene. My plan depends on being surrounded by hordes of conventional people doing conventional things.

Cassie is late. She does not apologise, because she is deliberately late. She sits down on the other side of the table.

'So what I can get you?' I say.

'G&T, thanks.'

'Sound.' I get up to go to the bar. 'The bag's under the table, by the way.'

From the bar I watch her rummage through the black refuse sack. I see her frown, puzzled. She is holding *Love in the Time of Cholera*. By the time I return with her coffee she has unearthed *Jean de Florette* and *Breakfast at Tiffany's*. She holds up the latter as I sit down. 'These aren't mine,' she says.

'No? So whose are they?'

'I don't know.'

'They're not mine, I know that. I thought they were yours when I saw your name inside.'

She says, puzzled, 'Yeah, I saw that too. But I don't remember buying them.'

'I thought you wrote your name on all your books.'

'Well, I do . . .'

'Hey, don't sweat it. If you don't want them, I'll take them. They're good books.'

But her instinctive reaction is to protect and cherish. To own. She stashes the books in the refuse sack. She doesn't mention the tapes of her singing in her sleep.

'Odd,' she says.

'We all get old, Cass. Maybe your memory isn't what it used to be.'

'Maybe it isn't. Maybe if it was,' she says, 'I'd stand up and walk out this very second.'

I nod. I allow my shoulders to sag. In this way I implicitly accept the burden of guilt for the failure of our relationship. This is what every woman craves: the illusion of absolution from responsibility. I believe they crave this because they understand, subconsciously, that on their shoulders – or hips, to be precise – falls the agonising responsibility for the propagation of the human race. Feminism is Christ in the Garden of Gethsemane, begging for the cup to be taken from its lips while knowing it cannot be.

Or maybe she's just happy to see me admit it was all my fault.

'Before you go,' I say, 'there's something I want you to know.'

She sips her G&T with her pinky finger aloft. She shakes her head. 'Save it, K. You'd be wasting your time. It's over. Oh-ver.'

'Don't get me wrong, Cass. I'm not trying to change your mind. I'd just like you to know why I am the way I am. There's a reason for everything, except maybe the universe itself.'

She holds herself stiffly. She sips again at the G&T, observing me across the rim of the glass. She is intrigued despite herself. Women should be sent to colonise Mars. In a straight choice, women will pick drama over oxygen every time.

'Go on,' she says.

I take a deep breath. 'I've never told you this, but I was in a serious car accident a few years ago. You know how I hate cars?' She nods. 'I'm not giving you any light at the end of the tunnel bullshit,' I say, 'but it was a near-death experience. It happened so fast it was over before I knew it was starting. But here's the thing. I had enough time to realise I was dead and to hope that it didn't kill the passenger too. I didn't mind so much for myself, but my last thought was a terrifically sad one, because I thought the passenger was going to die too. All that realising happened in a split-second,' I add.

'How come you didn't tell me this before?' From her tone I can tell that she doesn't believe me, but that she is desperately anticipating any evidence that might allow her to. She sips at her G&T. 'And what has this to do with us, anyway?'

'Well, obviously I didn't die. And the passenger was fine too. But the shock was traumatic. It's still ongoing. It's left me with an acute awareness of the fragility of life and a very shallow pool of emotional responses. Most of the time I only have enough emotion to keep me covered. I can't afford to make an emotional investment, otherwise I'd bankrupt myself.'

'K?'

'What?'

'Try speaking English. Just this once. I mean, I'm listening, but I'm not hearing anything genuine.'

'It's not easy to talk about this, Cass. The brain isn't really engineered to verbalise concepts relating to its own annihilation. But what I think I'm trying to say is, I sold you short on the emotional side of things. Because if I hadn't, I'd have wound up slitting my wrists.'

She flushes. 'I knew it. I can't believe you're threatening—'

'Cass? Relax. I'm not threatening anything. I'm explaining how it was then, not how I want it to be now. You've made your decision and I respect that. And to be perfectly honest, if one of us has to be happy, I'd rather it was you. No disrespect, but I think I can take the shit better than you.'

She sips her G&T. She says, in a doubtful tone, 'How do I know you're not spoofing?'

'What do I have to gain by spoofing? You're with Tony now. I'm only telling you this so you'll know why I was acting like a prick.'

'Don't flatter yourself. You *are* a prick.'

'I know. I'm thinking about counselling.'

This is the magic word. If there's one thing women love more than talking, it's talking about talking. 'Really?' she says. 'You're seriously thinking about that?'

'Thinking about it, yeah. But I don't know, it all sounds a bit faggoty to me. Want another one of those?'

'Yeah, go on. And don't be such a homophobe.' She drains her glass. 'Not so much ice this time,' she says.

From the bar I watch her rummage through the refuse sack again. Even from the bar I can tell that I am giving Cassie exactly what she wants, which is to be absolved of all blame, always. Even from the bar I can tell that the Rohypnol is already taking effect, and that Cassie is in for an interesting evening.

My line for tonight comes courtesy of Eugene Ionescu: *The basic problem is that if God exists, what is the point of literature? And if he doesn't exist, what is the point of literature?*

Sermo Vulgus: A Novel (Excerpt)

God has seen it all, Cassie. There's no shocking God. If there is an omniscient being responsible for the entire universe, its palate is by now irreversibly jaded.

God has seen ecosystems deliberately wiped out. He has seen races, civilisations and species obliterated. God has overseen the destruction of planets, taken bets on the exact time of a sun's winking out, coolly noted whole galaxies freeze to within a quark of absolute zero. Cassie, if the scientists are correct about the Big Bang, God has observed the destruction of at least one infinite universe to date.

Cassie, put your humiliation in perspective. On the cosmic scale, the fourteenth-century genocide of thirty-four million Chinese by the Mongol hordes wouldn't even make the Top One Million list of atrocities.

Tonight the last matriarch of an undiscovered Amazonian species of tree spider passed away. Tonight the ghosts of a vanquished galaxy waved placards as they marched in mute protest past the gates of God's many-roomed mansion. Tonight an infinite universe sweated blood and prayed that the cup of self-immolation be taken from its lips.

All, alas, to no avail.

Yasmin awaits, but first I must ensure Cassie will be comfortable for the evening. We walk back to my place with the intention of smoking a joint while listening to the new Antony and the Johnsons album. I allow Cassie to open the front door with the key she holds on my behalf. This is the ex-lovers' equivalent of two Verdun survivors symbolically signing the Versailles Treaty.

Cassie is under the impression that we are acting out a charade to prove how truly evolved human beings are: how we can love and hate, then shake hands and part with no hard feelings.

In reality Cassie is under the influence of three G&Ts and enough Rohypnol to make an elephant forget it has a trunk. She is merry, tipsy and determined to be sophisticated in a potentially embarrassing situation. Thus she will not – indeed, does not – notice the slightly acrid taste of two Nytols crushed into her glass of Pinot.

I put 'Swanlights' on the stereo. Cassie lasts until well into track four, 'I'm In Love', before she begins to slur her words. By track eight, 'Thank You For Your Love', Cassie is in a funny way. Her head slumps onto her chest. She emits a gentle snore. I allow the album to play out, then pick her up in a fireman's lift and carry her into the bedroom. There I rumple the sheets before undressing Cassie and carelessly strewing her clothes around the room, although I carefully place her pants atop the lamp on the bedside locker.

And now for the train station. Spare not the horses, James.

The pulse stutters and flares. Events march steadily on. Circumstance develops its own momentum.

The vacuum-sealed underground chamber is rapidly approaching its capacity to absorb silane gas. The moment is imminent.

Perhaps the old ex-mechanic's death was an omen.

Thus we make a feint designed to distract attention away from the hospital basement. Thus we draw Joe's prematurely grey gaze onto us. Thus we require an ex-lover's garbled and essentially unprovable accounts of disaffected lunacy, including that of alleged rape, the administering of illegal drugs, and the blowing up of hospitals.

Now is not the time to panic. Now is the time for cool heads and dry trousers.

My line for today is, *You should never have your best trousers on when you turn out to fight for freedom and truth.* (Henrik Ibsen)

•

'I'm curious,' I say.

Billy glances up from his notes. 'About what?'

'All this silane gas in the bunker. You said earlier on you'd been doing it for eight months, right?'

'So?'

'That means you had to have been doing it long before we started the redraft.'

'What's your point?'

'Well, were you? Or did you just write that?'

'What does it matter? The tank is gassed. We're ready to rock 'n' roll.'

'I'm not saying it matters. I'm just asking.'

'Ask no questions,' he says, 'hear no lies.'

•

I go to the station. *Quelle surprise*, the train is late. I smoke and observe the faces of those waiting on the platform.

Finally the train arrives. The passengers disembark. There is no twelve-year-old waiting with her mother for eleven-year-old Jennifer travelling from Dublin. This represents gross dereliction on Yasmin's behalf. For this she may need to be placed on the naughty step forever.

I leave the station and go outside to the car park, there to sit on the low wall, facing back towards the station and the hotel next door. I smoke another cigarette. I watch as the travellers disperse into the early evening. No twelve-year-old and her mother hove into view, running late and anxious that eleven-year-old Jennifer not be left alone at the mercy of men in shabby raincoats.

This is disappointing. This represents a significant blow to my plans. This represents a waste of precious Rohypnol.

I am about to leave when I realise I am thinking too literally. Too fixedly. And so I do not leave. Instead I take out another cigarette, then get up from the low wall and approach the maroon Mercedes parked in front of the hotel with a view of the station car park and the T-junction beyond. The man in the Mercedes is forty-ish, bald on top and shaved at the sides, with a bluey stubble. He pretends not to see me. I hold up the cigarette and tap on his window, then go through the motions of lighting a cigarette. He puffs out his cheeks and punches in the dashboard cigarette lighter. His window descends with a whining hum.

'There you go,' he says, passing me the glowing lighter. I spark my cigarette and hand it back, saying, 'Thanks, Yasmin.'

His reaction is nothing that would convict him in a court of law. A faint flush behind the bluey stubble, eyes that are quickly averted.

'No bother,' he says, reaching for the cigarette lighter.

'You can drive away,' I say, 'and have me track you down through your registration number. Or we can chat about it now.'

'Say again?' he says. He still holds the glowing lighter aloft, like a middle-aged devotee of *Star Wars*.

'I'm Jennifer,' I say. 'Oh, and happy birthday.'

'The fuck're you talking about?'

'You have options here, Yasmin.' Again, a barely perceptible flinch. 'You can try to explain away to the cops all those emails on your computer arranging to meet an eleven-year-old girl at the train station. Or maybe you're an IT whizz, you know how to deep-clean your PC, although you don't look like any kind of geek to me. Anyway, option two: you and I can have a chat, see if we can't come to some kind of arrangement.'

By now his jowls are an unhealthy shade of plum.

'Don't worry,' I say, 'I'm not after money. All I need is an alibi for this evening. Other than that, you're free and clear.'

'I haven't the faintest idea what you're—'

'Sound,' I say. 'On you go.' I step back from the Mercedes, glancing at its registration number. 'I obviously made a mistake. My apologies.'

He slots the lighter back into the dashboard and starts the engine.

'You'll appreciate,' I say, 'that as a good citizen it's my moral duty to report my suspicions to the cops. I don't know how seriously they'll take me, or how quickly they'll respond. So you'll have maybe a whole day to get your computer deep-cleaned. Maybe even a week. And maybe they won't come looking for it at all. A word of advice, though. Don't dump it and buy a new one. That'll look bad. A schoolboy error, that. Even worse than having your PC deep-cleaned the day before the cops come calling.'

I walk away, out of the car park and across the road towards Wine Street. I'm waiting at the traffic lights for the green man to show when the Mercedes pulls up. He reaches across and opens the door.

'Get in,' he says.

I get in. The lights go green. 'Have you ever seen *Raging Bull?*' I say. 'The De Niro flick, the boxing one.'

He nods tersely.

'Whatever happened to Robert De Niro?' I say. 'Huh?'

'What?'

'I'm guessing here,' I say, 'so correct me if I'm wrong, but I'd say you're a laptop man rather than a PC. So you can take it to bed with you. Am I right?'

A cherry flush beneath the bluey stubble.

'I'll be needing your laptop, Yasmin,' I say.

Two uniformed cops swing by my flat. One of them, burly, with a football-wide face and bright pink cheeks, says, 'William Karlsson?'

'That's right.'

'Sir, I'd like to ask you to accompany us to the Garda Station.'

'The station? Why? What for?'

'Purely routine, sir. So you can help us with our enquiries.'

'Yeah, but what's the enquiry about?'

'I'd rather we discussed that at the station.'

I bite my lower lip and swallow dry. 'Am I under, ah, arrest?'

'We're hoping that that won't be necessary, sir. We always prefer it when people come along voluntarily.'

This discretion is not for my benefit. This discretion is preferable to arresting someone and then filling out the relevant reports in triplicate.

'Yeah,' I say, trying to pitch my tone somewhere between anxious and dazed. 'Okay. Just let me grab my jacket.'

We drive to the station in a squad car. I am escorted to an interview room that contains one desk, three chairs, an ashtray and two detectives. I sit down on the chair opposite the detective sitting behind the desk. He is sallow, narrow-faced. Right now his expression is sour. His tie is loose but his hair is neatly coiffed. It glistens under the harsh sodium light.

He switches on a tape-recorder and announces the time, establishes who we all are. Then he tells me I'm entitled to have legal representation present.

I waive. 'Look, what's this all about?'

His lips thin. This is distasteful for him. 'There's been an allegation of rape.'

'You're what?' This meaningless ejaculation is designed to promote my innocence.

'Rape,' he says.

'But . . . I mean, who . . . ?'

'Cassie Kennedy.'

'Cassie? But me and Cass . . .' I shake my head violently, wipe my mouth with the back of my hand. 'No fucking *way*, man.'

'Watch the language,' growls the other detective, who is leaning against the wall.

I hold up a hand, an apology. 'Sorry, but . . .' I shake my head again. I meet the sallow detective's eye. 'This is . . . There's just no *way.*'

'Ms Kennedy says you met her last Saturday evening.'

'That's right, yeah. But I only met her to give back some of her stuff, books and shit. They were in a black rubbish bag.' I am attempting to babble. 'I gave her the stuff, we had a couple of drinks, then we went back to my place for, for . . .'

'For what?'

'To listen to music. A few glasses of wine.'

'Listen to music,' the Growler sneers.

'No, seriously. The new Antony and the Johnsons album. Cassie's a fan but she hadn't heard that one yet.'

'Then what?' the Sallow Guy says.

'She fell asleep halfway through.'

'Some fan,' sneers the Growler.

'What happened then?' Sallow Face says.

'I couldn't wake her so I went out again. I'd had a couple of pints, I fancied a few more. I didn't want to waste the buzz.'

'Where'd you go?'

'D—'s.'

'Anyone see you there?'

'Everyone saw me. I was sitting at the bar.'

'I mean, anyone who can verify you were there.'

'Sure. The barman, for one. And I ended up chatting to a bloke, he was sitting beside me.'

'About what?'

'Movies, mostly. There was boxing on the TV, we were talking about boxing movies. *The Fighter, Raging Bull,* y'know.'

'Did you catch his name?'

'I don't know. Sean, I think. Or Shane, maybe.' I shrug. 'I was a bit jarred at that stage.'

'You just left her in your flat?' the Growler cuts in.

'Why not? She used to live there. She had a key, she could lock up when she was going.'

'She says she woke up naked in your bed.'

'Maybe she did. I wasn't there. And it's not so long since that was *our* bed.'

'She says she can't remember getting into it.'

'Yeah, well, she'd had a few gins, some wine—'

'How about some Rohypnol, hey?'

'No fucking way, that's—'

'I already told you to watch the language.'

'Okay. But there's no way I gave Cassie anything she didn't want.'

'So how come she just fell asleep and doesn't remember getting undressed?'

I tug at my nose. I look from one detective to the other. I clear my throat. 'Did she mention smoking dope?'

'Say again?'

'We smoked a couple of joints. Nothing too heavy, but maybe on top of the gin and wine . . .'

'She didn't say anything about any joints.'

'Well, we smoked them.'

'Why wouldn't she say she'd smoked dope if she did?'

'Maybe she didn't want it coming out. Maybe she thought it'd affect her professionally. Or maybe she doesn't remember, Cass never was much of a drinker.'

The Growler says, 'We're going to want to take a swab.'

'Sure. No problem. Look, I never touched her.'

The Growler is fishing up a pole. He knows that the combination of Cassie's delay in reporting her suspicions and the red-tape of police bureaucracy, along with the fact that Cassie was drugged and thus physically relaxed if not actually compliant, means that any evidence of rape would be negligible at best. Ditto for Rohypnol.

This case will not be pursued on the basis of my guilt. It will be pursued on the likelihood of securing a conviction.

In my favour is the recent furore over the cops in Mayo who managed to tape themselves threatening rape against some Shell to Sea protestors. Now is not the time for any cop to toss around false rumours of rape.

Sallow Face says, 'Why do you think Miss Kennedy would make these allegations against you?'

'I honestly don't know.'

'You were in a relationship that ended recently. Is that correct?'

'What has that to do with anything?'

'Revenge is a common motive for rape.'

'Maybe so, but I didn't . . .' I pause, swallow thickly. 'Cassie and me, we split because she didn't want kids. Or not yet, anyway.'

'Miss Kennedy claims the relationship ended badly.'

'If they don't end badly, they don't end at all. One person wants kids, another doesn't . . .' I shrug. 'Being honest, we weren't even having sex that often by the time we split up. She'd had a miscarriage.'

'So you went and raped her,' the Growler says, 'because that was the only way you could exert any influence over the situation.'

'Look,' I say, 'rape is a hate crime. As far as I know it has nothing do with sex and a lot to do with power.' Sallow Face nods along, hoping to encourage me into an incriminating statement. 'What I'm saying is, if anyone was feeling powerless, it was Cassie. She couldn't convince me to keep things going without kids. And to tell you the truth, I was worried about her on Saturday night. How would I flip over from that into hating her enough to rape her?'

'How come you were worried?'

'That carry-on with the books.'

'What books?'

'The books and the other stuff she left behind when she packed. There were a couple of books in there, she didn't recognise them.'

'So?'

'Cassie signs her name on her books, every book she ever bought. That's how I knew they were hers when I was clearing out those shelves. But when she took them out of the bag she went into this whole thing about how they weren't hers, she couldn't remember buying them.'

'It's easy enough forget about a couple of books,' the Growler growls.

'For some people, maybe. But Cassie's a reader, she loves books. And she'd signed these ones.'

The Growler doesn't like my 'some people' jibe. 'Why would you be so worried about her forgetting a couple of books?' he persists.

'It's not just the books. I'll be straight with you – when I saw the cops at the door tonight, I thought they were coming to arrest me for blowing up the hospital.'

The Growler half-chokes, but Sallow Guy only squints. He's heard about the hospital before. 'Go on,' he says.

'Cassie and me, we had a lot of arguments before we broke up.' He's heard about this too. 'My job is crap, but it gives me plenty of time to write.'

'What's this about blowing up a hospital?' the Growler growls.

'This story I was writing, it's about a guy who wants to blow up a hospital. Cassie read it and accused me of wanting to blow up *the* hospital.'

'What – the hospital here?'

'Exactly.' I half-grin, then bite on my inner lip. 'I mean, she accused me of planning to blow up the place where I work.'

The detectives exchange glances. Sallow Guy says, 'Go on.'

'I gave Cassie the story to read, I thought she'd like it. But she went ballistic.' I shrug. 'Sometimes Cassie wasn't so good at picking up on irony.'

'What's that supposed to mean?'

'Well, the story's about this porter who gets so freaked out at being on the bottom of the shit-pile, not being appreciated, that he decides to blow up his hospital. Reading between the lines, it's a parable about how writers are demented by their own egos. The hospital coming down is supposed to be this impossible pursuit, like the whale in *Moby-Dick*. Because, at the end, the hospital never blows up. He's just this sociopath fantasist.' I shrug. 'But Cassie didn't get any of that. She just freaked. I don't know, maybe she didn't read all the way to the end.'

'What has that to do with her claiming you raped her?'

'All I'm saying is, Cassie took things too literally sometimes.'

'Things don't get much more literal than rape.'

'You're singing to the choir on that one, man. Look – I *like* Cassie. I trust her, she still has the keys to my flat. We just want different things.'

The detectives exchange glances.

'This guy she's hooked up with now,' I say, 'Tony, her ex. I met him, he seems a good guy, he's going to make her happier than I could and good luck to them both. I'm happy she's happy, I told her that on Saturday night. The last thing I want to do is go raping her.' This much, at least, is true. 'I don't know,' I say. 'Maybe I should just have told her I was pissed off. Maybe she got pissed off I wasn't pissed off it all ended.'

This statement meets with silence. This is not exactly misogyny in action. It is not exactly three men in a room not fathoming the impenetrable workings of the female mind. It is not exactly worth an alibi in itself. But every little helps.

Sallow Guy says, 'We'll need to take that swab.'

'Fine. Take whatever you need, I have nothing to hide.'

'We're also going to want to have a look around your flat.'

'For what?'

'We'll know that,' the Growler growls, 'when we find it.'

'It'd also look good,' Sallow Face says, 'if you voluntarily surrendered your passport. To show willing.'

'No problem. I'm not going anywhere.'

Sallow Face sniffs. 'We appreciate your co-operation, Mr Karlsson.' He sounds mechanical, as if speaking by rote. 'This must be a difficult situation for you.'

'It's no picnic for Cassie, either.'

The Growler coughs. Sallow Guy announces for the benefit of the tape that he's terminating the interview, then switches off the recorder. He says, 'Get this guy signed out.'

The Growler leaves. Sallow says, 'This book.'

'Which book?'

'The one about the hospital. We'll need to see it.'

'Sure thing.'

He stands up. 'By the way,' he says, 'where'd you get your hands on that dope you smoked on Saturday night?'

My line for today is, *A genius working alone is invariably ignored as a lunatic.* (Kurt Vonnegut, *Bluebeard*)

The protocols must be observed. Cassie must now be questioned as to the motives behind her allegation of rape. The issue of illicit drug-taking will be raised. Her ability to remember details as basic as the ownership of her own property will be queried.

For my part, and given my position in a public health institution, my employers must be notified of my illicit drug-taking. The police will also make enquiries as to my previous behaviour in the workplace, in particular the possibility that I have been chastised for sexual harassment, improper suggestions, or a malignant attitude towards women in general. This represents the opportunity my supervisor has been praying for. This is manna indeed.

He stands behind his desk rocking on his heels. He makes no attempt to appear caring, understanding or compassionate about my situation. This is progress. This is the instinctive outworking of the selfish gene that propelled the *Homo sapiens* species to the top of evolution's queue. This is the human race winning a game defined and understood only by the human race.

'There's rules, Karlsson. Even if this was not a multi-gendered workplace environment it would still be necessary to suspend you pending the outcome of this investigation.' A December dawn glows in his prematurely grey eyes. 'Don't consider it as a vote of confidence or otherwise. Try to see it as an opportunity we're affording you, to take some time out in order to deal with what must be a difficult situation.'

'Joe, that thing I said about your kid . . .'

He waves me off. 'Karlsson, you and I both know you said what you said at a time of great personal stress.' He bares his teeth in a dry canine smile. 'I've told you before, anything said in this office stays in this office. You and I, we have a confidential relationship.'

'You're missing the point, Joe.'

A smirk. 'About what, the Polynesians?'

'The point is, even if you tell the cops about our conversation, and even if they arrest me, I'll be back out on bail inside twelve hours. Don't doubt it. I'm thinking of your kid here, Joe. What you have to do is decide what's more important, personal revenge or a daughter growing up with a face like torched chip wrappers.'

He leans on the back of the orthopaedic chair. He seems to sag. He tries to work the canine smile again but winds up looking like a sick puppy.

'Karlsson . . .'

'You're out of your depth, Joe. Get back to the shallow end where the kiddies play. The big boys play by different rules and even the rules would make you vomit. Joe,' I say, 'when you write that report for the cops, imagine you're writing it on scorched chip wrappers.'

His eyes glaze over.

'If you want my advice,' I say, 'then you'll tell the cops that I'm innocent until proven otherwise, and you'd be setting up the hospital for bankruptcy if anyone here so much as looks crooked at me over these outrageous allegations. Trust me, you'll sleep better.'

I leave, closing his door quietly behind me. The blood roars in my ears. Tomorrow I rouse the Mongol hordes from hibernation and point them south-west, complete with the Black Plague fleas that infest their horses.

•

'You don't look convinced,' I say.

'I'm not.' Billy scratches under his chin. 'To be honest, I don't like the idea of Cass being even allegedly raped.'

'It's better than killing her off.'

'Sure, yeah. But still . . .'

'What?'

'She's going to look a fool, isn't she? Humiliated. She's gone to all the bother of reporting it, and that couldn't have been easy. Now it's looking like the cops aren't going to take her seriously.'

He's been a moody sod all day. 'What's on your mind, Billy? I mean really.'

He shrugs. 'Would it have been so difficult,' he says, 'I mean the first time around, to have written a story about K and Cass just sailing a yacht in the Greek islands? People like happy endings in the Greek islands. Look at *Captain Corelli's Mandolin*.'

'I can't write fat books, man.'

'It wouldn't have had to have been a whole novel,' he says. 'A short story would have done the trick.'

'What's done is done, Billy.'

'Except,' he says, 'Karlsson was never Karlsson, was he? He was you. You without the choice to be you or not.'

'Choice?'

'Sure. The freedom to be whatever he wanted to be.'

I laugh. 'And what makes you think I have free will?'

'You've a lot more of it than K had.'

'I'm just a character in everyone else's story, Billy. They're just characters in mine.'

'Bullshit.'

'Read up on your Buddha, man. The whole world, the whole universe, it's all just an illusion.'

He pats the table. 'Seems a solid enough illusion to me,' he says.

'Let me put it this way,' I say. 'If I had free will, I'd be the one sailing a yacht around the Greek islands. Except I'm sitting here talking to you.'

He makes a fist and pounds the table. 'You made a *choice*, man. That's different. That's my whole point.'

'Billy,' I say, 'the whole idea of free will, it's pie in the sky. The Hindus, the Muslims, the Buddhists, the Christians – they all believe it's all pre-ordained. And they can't *all* be wrong.'

'They can, y'know,' he says. 'I mean, if it's all mapped out, what's the bloody point of being alive in the first place?'

'Maybe so you can accept that it's all pre-ordained and acknowledge your place in the grand scheme. Appreciate the beauty of the design. Imagine for a second you're a single tiny tile in a huge mosaic and you're—'

'Gimme a break,' he groans. 'What're you on, PCP?'

'Hey, Hemingway?' Deborah steps out onto the patio, shading her eyes with one hand. 'It's nearly ten-past and your parents are expecting us for seven. Can you get Rosie changed and put her in the car?'

'Sure thing, hon.' Tonight is a rare night for us, dinner for two over flickering candles, and Debs doesn't want to lose a single second of it. 'Be right with you.'

She raises a sardonic eyebrow, then taps her wrist with one finger and goes back inside.

'There you go,' I say. 'That's how much free will I have.'

'You could have said no,' he says. 'Told her you were too busy.'

'To Debs?' I laugh as I stand up. 'Free will's a marvellous idea, Billy, but I'd rather keep both balls, cheers all the same.'

He grins, then gathers his notes together. 'If you're going to be out and about,' he says, 'd'you fancy a pint later on, after dinner?'

'Yeah, maybe. I'll see how it goes. Debs might be tired.'

'I'll text you, we can take it from there.'

'Do that.'

•

We need to think Greek, people. We need to think Egyptian and Roman. Who now speaks the language of Cheops, Aristotle or Julius Caesar? Who today worships Amun-Re, Athena or Vulcan?

Think instead of the pyramids, the Parthenon, the Coliseum. A civilisation defines itself by its buildings. Eras are marked – literally and figuratively – by their physical constructs.

Forget literature, language, religion. If you want to be remembered, become an architect. A civilisation leaves behind nothing but its buildings and its prejudices. If you start taking down their buildings, they're going to sit up and take notice.

There's nothing to pique the imagination quite like a missing hospital.

My line for today is, *Politicians, buildings and whores achieve respectability if they survive for long enough.* (Robert Towne, *Chinatown*)

September 14th

Dear Mrs Kerins –

There is a bomb planted on the third or fourth floor of the hospital, depending on whether you count the basement as an actual floor. This bomb is of a sensitive nature. Any attempt to defuse it will result in premature detonation. It is timed to explode at precisely 22.55 on Saturday night, September 17th. I advise you to sign your husband out of the hospital before that time on that date.

Yours sincerely,

A Friend

Naturally, I do not choose Mrs Kerins at random. According to the files, Mrs Kerins is the young wife of a long-term in-patient with a pancreatic tumour. By a stroke of good fortune, however, when cross-referencing the files, I discover that Mrs Kerins is seven months pregnant.

This represents instant pathos. This ensures that Mrs Kerins will not spend very long wondering if my note is a hoax. It ensures that she will immediately panic and then attempt to dilute her misery by telling anyone who will listen to her dreadful news.

Inevitably, news of the bomb warning will reach the ever-twitching antennae of the Fourth Estate. This in turn ensures that the Health Service Executive will not have the luxury of presuming that the warning is a hoax, or of quietly searching the third and fourth floors in order to establish the validity of the warning before evacuating the hospital. Further, it ensures that the HSE will not be responsible for the premature explosion of a bomb, and thus will not have the blood of innocent civilians on its hands, or no more than it currently has.

I hope you are not disappointed. Perhaps you presumed I would incinerate all patients, staff and visitors along with the hospital building itself. But this would not be a logical move. The point of a terrorist bomb, as is the case with a land mine, is not to kill per se. A good novel and the terrorist bomb have this much in common: they are about questions, not answers.

The terrorist bomb is the first wave of paratroopers parachuted in to establish a bridgehead on a front page near you, behind whom arrive the justifications, the context and the irresistible moral relativism. The point of the terrorist bomb is to force a crack in the façade of the status quo, through which trickles those all-essential rumours of suffering, agony and victimhood.

I have no desire to annihilate those who are already suffering. If I had I would have helped the ex-mechanic to die. I would have bludgeoned the non-contributing homeless with lump hammers. I would have suffocated old Mrs McCaffrey with her embroidered pillow. But I did not.

It is my fervent wish that the hospital is evacuated before the silane rips through the superstructure, igniting every atom of oxygen it encounters. It would be utterly illogical to create a pantheon of counter-martyrs to my cause.

Of course, the hasty evacuation of the hospital may result in collateral damage, a.k.a. the untimely demise of certain patients who are currently hooked up to the various machines sustaining them. This is unfortunate and regrettable, although in time those men and women may come to be revered as the first martyrs in the cause of rejuvenating the ruthless streak that has sustained the human race for over a million years now.

I expect no thanks for this.

No thanks, please.

•

While Debs adds a few more strokes of blusher to the masterpiece-in-progress that is her perception of herself, I get Rosie settled in the spare room of my parents' house. I powder her bum and apply a little cream to a red patch, then get her nappy on snug and slip her into the one-piece with the picture of Pooh Bear and Piglet on the chest. Then I sit on the edge of the bed and cradle her, her head nestling in the crook of my arm, and bounce gently left and right while she sucks on her bottle. Some nights it can take ages to send her off, as Rosie struggles to drink her bottle on a wheezy chest. Tonight, though, it's as if she senses that her Mum and Dad need her to go down quietly. She lies in my arms virtually inert, her blue eyes unblinking, while I croon my version of the lullaby:

Rock-a-bye baby, in the tree-top
When the wind blows, the cradle will rock.
If the bough breaks, the cradle will fall,
And down will come baby, Daddy break your fall.

Halfway through the fifteenth rendition, her eyes finally close and the almost empty bottle falls away from the tiny pink lips. I raise her up in my arms to allow my nose to touch the warm peach of her cheek, listening for any sound of wheezing, but tonight she is calm, untroubled.

I lay her in the cot and place Sleepy Bear beside her, outside the blanket so that its weight prevents her from tossing the covering off, but close enough for a snuggle if she reaches out in her sleep.

Then I watch her until Debs decides we are fashionably late for our own date. I decide that the childless ascetics may preach until their tongues fall out, but a sleeping baby is the warm lie to their truth of free will.

•

One of the benefits of being a hospital porter is the freedom that comes with being systematically underestimated. Thus, for example, no one will suspect that a hospital porter might possess two computers, the better to hide incriminating material, such as evidence of a hasty departure from the country. Thus no one suspects that a hospital porter might have the wit and wherewithal to secure two passports, one of which he can hand in to the police when requested to do so.

I ring Yasmin.

'Hello?'

'It's me,' I say.

'Shit.'

'We have a problem.'

'What's wrong?'

There's a faint sibilance, a slight slurring, that suggests Yasmin has been drinking.

'It's your laptop,' I say.

'What about it?'

'I hid it at work where no one would find it. At the hospital, I mean. Down in the basement.'

'So?'

'They're about to find it.'

'Fuck.'

'You heard about the hospital?'

'No. What about it?'

'There's some kind of bomb alert.'

A low moan. 'A fucking bomb?'

'They're pretty sure it's a hoax but they're evacuating everyone anyway. Then they're going to search the whole building.'

'Fuck. Fuck-fuck-*fuck*.'

'I want that laptop, Yasmin. And you're going to get it.'

'But if they're evacuating the—'

'Who's going to notice you? One more guy in all that confusion.'

Right now, if I were Yasmin, I'd be weighing the pros and cons. The main con, obviously, being that the bomb is real. The main pro being the opportunity to destroy all evidence of his life-ruining perversion.

It is all I can do not to murmur that it's all a con.

'But how would I get in?' he says.

'That's the easy bit, Yasmin.'

'Stop fucking *calling* me that.'

'You'd rather I called the cops instead, left an anonymous tip?'

Even over the phone I can hear his teeth grinding.

'So where is it?' he says.

'A janitor's cubbyhole, in the basement, it looks like some kind of old bunker. There's a light-switch to the left when you go in. The laptop's on the top shelf, the shelves against the back wall. Look for the cardboard box with Granny Smith apples on it. Got it?'

'Granny Smith, yeah.'

'Good. Now listen, this is how we get you in . . .'

September 15th

Dear Cass –

I appreciate that you will understand my suicide to be an admission of guilt, as will the police. But I did not rape you.

Yes, I took advantage of your generous nature, and yes, I undressed you and placed you naked in the bed that was once ours. Yes, it is true I forced you against your will to become my unwitting accomplice. But I did not do anything else you might construe as immoral, physically invasive or humiliating.

You should also know that my suicide has nothing to do with the failure of our relationship. Neither has it anything to do with the hospital.

I choose suicide as the only logical option open to a sentient creature in a meaningless universe. By the time you read this I will have already chosen suicide. In effect, you are reading the words of a dead man.

There is no reason you should consider this a ghoulish experience. The novels of Durrell, Golding, Hemingway and Joyce are all suicide notes written by dead men. Words only truly come alive, if they ever do come alive, when their author is dead.

To paraphrase Norman Mailer, it's tough to dance when your father is watching.

At this point I would like to apologise for all those actions of mine that caused you pain and grief. Unfortunately, I can't. I say this knowing that honesty is wasted on the living. It is possible to be truly honest only to the dead, and the dead could care less about what we believe to be truth.

I say these things because I know that your narcissism will not allow you to leave this letter unopened. Yours is the narcissism of the age, which demands that everyone see their reflection in everyone else's mirror too. It is the narcissism that has stunted the collective imagination to the point where you cannot envisage the world existing without your presence to inspire it. In every mirror you see the fulcrum upon which the universe turns.

It is for this reason that the novelist hesitates before printing his final full-stop. The good novelist is all mirror. A good novel is an indefinitely protracted suicide.

I am not, sadly, a good novelist. Hence my suicide.

Cassie, believe me when I say that I did not rape you. Believe me too when I say that I would have murdered you and every last one of the seven billion liars to be considered a good novelist.

But then, where would I have found the time to write?

Yours,

K

•

Debs finds my Billy dilemma amusing.

'If you didn't want to meet him for a pint,' she says, 'why didn't you just say so?'

'You don't know Billy. He'd think I'm ashamed to be seen out with him or something.'

As is usual in these straitened times, the restaurant is only half-full, despite it being a Saturday night. Conversations murmur, tiny streams filtering into a placid pond. Deborah swirls her red wine. 'No reason you should be,' she says, 'just because he's some fruit-cake who wants to blow up a hospital.'

I've spent the evening bringing her up to speed on the latest developments. She's particularly fascinated by the idea that Billy wants to evacuate the hospital before he blows it for real. 'Albert Schweitzer, this guy,' she reckons.

'If he rings,' I say, 'we can say we're on our way home, Rosie got sick.'

'No way,' she says. 'Don't you dare tempt fate like that. And what if we bumped into him afterwards? Unless you think we should actually go home early, on the first night out we've had since God was a boy?' She shakes her head, sets her napkin aside. 'If you want to meet him,' she says, 'then meet him. But we're not going home early, and you're *not* to use your daughter as an excuse. Hear me?'

She crosses the restaurant, goes out through the glass doors and turns towards the Ladies. I wait until she is out of sight before turning on my phone, which she has asked me to switch off so that we can enjoy our rare night out in peace.

A beep-beep tells me I have a text message. It's from Billy.

It reads: 'The shark has jumped. Repeat: THE SHARK HAS JUMPED.'

The shark?

The phone vibrates in my hand, letting me know I have a missed call. I dial 171, hear my father's voice.

'Son? *Son*? Shite, it's his answering thing . . . Listen, Rosie's took sick, she's . . . she's turned *blue*. She was wheezing bad, and now she's hardly breathing. We're on our way to the hospital now, so ring us as soon as you get this.'

For a moment I go blank. When the waitress asks if everything is alright, I even say, automatically, 'It was lovely, thanks.'

And then I see the expression on her face, something wary about it, and I realise where I am, what it is she must be looking at. I scramble out of my chair and rifle my pockets for money, telling the waitress that there's an emergency and my wife is in the Ladies and would she mind telling her we need to leave immediately, please?

Debs sees me from the Ladies and sprints back to the table. 'What?' he says. 'What is it?'

'Rosie. Mum and Dad have taken her to the hospital, they're saying,' I choke up, 'they're saying she's turned blue.'

'Fuuuuuuck.'

Down the stairs, out to the street, hail a taxi.

'The hospital?' the guy says. 'No can do, chief. They're evacuatin' it.'

'They're what?'

'Evacuatin'.' He enunciates each syllable, relishing it. Cabbie gossip doesn't get any juicier than this. 'A bomb scare. Fuckin'

Real IRA, they're sayin'. Bastards.'

'Just get us as close as you can. There's a fifty in it.'

The guy takes us up Connaughton Road, past the tinkers' caravans, and drops us within sight of the hospital's entrance. It's chaos. A hovering helicopter whump-whumps overhead, its back-wash sending up mini-cyclones of dust and paper wrappers. A steady stream of patients come out, squinting against the blasting dust, on crutches and swathed in bandages, some limping and supported by others, all dressed in pyjamas and dressing gowns, some pushing wheeled frames and holding aloft IV drips. Porters push beds while nurses direct the traffic. Cops in fluorescent yellow jackets try to clear a path, to allow the patients out while keeping the swelling crowd back. Walkie-talkies crackle. Blue lights flash, ambulances and fire engines. Despite the chopper's clattering, Eileen Magner bawls her breathless schtick to an RTE camera. I'm screaming at a cop that our daughter is in there but he's not listening.

'There!' Debs points over my shoulder, and I see Mum and Dad being herded away, funneled by the surging mass. They're shouting something at the nearest cop but he's turning away, his broad back a solid wall.

No Rosie.

I struggle through the crowd, grab at Dad's sleeve. 'Where *is* she?'

'We got her to a doctor,' he shouts. 'Just outside the emergency room. Then they started pushing everyone out . . .' A helpless agony glittering in his eyes.

A hand grips my shoulder. I turn, expecting Debs, but already she's trying to force her way through the crowd in the direction of the ER, a salmon leaping at a tidal wave.

The hand is Frankie's. 'What's wrong?' he shouts.

'My baby girl, Frankie. She's in there. She's still *in* there.'

'Fuck,' he says. '*Fuck.*'

In his eyes I see the frantic calculation, the adding up and taking away, black marks being wiped, laurels conferred.

'Come on,' he says, pulling back, going with the surge away from the hospital.

Now, moving away from the seething mass, circling the hospital uphill, there is no resistance. No crowds, no cops, no blue flashing lights. A pain in my chest like I've been shot. Frankie panting, explaining as we go. An escape hatch, built into the hospital's basement in the time of Cuban crisis. The one that's off the CCTV map, the one the porters used for ducking in and out for sneaky tokes. We scramble down the steep grassy incline, come out in a small courtyard amid rusting ambulances, the unseeing X-ray machines, one-wheeled wheelchairs, the bric-à-brac of decades' waste.

Frankie fumbles for a key.

'*Christ*, Frankie.'

'I have it, K. I *have* it . . .'

The key goes in the lock. The tumblers turn. We're in.

A long dark corridor, dimly lit by strip lighting.

'The emergency ward,' I say. 'That's the last place they saw her.'

'This way,' he says.

•

I sense that some of you still anticipate a happy ending. My invisible antennae twitch as they scent the precious few molecules of optimism in the ether.

This is not to sneer. I understand and appreciate your desire, your need, for upbeat conclusions. I am moved to applaud your longing for some form of natural justice to materialise from the great indifference. I am proud to own up to my role in the human conspiracy when I recognise my own reflection in your contradictory wish to see the hospital vaporised and the miraculous escape of everyone therein, with the obvious exception of Yasmin the Paedophile.

But we must adhere to logic at all times. The hospital is doomed. The bomb disposal wallahs are doomed. The human race is doomed. All of these things are so inescapable as to render futile the very recording of their inevitability.

All that is left now is the possibility of wonder. Logic and wonder are not mutually exclusive.

Cling to your faith, if you must, when the night comes on and the universe reverts to its default setting of cold and empty darkness. In this much, at least, the universe is a magnanimous parent, allowing a fretful child its soother for one last night. But it is time to grow up, people. Time to put away the rubber sheets and spinning tops.

Meanwhile, it being impossible to evacuate a hospital without attracting attention, the media has arrived in force. A nation is alerted to the asp at its bosom. News being news, the venom spreads. Other nations are alerted. Other nations swoon in horrified ecstasy before the altars of their TV screens.

I too am fixated on a TV screen, watching the drama unfold as the announcer speaks words I do not understand. I see miles of fluttering yellow tape. I see men in bulky jackets wearing truncated submachine guns strapped to their chests. I see the bomb disposal squad arrive and disappear into the hospital. I note the heavy trudge of the truly aware and dedicated. Only I know for sure that they will never reappear.

This is how the scriptwriter feels when the hero's car plunges off a bridge. This was how God felt as He watched the Jews file into the showers and reach for a soap fashioned from the sludge of their brethren.

The doors close behind the team. From this moment on we must close our eyes and surrender to the imagination, the better to identify with those men now descending into the bowels on our behalf. We must strain every nerve and sinew to consider ourselves worthy of the sacrifice of every single man who charged across No Man's Land, with the obvious exception of Hitler. We must want to be them, to empathise with their imminent annihilation, if we are to be worthy of what comes next.

I close my eyes. I see them descend the stairs one heavy step at a time, burdened by their equipment and the weight of their mortality. I hear them speak in hoarse tones. I hear them deploy coarse humour to deflect their fears. I hear them speculate on the nature of the explosive device they are about to confront. I hear in their irreverent jocularity the confidence of men who have made an art of probability.

I swoon as they run through their poignant routine of superstitious gestures. They shake hands. They make the usual promises to one another, to convey final words to loved ones should the worst materialise.

Meanwhile, down in the basement, Yasmin lays Rosie on the ground and contemplates the sealed bunker door. He wipes his sweating palms on his white coat.

•

Frankie charges ahead. He seems to know his way instinctively in the dark, anticipating corners, dodging around pieces of equipment parked against the walls. Meanwhile I'm banging into beds, barking my shins, the pain in my chest white-hot, the sweat icy cold.

We cross the atrium, hurdling the low benches, past the reception area. Turn into the deserted A&E, ghostly and draped in shadow, the emergency lights casting pale glimmerings. We each take one side, go past the cubicles whipping back the curtains, ducking down to peer under the beds. Nothing.

'Are you sure she's still in here?' Frankie pants.

'She didn't come out, Frankie. Check everywhere.'

Faint beep-beeps sound over the blood pounding in my ears, a flat-line beeeeeeeeeep from somewhere off the main ward.

'I'll do the nurses' station,' he says, pointing across the ward. 'You check the—'

The faintest of shudders, an almost imperceptible brightening, is our only warning.

'Get *down*, Frank—'

Too late. The ward erupts. Beds, chairs, humans, machines: straws in a twister.

A whirlwind, reaping.

•

Were this *Moby-Dick* we might say, 'Thar she blows!'

The sudden flaring blinds. The flash of flame precedes the explosion by a micro-second. Yasmin is incinerated in less time than it takes to say *whoomph*.

In the same micro-second the explosion reverberates within the underground chamber. Constrained thus, it turns in on itself. The support pillar to the rear of the chamber buckles. Even above the boom of the explosion I believe I can hear the scream of rending steel. Perhaps this is the scream of the plucked radish.

The hospital groans. Perhaps it is a frisson anticipating sexual release.

The convulsion shatters every window in the hospital. Outside, behind the ribbons of fluttering yellow tape, the instinctive gasp of the watchers creates its own sonic boom in response. Then the yelps and yowls as shards of flying glass begin to shower down.

Distracted, the watchers do not see the hospital tilt. They do not see the hospital rend itself from its foundations like some huge concrete Samson. They panic nonetheless, as brick, mortar, glass and chrome crash down in random revenge on their erstwhile tormentors like so many cluster bombs.

Where I am, I see the camera lens shake. Where I am, I hear the commentator attempt to articulate terror via a strangled yelp. This is no easier in Greek than it is in English.

I see a cloud of dust and smoke rise from the smouldering rubble. This is the logic of poetry carried through to its inevitable conclusion. *I think that I shall never see / A poem as true as a fallen tree*, etc.

Pandora you witch, Narcissus my old friend: can you hear what I hear?

Tonight the Great White will convene an emergency war council and there shelve its plans to grow legs and invade.

Tonight Herostratus howls again at the moon.

Tonight I hear Pilate's sigh, Prometheus croon a lullaby.

Tonight the Jews drag Hitler from his bed and inject his eternal veins with his own faeces.

•

When I come-to I have no idea of how long I've been out. It can't have been long or I wouldn't have come-to at all; the swirling smoke would have killed me in minutes. Coughing hard, trying to work out if anything has been broken, if the damage is—

Rosie.

I haul myself to my feet, banging my head on the overhang of the nurses' station. Eyes streaming, I lurch forward and stagger out of control, lose my footing. The floor has reset at a weird angle, dropping away. Careful now, impossible to see the floor through the smoke, I inch across the ward.

'Frankie?'

My voice sounds comes out a croak, but even that much effort is enough to get my scorched lungs heaving.

But even as I choke on the roasted air, it occurs to me that Billy's theory about the silane gas igniting every last atom of oxygen is a bust. That his idea of—

The basement.

A voice in the back of my head telling me it's pointless, it's too late.

Sabotage.

No, *self*-sabotage. The future operating behind the enemy lines of the present.

'*Now listen good. This is how we get you in.*

'*There'll be an elderly couple carrying a baby, it'll have breathing problems.*

'*She's your ticket inside.*

'*Once you're in, make for the basement.*'

If I am to die, it will not be smoke that kills me.

If I am to die, I will die of being a man.

The stairwell to the basement is a chimney funnelling hot, oily smoke. A permeable barrier I have to lean into to penetrate, the banister too hot to touch. Stumbling blind, eyes streaming, I expect to be fried alive when I burst through the double-doors into the basement proper, but the bizarre thing is that it seems cooler, the smoke thinning out.

Then I'm hurtling around the corner towards the bunker. A faint wail from the murk, a baby's cry. Hope shoots through my chest just as my feet connect with something solid and down I go, face-first into the concrete.

No pain, not at first, just shock. I kneel there coughing, so weak I can barely hold myself upright, but then the smoky haze shifts and I see him: Billy, kneeling close enough to touch, his face contorted as his hands pump Rosie's chest. Then he's gone and I hear a ragged scream, and he looms into view again, his wild eyes bloodshot and streaming, and I understand that he is not giving Rosie CPR.

He's trying to crush her tiny chest.

I hurl myself across Rosie, smash my forehead into his face.

The impact is cold, hard. A crash, then splintering.

When I open my eyes again, Billy is gone.

When I open my eyes again, Billy was never there.

In his place a reflection, a crazy-paved Picasso portrait of the author as agent provocateur. In his place a shattered pane of glass, the wall mounting that houses the coiled rubber hose.

In Case of Emergency, Break Glass.

I look down to see Rosie's pale blue eyes goggling. Her mouth pursed open in a perfectly round O. My hands on her chest, the fragile ribs beneath, and beneath that, nothing.

No heartbeat.

Instinctively I place one hand beneath her neck, tilt her head back. Bend down and place my lips on hers, breathe into her mouth, then gently pump her chest once, twice, three times.

Does she stir? Or is it my hands trembling?

If not now, never . . .

I untuck my shirt, get Rosie underneath it, go. Stepping across Yasmin's prone body, his face and hands melted into blackened lumps. Back across the underground car park, out into the smoke-choked stairwell. Staggering blind. The heat roasting now. I can hear my eyebrows crisp, smell the acrid whiff of burning hair.

Out into the reception area, wheel right. I trip over some rubble in the corridor, come down hard on one knee. The pain shoots up through my hip, whiplashing my spine.

Dim daylight to be seen at the end of the corridor, the hospital's main doors. On. *On.*

The glass doors have been blown out, the automatic sliding mechanism melted. I duck under and step through, collapse to my knees. The weight of Rosie dragging me down.

A dazzle, a blaze of lights. Screams. The smoke-filled muck tastes like the purest Arctic air.

I hear a croaking, barely audible: 'I need help here. Help.'

Then a rushing, footsteps pounding. Arms around me. I'm falling.

'I have her, man. I *have* her. You can let go now. LET GO!'

I let go and she's gone and I fall.

For a moment I can only lie there, stunned. Choking, eyes streaming. Stick figures swimming in a blurred glare. A jealous spasm as I realise the professionals are swarming Rosie. A nurse, two paramedics. The plastic gleam of an oxygen mask as it disappears into their midst.

The child, of course.

Nothing matters but the child.

It is as if the decision is made for me. As if it has always been made.

I get one knee underneath me, then the other. A crippled sprinter waiting for the gun to crack.

The hospital's smoking maw awaits.

One last glance over my shoulder. Rosie nestling in the nurse's arms. Bawling, now. Both of them.

I drift away into the hospital, wraith-like, disembodied.

•

Sermo Vulgus: A Novel (Excerpt)

Cassie, I would have eaten of the fruit too. Who would be daughtered to the fool who would not eat to know Everything?

The whole point of being alive is to store away enough answers to last an eternity of questions.

Cassie, the universe is eighty percent composed of dark matter, of which we know Nothing. Cassie, my one love, the energy of the universe is three-quarters composed of dark energy, of which we know Nothing.

Tonight my universe comes to an end. Tonight, on this remote and lonely beach, my infinity will suffer its fatal inversion. Tonight I back away out of the story, quite literally.

The sea is calm tonight, Cass. The Aegean usually is. There is an almost full moon. The sand is black and cold, coarsely grained. I sit on the beach and watch the stars and imagine each grain of sand as a microscopic diamond.

Cassie, you said you would never wear diamonds. They are too hard, you said, hard as the bones our yesterdays gnaw. You said only braided lightning would grace your finger. Can't we at least try, you said, to draw a straight line through the heart of every sun?

This moment is timeless. In this moment meshes everything I might possibly be and everything I might once have been.

Cassie, I am reaching back to that moment when sperm and egg engendered the latest in an infinite number of unique infinities. I am wondering at how the shockwaves of that collision still oscillate. The ripple is eternal.

Cassie, my ripple is only one of an infinite number of unique oscillations eternally intersecting with all other ripples. I am tempted to throw a stone into the calm Aegean just to watch the ripple fade and mutate into another, more appropriate, form of energy.

But I am my own stone.

I strip off. I arrange my socks and shoes neatly. I tuck my wallet into one shoe. I walk to the water's edge. I stand there for a moment, looking up at the almost full moon.

Cassie, the dilemma is this: to commit suicide is to renounce the flesh. But I am flesh forged of flesh, will forged of will, choice forged of choice.

I retrace my footsteps, walking backwards in the footprints already made in the sand. Past my neatly folded pile of clothes, my wallet, the rented scooter, the deserted shacks of this remote fishing village on the northern coast of a small Aegean island.

And so I retreat, step by step. Back I go, to melt into the limbo of a universe which is overwhelmingly composed of dark materials we cannot comprehend.

Cassie, what if the universe is made of love?

Nothing left now to say. Nothing, except that it would have been enough to see, just once, that miracle when the quantum chaos prompted the unknowing child to smile up at me. To conjure even a boson's worth of illusion from the pitiless void, to justify the miles we crossed to come so far. The light-years. The thirty thousand billion cells. The trillions of particles, the unimaginable number of random collisions required to create a thinking thing.

All gone, wasted, lost.

We should have made babies, Cass.

One would have been enough.

•

'So that's pretty much that,' Billy says. By now the shadows have lengthened so far that the gecko in his Irish racing green clings to last patch of sun above the door. 'I mean,' he flicks dismissively through the final few pages, 'there's a whole section here, the big Poirot reveal when Debs tells the cop, Sallow Face, how you worked as a hospital porter to research your book, except you were sick, suffering from male post-partum depression, under pressure with deadlines, couldn't pay the mortgage, all this. Sick as two small hospitals, Sallow Face tells her.'

The sheets are white, the walls are white, the tiles on the floor are white.

'But if you ask me,' he says, 'you're only pandering there.

Anyone who didn't pick up on all that won't have read this far anyway.'

I scribble on the pad, hold it up.

Rosie?

'Oh yeah,' he says, flicking back a page or two. 'There's a good bit here about how the X-rays showed some deep-tissue scarring. Smoke damage, but not from the hospital. More like someone had been blowing smoke directly into her lungs over a period of time. D'you want to leave that in?'

I nod.

'Consider it done,' he says, making a note. 'And if you're leaving that in,' he says, 'you might as well leave the sappy finale. Make it a proper crime novel, like, all that liberal angst curdling into conservative bile.'

I scrawl on the pad.

Read it.

'You sure?'

I nod.

'Okay,' he says. He flicks forward through the pages. 'So this comes after the big reveal,' he says, 'the smoke-scarred lungs, and you ask to hold Rosie one last time, except you can't, you're cuffed to the bed, but Debs makes this big gesture of forgiveness and absolution, holds Rosie close to you. Ready?'

I nod again.

A wry grin, a self-conscious clearing of the throat.

The little girl senses me, some instinct turning her head.

'The little girl senses me,' Billy says, 'some instinct turning her head.'

Her face comes up to meet mine with a faintly quizzical expression.

'Her face comes up to meet mine,' Billy says, 'with a faintly quizzical expression. Her wide eyes blue as heaven all over.'

Her wide eyes blue as heaven all over.

O my love, I say. O my one true and precious love . . .

And she smiles her hapless gummy smile, and gurgles, just the faintest of wheezing to be heard, and a flailing hand catches my lower lip like a tiny grappling hook, the fingers so frail and translucent, yet strong enough to grip my lip and pinch so that all that is left to do is lower my face until my nose brushes her cheek, the warm peachy down of her skin, and I inhale her sweet baby smell and it's enough to finally melt something within, so that there's a snap and a sudden trickle, and then a gush, a flood, and swept away I understand at last and far too late all that is lost and gone, gone and lost forever.

'. . . lost and gone, gone and lost forever.'

All that is left now is the small but perfectly formed matter of ritual sacrifice. A token gesture. A sop to those who like their absolution painful and gory. A bloody charade of repentance.

Tonight we sever the only muscle in the human body that is attached at only one end.

This room, appropriately enough, has the appearance of a hospital theatre. White walls, white tiles on the floor, the ceiling, the sheets on the bed. All white.

From beyond the shuttered windows and the balcony overlooking the Aegean I hear the burred *thrip-chip* of the cicadas. Homer would have heard their ancestors. There is a blessed relief in the prospect of no longer having to make any more sense than the average cicada.

There is a perverse joy too in the idea of sawing through the ligature at the muscle root. The operation would be bloody and painful, it is true, and the benefits are undeniable. Sadly, steak knives and scissors are non-runners, and the perverse joy will have to be deferred. After the excision the wound will need to be staunched and perhaps cauterised, lest I bleed to death. For this reason the severing must appear to be accidental.

Deliberate severance of any human appendage is generally regarded by emergency ward staff as suspicious enough to warrant reporting to the appropriate authorities. By contrast, an accident will be regarded as unfortunate enough to warrant professional but heartfelt sympathy.

My cunning plan runs thusly: I will clamp my tongue between my teeth, as far back as nature allows. Then I will dive headfirst down the marble staircase outside my bedroom door, holding my chin high in the air.

The difficult part, I think, will be the not screaming halfway down.

The bonus in this method is the potential for smashed bone, disfigurement and permanent scarring. The most effective disguise is the one nobody wants to look at.

Would an eyeball gouged from its socket be too much?

On discharge from hospital, I should be to all intents and purposes invisible and mute. From this moment on we must rely solely on the written word. Our tools will be silence, cunning and exile.

Why not? No one was listening anyway.

My line for today, for tonight and forever, comes courtesy of Seamus Heaney: *Whatever you say, say nothing.*

Acknowledgements

Heartfelt thanks are due to Sean O'Keeffe at Liberties Press for publishing this novel; to Daniel Bolger for his diligent editing; and to the superb marketing department led by Caroline Lambe.

I would like to thank my agent, Allan Guthrie, and my former agent Jonathan Williams, for their unflagging support at various times, and for their always helpful suggestions. I would also like to acknowledge the assistance of the Irish Arts Council, and particularly that of Sarah Bannan.

Thanks are also due to those who were generous enough to read the novel and offer their advice and encouragement. These include, in no particular order, Ed O'Loughlin, John Banville, Ken Bruen, Deborah Lawrenson, Adrian McKinty, John McFetridge, Scott Philips, Reed Farrel Coleman and Donna Moore.

I would also like to thank the writers and readers who, through the pages of the blog Crime Always Pays, have been so blindly optimistic on my behalf over the last number of years. You are too many to name, but be assured that I am very grateful indeed.

Finally, a special thank you is due to my family, and particularly my wife Aileen, without whose sacrifices I would be unable to find the time and space in which to write.